Read

"Does your
unchaperor

"No, and I'd like to k
believe it. Six long mo
and in less than an hour, she'd opened up her heart and
her life to a man she didn't know—to a doctor, no less,
to the kind of man she was running from.

"I know how to keep a confidence." Trey—she didn't
even know his last name—flashed her a wink. The devil
shone in his eyes and in the cut of his one-sided grin.
"I'm a doctor."

"I know what you are."

"Handsome, charming, debonair. Kind to children and
damsels in distress." Twin dimples danced and beguiled,
and he was far too sure of himself, yet, with those
wicked eyes and the mesmerizing cut of his muscled
body, he was that and more!

Praise for Jillian Hart's previous titles

COOPER'S WIFE

"Well-crafted and poignantly funny…this is a feel-good
story for both veterans and newcomers to the genre."
—*Romantic Times Magazine*

LAST CHANCE BRIDE

"It will touch you deeply."
—*Rendezvous*

"The warm and gentle humanity of *Last Chance Bride* is
a welcome dose of sunshine after a long winter."
—*Romantic Times Magazine*

Montana Man
Harlequin Historical #538—November 2000

DON'T MISS THESE OTHER
TITLES AVAILABLE NOW:

#535 THE STOLEN BRIDE
Susan Spencer Paul

#536 SILK AND STEEL
Theresa Michaels

#537 THE LAW AND MISS HARDISSON
Lynna Banning

JILLIAN HART

MONTANA MAN

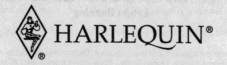

HARLEQUIN®

TORONTO • NEW YORK • LONDON
AMSTERDAM • PARIS • SYDNEY • HAMBURG
STOCKHOLM • ATHENS • TOKYO • MILAN • MADRID
PRAGUE • WARSAW • BUDAPEST • AUCKLAND

If you purchased this book without a cover you should be aware that this book is stolen property. It was reported as "unsold and destroyed" to the publisher, and neither the author nor the publisher has received any payment for this "stripped book."

ISBN 0-373-29138-8

MONTANA MAN

Copyright © 2000 by Jill Strickler

All rights reserved. Except for use in any review, the reproduction or utilization of this work in whole or in part in any form by any electronic, mechanical or other means, now known or hereafter invented, including xerography, photocopying and recording, or in any information storage or retrieval system, is forbidden without the written permission of the publisher, Harlequin Enterprises Limited, 225 Duncan Mill Road, Don Mills, Ontario, Canada M3B 3K9.

All characters in this book have no existence outside the imagination of the author and have no relation whatsoever to anyone bearing the same name or names. They are not even distantly inspired by any individual known or unknown to the author, and all incidents are pure invention.

This edition published by arrangement with Harlequin Books S.A.

® and TM are trademarks of the publisher. Trademarks indicated with ® are registered in the United States Patent and Trademark Office, the Canadian Trade Marks Office and in other countries.

Visit us at www.eHarlequin.com

Printed in U.S.A.

Available from Harlequin Historicals and
JILLIAN HART

Harlequin Historicals

Last Chance Bride #404
Cooper's Wife #485
Malcom's Honor #519
Montana Man #538

Please address questions and book requests to:
Harlequin Reader Service
U.S.: 3010 Walden Ave., P.O. Box 1325, Buffalo, NY 14269
Canadian: P.O. Box 609, Fort Erie, Ont. L2A 5X3

Chapter One

Montana Territory, 1884

Please, don't let them find me. Miranda Mitchell glanced over her shoulder at the snow-covered town street that stretched out behind her. Breathing hard, she kept running. She might not be able to see them, but she could *feel* them coming closer. A crowd surrounded her, blocking her view of the street. She was still safe. For now.

Driven by fear, she swiped at the snow gathering on the brim of her bonnet and kept running, her shoes tapping on the slippery ice toward the train at the end of the platform. The conductor's last call to board rang in the crisp morning air, carried by the bitter wind that knifed through her clothes as she picked up her skirts and sprinted across the slick platform, her ticket crumpled in one hand.

Dark smoke plumed into the air, ash mixing with snow, and the train gave one long departing whistle. Miranda kept running. The platform seemed to go on forever. Well-wishers crowded next to the train, waving to loved ones safe inside, blocking her way.

Determined, she shouldered through a break in the

crowd only to see the doors shut tight, the train ready to leave. Her faint hopes tumbled, and she simply stared. It couldn't be. She *had* to make this train. Her entire life depended on it.

"They're still taking passengers down there." A kindly woman touched her elbow and then pointed with one gloved hand. "Maybe you can still make it aboard."

"Oh, thank you." Miranda gathered up her hopes and her skirts and ran, barreling down the edge of the platform with all her might. She still heard no commotion on the street, but wouldn't be able to hear anything over the deafening roar of the train's engine. If they saw her, would they shoot? No, not in a crowded place. Surely even a bounty hunter would have that much sense.

Then again, the man who'd tracked her down didn't have the look of wisdom about him. Hard-eyed and ruthless, he'd kicked in the back door of the boardinghouse, both guns already drawn. The sound of wood breaking had given her enough time to grab her satchel and run out the front. Without this warning, she would be in his custody now, enduring Lord knows what kind of treatment.

Her stomach turned to ice, and she skidded to a stop at the end of the line. A conductor was helping an old man board, and the train waited impatiently, engines rumbling. Miranda glanced over her shoulder but couldn't see the street. There were too many people. She eased up on tiptoe, but still couldn't see much more than an array of hats and a slice of the icy platform. The bounty hunter and his men could be out there, maybe as close as the ticket window, and she wouldn't be able to see them, wouldn't even know they were near.

Fear tasted cold and metallic on her tongue, and her heart thudded so hard in her chest, it hurt. The line in front of her was growing shorter, but not fast enough.

Please, hurry, she prayed, her fingers curling around the tiny gold locket at her throat. *Please, keep me safe.*

''No-o-o-o. No train.'' A little girl's voice cut above the din of voices, the rumble of the engine and the clang of baggage being loaded, her heartbreak and terror keening on the wind.

Miranda turned and noticed a man, not three paces away, kneeling on the platform before a fragile child, holding her tenderly in his solid arms. He had the look of a lawman—broad shoulders and intelligent eyes, strength and a hint of danger. He radiated might and competence. But there was no badge on his chest and nothing more than a six-shooter strapped to his muscled thigh. Two train tickets peeked out from his jacket pocket too fine to be bought and paid for with a sheriff's salary.

She shuffled a step forward in line, but she couldn't take her eyes off the handsome man made stronger by his tenderness for a child.

He brushed at the layer of snow that clung to the girl's wool cap. ''Josie, if you and I don't board this train, then how are we gonna get to my house?''

The girl's brow wrinkled as she thought. ''We can walk right on down the road, Uncle Trey. Then we don't gotta take no train.''

''You want to *walk* all the way to Willow Creek?''

''I won't complain none. Not once.''

''But it's a hundred miles from here to there.''

''I ain't afraid to walk.'' Josie tilted her head to one side, pure fight.

A sharp, high sound split the air. Miranda jumped, ready to bolt, expecting to hear the clatter of galloping horses on the frozen ground or shouted threats from the bounty hunter and his men. When the sound shrilled again, she realized it was only the train whistle. Goodness, she felt foolish.

The conductor reached down to help a frail old woman onto the bottom step. She moved carefully, and while Miranda didn't want the woman to fall, she wished the line would move a little faster. The back of her neck started to prickle—she could feel those dangerous men gaining ground. She couldn't let them find her, she couldn't—

"Well, now, Josie." The man's voice, deep and tender as twilight, again cut through Miranda's thoughts and the noise surrounding them. She turned just enough so she could see him lean closer to speak with the small child in his arms, forehead to forehead. "I got a confession to make. I'm afraid to walk all that way."

"You ain't afraid of nothin', Uncle Trey, not even the train."

Miranda couldn't help herself. Unable to tear her gaze away, she peered past the brim of her bonnet at the man's profile and the charming grin that turned his chiseled face from handsome to breathtaking. She felt drawn toward his tenderness, something she'd seen so little of in her own life or in her years volunteering at Children's Hospital.

And she was amazed that this man, so big and strong, didn't seem diminished, less masculine, for his gentleness. It tugged at her heart like a thousand midnight dreams. The anxiety cold in her veins felt small when compared to the warmth of this man's treatment of the child he held—a niece, not a daughter of his own.

"Suppose we do decide to walk through the mountains all the way to my house. Now, there's all sorts of dangers to a man on foot," Josie's Uncle Trey confided. "A wild buffalo herd could trample me. A bear could decide I'd make a fine supper. I could develop a bad case of bunions from walking in these new boots. You wouldn't want that, now, would you, Red?''

''Yes.'' Josie looked up at the train, tears pooling in her big green eyes. Fear lived there—true as a spring morning, fresh as rain.

''Now, how am I going to do my job with bunions?'' He tried to keep his voice light, but he glanced up at the diminishing passenger line and the sound of the engines ready to go. Miranda saw his panic and more, much more. ''If I get a whole lot of bunions, I won't be able to do more than limp. How would I make house calls? When Mrs. Watts gets another rash, I'll have to say 'Sorry ma'am, I won't be able to limp over and ease your misery.' C'mon, do your old uncle a favor and get on the train.''

''But the tr-train m-might c-crash again.'' The little girl laid her cheek against his wide chest and sobbed. ''That's how Ma and Pa died.''

''I promise it won't happen again.'' Deep lines of anguish matched the choked sound of his voice. ''Honey, there's no other way to get to my house. Not this time of year. There's a storm coming up, and the mountain passes are closed—''

''I don't wanna new home.'' Although the little girl's voice was quiet, hardly more of a sound than the wind, the suffering in her voice rang as loud as the biggest bell—sharp, pure, true. ''I want my ma.''

''All aboard!'' the conductor's call pierced like a knife, and Miranda realized everyone had boarded the train except for her and this man and child.

''I don't want to force her.'' The doctor's voice drew her gaze and she realized he'd noticed her watching them—it was hard to miss. She was standing with her back to the train, her hands to her mouth, tears pooling in her eyes when she should be safely hidden on the train. Standing in plain sight like this—

Her toes slid forward, bringing both feet and all of her closer. What was she doing? Every instinct screamed at her to turn around, that this wasn't any of her concern, that she had her own life-and-death problems.

And yet deep in her heart, the little girl's words resonated over and over. *That's how Ma and Pa died.* All her life, she'd never been able to walk away from a child who needed help. Not one.

"I could use a hand." His gaze flickered with relief, and she could see the anguish in those eyes as dark as a moonless night, deep like shadows. "This train is about to roll down those tracks, and I've got to find a way to get her aboard. I hate to force her after the accident."

Miranda saw the brace wrapped around the child's stick-thin leg, the steel still shiny and new. She remembered the train wreck of a month ago—twenty-seven days, to be exact.

She'd disembarked from that fated train here on that same day. She'd been asking the ticket clerk directions to a respectable boardinghouse when she'd heard the crash in the distance. Minutes later, a ball of fire rose on the western horizon.

Thirty-six people died and many more were injured. This little girl had been one of them. Agony twisted through her, her goal to escape unimportant. She turned her back on the street.

"Don't be afraid." Miranda took a step nearer, unsure if there was anything she could do for this frightened, hurting child. She had to try. "Your uncle is right. Trains don't always crash."

The little girl didn't look up. She clung to the strong doctor, her light red curls shaking with each tortured sob.

"Josie is a very brave little girl." Grief darkened the uncle's eyes, revealing a steady substance that drew Miranda closer, and she lowered her defenses just a little.

"I can see that. But the train is starting to move." Her heart gave a little jolt when she saw the wheels turn once, and then again. The creak of steel upon steel and the groan of the loaded cars on the tracks filled the air.

"Looks like I'll have to carry her on—" Regret laced his voice as he straightened, holding the girl captive in his arms.

"No-o-o-o, Uncle Trey, don't m-make me." The sobs came, genuine and sharp with fear. "I don't wanna get hurt again."

"Hurry." Miranda's hand tightened around her satchel's grip, not sure how best to help the frightened child. She saw a black bag alone on the platform and grabbed that up, too. "We still can make it."

"We have to. I'm sorry, Josie." Anguish drew deeper lines across his face as he began jogging with the child, who struggled in his arms.

Miranda saw his remorse in the pinched lines around his expressive eyes and the fine cut of his mouth, drawn tight with worry for the child. He ran along the edge of the platform toward an open door.

As the long line of cars continued to slide away, one by one, Miranda saw in her memory the train wreck, surging back like the leading edge of a Montana blizzard—harsh and swift and without mercy. She smelled the acrid scent of smoke, imagined the stillness after the world-altering screech of steel impacting steel, heard the passengers crying out in grief and fear and pain.

She'd hurried to help those she could then, and she ran to the uncle and niece now, her hand brushing the hard, lean curve of the doctor's upper arm. She felt a flash of heat through his wool coat and her kid gloves where they briefly touched. But her gaze was only on the child, a little girl so fragile it looked as if the wind could blow her away as easily as it drove delicate snowflakes to the ground.

"I know what you need." Miranda heard an explosion of gunfire behind her, pivoted, and saw the band of men riding hard down the nearby street.

The train continued snaking away, car after car lumbering by as Josie's Uncle Trey stopped running and turned to study her with eyes dark with hope. "What you need is a good-luck charm."

"Ain't no such thing." The child's eyes shone with unshed tears.

"Sure there is. I have one hanging around my neck right now."

"It's just a locket."

"Just a locket?" Her hands trembled as she heard the approaching thunder of horses growing louder and closer. She lifted the chain over the knot of hair pinned at the crown of her head and the peak of her bonnet.

"Sounds like some trouble's headed this way." Trey straightened his broad shoulders and gazed quietly toward the street, where a handful of rough men drove lathered horses through the crowd of departing people straight toward the platform.

Trouble? It was the end of her life. Her instincts told her to run, but it wasn't the right thing to do. She placed the gold chain over Josie's strawberry blonde curls and laid the small locket against the placket of the girl's fine dress. "I promise, Josie, this will keep you safe. It's always worked for me."

"Really?" Doubt-filled eyes blinked away tears.

"I've ridden on probably fifty trains, and look at me,

I'm as safe as can be." She might be trembling and might be looking danger in the face, but she had to help this child. It mattered more to her than she could explain. "I promise, if you wear this, you'll be safe."

"Looks like this is the last car." The doctor's voice sounded gruff, raw with emotion, as he started running. "C'mon, hurry. We can still make it."

Miranda heard the drum of shod hooves on the platform and felt the boards quake with the force of the galloping horses. She took off at a dead run as the caboose ambled past and caught up with the doctor as he handed his niece to the conductor inside the train.

"Hurry. You can do it." He held tight to the metal bar at the open door and reached out for her with the other.

Gunfire pierced the air, a warning shot from not three feet behind her. Fear drove her forward and she caught the tips of the doctor's fingers.

Strong and sure, he clamped on and pulled her to him. She pitched into his arms and somehow the toe of her shoe caught the bottom step. She stumbled, but the strong man's grip on her shoulder guided her into the car.

She looked back to see the caboose slipping away from the edge of the platform, leaving the armed bounty hunter and his men at the edge.

Gaining speed, the train eased around a slow curve, breaking away from the bustling town toward the steep peaks of the Continental Divide.

Trey closed the door behind him, gazing at her with eyes wise and wondering, with a hint of a smile touching the left corner of his mouth. "Looks like your friends didn't make the train."

"They weren't friends I wanted to travel with."

"Then you're in luck." He reached past her to heft

Josie up into his arms. "Those bullets could have hit someone. Are you hurt?"

"No, I don't think they would have actually shot me." She righted her bonnet and tried to take a step back, to put distance between them. "Thank you."

"Well, I want to check on the caboose. Those might have been warning shots, but bullets fired up in the air have a way of coming right back down. I want to make sure no one's hurt. Would you do me a favor?"

"If I can."

Steady warmth snapped in his eyes, drawing her closer even when she wanted to escape. "Would you stay with Josie? Josie, would it be all right if our mystery lady stays with you for a few minutes?"

"I'm no mystery, believe me." Miranda dropped her eyes to the child's peaked face, pinched with worry, and tried hard to ignore Trey's measuring gaze. "My name's Miranda."

"No last name to go with that?" His grin dazzled, carving twin dimples in his left cheek. "Or are you on the run from the law?"

"That's right. I'm fleeing from justice and it's best for both of you if you don't know my last name." Her chest tightened, for that wasn't far from the truth. She was an heiress, not a fugitive, but she *was* fleeing and from far more than the price on her head.

Remembering her pursuers, she glanced out the window at the heavily falling snow and saw nothing but rangeland, the town and the bounty hunter left far behind.

"I would love keeping an eye on your niece." She was safe, for now at least. The men who hunted her would wire ahead to the next major town, she had no doubt of that. But somehow she would figure a way out. She'd been doing it all the way from Philadelphia.

"Miranda." Josie tilted her head to one side, fear still glittering in her emerald eyes, but at least the panic was at bay. "Wanna see my baby doll?"

"Sure I do." She stepped forward to lift the child out of her uncle's protective hold. The scent of him enveloped her, leather, wood smoke and man, the blend attractive and pleasing, making her wish…well, for things that she could never have if she were caught.

Miranda knew it was a risk to speak with anyone who would remember her, especially to tell them her first name, but she knew what it was like to be a child, defenseless and alone, with a broken heart and a sorrow big enough to drown in. She cradled Josie close, careful of her braced leg. "Let's go find your seats."

"First class." The doctor handed her the tickets, and she noticed for the first time as their fingers brushed how well shaped his hands were, thick and strong, but sensitive. Healer's hands.

Just like her father's.

Her stomach snapped tight at the memory, pain and regret gripping her hard. She nearly dropped the tickets as she spun away, closing her mind off from a past she'd vowed never to remember again.

Chapter Two

"No one was hurt." Trey Gatlin knelt down beside the plush seats where the mysterious Miranda cradled his little niece. "Lucky that bullet hit the caboose. The men after you didn't hesitate to fire a gun near a train full of people."

"I never should have—" Miranda closed her eyes, and a dark lock of hair tumbled down from her bonnet to caress her porcelain cheek, but her softness and beauty paled next to the concern and regret that gleamed in her eyes when she opened them. "I just wanted to get away. I thought I would have enough time."

"And you would have." Trey slipped his black bag under Josie's seat. "If you hadn't stopped to help us, you would have been safely on the train and out of sight. Who were they?"

She bit her bottom lip, indecision on her face warring with regret. "I don't know them personally."

"The West is a rough place for a woman alone." He'd noticed only the single satchel she carried. What kind of trouble was she in? In his profession he'd seen far too much of the hardship that could befall a woman, and he'd always done his best to help.

With an angel's face and the way she'd comforted Josie, Miranda wasn't running from trouble with the law, he knew that. But who was she running from?

The train jarred. Josie gave a cry of alarm, and he dropped to his knees to take the child in his arms. All fear and fragility, she fit against his chest, under his chin, and clung to him.

Trey's heart cinched tight, and pain sheared through him. He missed his sister. But his loss, as painful as it was, did not equal Josie's. "The train is just slowing down because of the storm, that's all."

Her tears fell hot and wet against his shirt. "Th-that's what happened last time."

"Just hold on to your good-luck charm," Miranda advised above the rustle of her skirts as she stood. "Do you know why my locket is special?"

Josie shook her head, not quite willing to believe.

"Because it's full of my mother's love. And you know that a mother's love will always keep a little girl safe." She smiled up at him, a slow, shy curve of her pretty mouth that drew his gaze and made him measure the fullness of her bottom lip. She had a sensitive mouth, shaped like a cupid's bow, and his chest clamped tight as she slipped past him.

"I don't know what to say, Miranda." Trey cleared his throat, unable to lift his gaze from this woman who spoke like an angel. "Thank you."

"My pleasure." She smiled, and all the air fled from his lungs. "Take care of little Josie," she told him, her voice resonating with a hollow sound that made him wonder again who she was and what she was running from.

Not a family—no woman that compassionate could leave a child behind her. Not a husband—no ring marked her fourth finger, not even the imprint of one was visible as she grabbed the sides of her skirts to better maneuver in the aisle.

"Miranda."

She turned. The train bucked again as the swift edge of a blizzard hit. The car rocked as the light drained from the windows. Alarm widened her eyes, and she looked vulnerable and young. He remembered the men racing to the edge of the platform, the dangerous ruffians who'd fired loaded six-shooters, trying to intimidate an innocent woman.

Josie sniffled against his chest and held him with bruising force. He had a child to comfort, and he knew next to nothing about children. He had his own problems back home. But something about Miranda drew him, and he wanted to pay back her kindness to Josie. Or maybe he simply couldn't bear to let her go.

"Come sit with us." He held out his hand.

"No. I have my own ticket." She turned, chin set, her knuckles white around the walnut grip of her expensive satchel. There was no mistaking the softness of her hands; they bore no calluses from hard work or redness from lye soap. She was a gentlewoman, city bred, and she was alone. A young woman of means did not travel this rugged land without an escort.

Again, Trey thought of the men following her. The train crept along the tracks as the furious north winds and icy snow battered it. He figured if a man was determined enough, he could race a horse down the tracks and catch up to the now slow-moving train.

Judging by the look on Miranda's face, the same thought occurred to her.

Trey took another step, leaving his hand outstretched, waiting for her touch. "This storm has both me and Josie scared. We could use a little of your good luck up here with us.''

''I thought your niece said that you weren't afraid of anything.''

''She lied.'' Dimples cut into his cheeks, a grin hinting at the corners of his mouth.

But it was his gaze that drew her—the steady, warm concern that made him feel so substantial. That made her palms turn moist and her heart knock against her ribs.

She was on the run—the men hunting her would be watching the train routes, would question passengers, one could even be in this very car.

Of all the people she'd come across since she'd fled her father's home with only the contents of one small satchel and her savings, she'd never told a single soul, living or dead, her name. She had a better chance eluding her father's men alone and unnoticed. How could she accept Trey's invitation? Even if the hardship of six months on the run and the loneliness in her heart tugged at her.

Her gaze strayed to Trey's outstretched hand, palm up, offering more than someplace to sit on this slow-moving train. He'd seen the men after her. He must have been able to read the panic in her eyes. Even in the dim lamplight the revolver holstered to his hip gleamed.

''Come on,'' his rum-rich voice soothed, a contrast to the fast rat-a-tat of her pulse and the brutal howl of the blizzard battering the north windows. ''Josie and I need a little more of your good luck, don't we, honey?''

The little girl tucked safe in his arms nodded fiercely, scattering strawberry blonde curls around her pale face. How vulnerable she looked, how needy.

Everything lonely and hurting in Miranda's heart ached. She had a weakness for children—a gigantic pillowy soft spot that had always been the reason she'd worked so hard in her father's hospital. She'd done what she could for the sick and suffering children when her friends were busy counting up the number of their beaus, attending parties and filling hope chests with fine lace, linens and dreams of happy marriages.

Regret slammed so hard into her chest it might as well have been the gust of bitter wind that rocked the car. How she missed the children. Even now, that sadness filled her.

"Please, Miranda." Tears glistened in Josie's emerald eyes, as precious as those rare gems. "I'm awful scared."

She couldn't do it. Every instinct she had screamed for her to head back to the third-class cars, the cheapest ticket available. She had to be alert. The blizzard could mean the men after her had given up. It also meant the train was now crawling blindly, making a diligent bounty hunter with the hopes of a substantial cash reward more determined and bold.

One of those men had been without enough of a conscience to shoot at the train to stop her—not caring whom he might injure. Could she be a danger to everyone on this train? To the very people she sat beside?

"Josie, please, don't be scared." Miranda ignored Trey's steady hand, offering her much more than she could accept, and traced her fingertips across the etched roses in the center of the polished locket. "You have my mother's necklace to keep you safe."

"But what will keep you safe, Miranda?" Trey asked, his words resonating with a blend of concern and knowledge that slashed through her defenses and her arguments.

It had been a long time since she'd felt anyone's concern. "I'm not a little girl. I'm old enough to make my own luck." She stubbornly took a step back, watching tears spill down Josie's face, torn. She hated that she had to go. She wished she could do more to stop this child's pain.

"I admire that." Trey lowered his hand and squared his shoulders.

Of all the men she'd come across in her life, she'd never seen a man more mesmerizing and captivating. Trey was sure of his strength, and he created a presence so strong that the light and noise in the car faded until all she could see was him. His gaze latched onto hers.

"I'm armed." He laid his well-formed hand over the gleaming wooden grip of the Colt. "Are you?"

She shook her head. She could not tear her eyes away from the breadth of his thigh, where the holster hugged what looked like rock-hard muscle.

This was a man who didn't spend his life indoors away from the sun and wind, his body growing soft with leisure and time. No, Josie's Uncle Trey looked like a man who rode the range for a living, from the hard ridge of his shoulders down to the tips of his well-worn but polished riding boots. Every inch looked as tough as nails, like the lawman she'd first figured he might be.

"Then stay with me. You'll be safer." He laid one hand on her shoulder. "I doubt those men would be foolish enough to brave this storm, but if they do, they could catch up with us in no time. I don't know what you're running from, Miranda, and it's none of my business."

"Then why—"

"Because where I come from, a man worth his grit protects a woman. He doesn't fire a gun at her on a crowded platform with a train full of people behind her." His grip tightened.

Miranda instinctively tried to brush him away, but stopped when she realized his hold on her wasn't bruising or possessive, like Lewis's had been. Nor was it controlling like Father's. Trey's touch was firm and binding, but as respectful as a promise made and kept.

"I could put you and Josie in jeopardy—"

"Don't you worry about that. We're tough, aren't we, Red?" He gave the little girl wrapped in one arm a slight squeeze.

"That's right. We're real tough." Josie bobbed her small chin once despite the heartbreak in her eyes.

"So am I." Could she stay? Should she?

For the first time in months, Miranda felt the mantle of fear slide off her shoulders, leaving her weak and tired and strangely at ease. The longing in her heart spurred her. She stepped forward, twisting away from the burn of Trey's fingers curling into the rise of her shoulder.

She was lonely, after all. Miranda eased along the seats flanking a window made dark by the brutal storm. "I usually travel alone, but just this once, just for you, Josie, I'll make an exception."

She avoided Trey's gaze, but felt it heavy on her back as she grabbed her skirts and slid across the plush velvet.

"Wait." Again, his touch stopped her, leaving a hot, aching feeling where the weight of his hand settled on her forearm. "I'll take the window. It's colder."

"I'm no delicate female." She turned her shoulder and settled into the seat, brushing off his concern as if she didn't need it.

But in truth, it had been so long since anyone had known or cared if she were warm or cold, safe or in danger. Her chest squeezed tight. She felt grateful as this man settled beside her. She tingled deep inside when his broad shoulder brushed hers.

Surely, she wasn't making a mistake in staying. In trusting that the bounty hunters, or their hired men, couldn't follow in this storm. But as Trey dug Josie's doll from his bag, Miranda didn't relax, or stop fearing the ruthless men on her trail.

The lamplight, meager in the first-class cabin, played across Miranda's face, highlighting the soft slope of her nose and the rosebud softness of her lips. She turned from the window to answer something Josie had asked.

Miranda's voice was like music, like melody and harmony, and flowed as sweet and quiet as a Brahms lullaby. Low and spellbinding, the sound moved through him. The clack of the wheels on the track and the scouring blast of the blizzard faded into the background until all he could hear was Miranda's alto sweetness as she agreed to braid her doll Baby Beth's hair.

The door swung open in front of them and, propelled by the severe wind, crashed against the wall with force enough to shake the car. Miranda jumped with a look of panic, and her pupils became big black disks. Her slim body tensed, ready to run or fight, he didn't know which. When the conductor stepped into the car and pulled the door back into place, Trey watched the relief soften Miranda's face, but the tension squeezed tight in her shoulders and spine did not ease.

"Don't worry." Trey laid his hand over hers, felt the cold, silken texture of her skin and the bone-hard tension of muscles bunched, ready to fight. "He isn't armed."

"Oh, really?" She lifted one brow, the sardonic twist of her mouth somehow endearing. She was afraid, but she wasn't cowering. Or, he guessed, willing to admit it.

"This is one threat I can handle." He winked at her, pulling out the ticket cards from his breast pocket.

"I'm not here because I need protection."

"Of course not. A woman traveling alone is an even match against six armed ruffians."

"I'm not helpless." Her chin shot up. "And those brutes may be armed, but so far I've been able to outwit them."

"Until you stopped to help us."

"It was torture, but someone had to do it." She flashed him a quick smile, wavery but true.

He was dying to ask what she was running from, who the men were on her trail—bounty hunters, by his practiced eye—and why they wanted a woman with eyes as gentle as dawn. She was from money—he'd learned to read a person at a single glance in his line of work—her hands were as smooth as watered silk and her face appeared as soft as morning. The cut of her gray cloak was simple, but the worsted wool was of a high quality. Every stitch, every garnish, every button, no matter how sedate, spoke of her station in life, one high above his.

Women well born and gently raised were never found alone on a Montana mountainside. Curiosity burned, but he'd learned patience in his profession, too.

He explained Miranda's absence of a first-class ticket to the conductor and offered quietly to pay the difference. But the kind-eyed man only waved his hand, his gaze falling on Josie's brand-new leg brace and moved on, the understanding quiet but unmistakable.

The train inched along through the towering peaks of the Rockies, invisible from the window where the gray and white of the unrelenting blizzard blocked everything from their view.

"We're going so slow, will we be able to climb through the mountains?" Miranda pocketed her ticket stub, directing her attention away from the doors to Josie, who held out her doll's miniature hairbrush. Despite the interruption and the storm, Baby Beth still needed to look her best.

"Hard to tell. They may take us only as far as Pine Bluff." Josie shifted on Trey's knee, and he felt the stiffness easing from her little spine. He watched Miranda take the brush and begin grooming the doll's flyaway hair. "The telegraph wires could go down in a storm like this."

Miranda dropped the brush. It clattered to the floor with a thud, but the sound was lost in the friendly noises inside the car as passengers talked. She shrugged one slim shoulder. "I can only hope those wires are down."

"I doubt the telegraph people would share your hopes, but then, sometimes modern inventions can work against a person." With one hand on Josie's shoulder to balance her, he reached with his free hand just as Miranda bent forward at the same time.

Their foreheads brushed. He could feel the wisps of a few rebellious tendrils, breezing across the skin of his brow as brazenly as a lover's touch. His body reacted hot and hard, but he didn't move away even as the blood thundered through his veins and his breath grew short and choppy.

"I can't reach it." She didn't blink, and a small frown tugged down the soft corners of her mouth, drawing his gaze and making him wonder just what her soft, bow-shaped lips would taste like if he kissed them. Her grin grew. "Your big head is in the way."

"My head is big?"

"Bigger than mine." A wicked smile teased at one dimple, and his stomach felt as if it were falling straight down to his tailored boots. "In my experience, the amount of charm a doctor exudes is in direct proportion to the arrogance he's trying to cover up."

"You have a lot of experience with doctors?" Now he had to know. He had to get a little more personal with this woman who made even an affirmed bachelor like him feel more hot and bothered than he'd been in a decade. "You look healthy to me."

"My father is one." The words popped out of her mouth before she thought, and she sat up, forgetting Josie's hairbrush. "I'm engaged to one."

"Engaged?" He quirked one dark brow, as if to say, now, *that's* interesting, before he knelt a little farther, stretching those magnificent shoulders and arching his broad, well-constructed back to rescue the brush beneath the seat.

Miranda watched as he straightened, nodding easily at Josie's "Thank you, Uncle Trey." Curiosity twitched at his mouth. "Does your fiancé know you're unchaperoned and in trouble?"

"No, and I'd like to keep it that way." She couldn't believe it. Six long months she'd kept her secrets safe, and in less than an hour, she'd opened up her heart and her life to a man she didn't know—to a doctor, no less, to the kind of man she was running from. She couldn't believe it, couldn't stomach her weakness.

She'd been alone too long. She felt starved for someone to talk to, someone with kind eyes, or a child who needed a little help. She'd just opened up like this, without control, without consideration to what would happen to her if those bounty hunters found her.

They would drag her back to Philadelphia, to a wedding she did not want, and to a father she could never stand to look at again.

"I know how to keep a confidence." Trey—she didn't even know his last name—flashed her a wink. The devil shone in his eyes and in the cut of his one-sided grin. "I'm a doctor."

"I know what you are."

"Handsome, charming, debonair. Kind to children and

damsels in distress." Twin dimples danced and beguiled, and he was far too sure of himself. Yet with those wicked eyes and the mesmerizing cut of his muscled body, he was that and more.

"See?" She tugged at her bonnet strings. "I knew the arrogance was in there somewhere."

"No man is perfect." He winked a second time. He was humoring her. Or maybe he could feel it, too—the way the train slowed.

They must be approaching the next station. A whistle blared faintly above the blast of ice, muted by the ever-present howl of the wind.

Was she in luck? Had the vicious storm knocked down the telegraph wires? Or would someone looking for her board this train? Her palms turned clammy and her fingers felt wooden and stiff as she began French-braiding Baby Beth's hair in accordance with Josie's careful instructions.

Beside her, Trey turned in his seat to watch as the station eased into sight, the storm broken by the shelter of tall buildings.

Snow still swirled, but Miranda could see the faces of the waiting passengers blur on the other side of the frosted glass. Men, women, children. Trepidation curled around her heart, cold and foreboding.

Somewhere in the crowd was a man searching for her. She knew it. She could *feel* it.

"Miranda, use this barrette." Josie's grip was warm against the back of Miranda's knuckles.

She turned to see trust as true as the shine on her mother's locket. "This is mighty pretty for a dolly to wear."

"It matches her traveling dress." Josie tugged at the buttons on her coat, revealing a dark dress made of the same beautiful fabric.

A fancy doll, fine clothes, barrettes made of lustrous mother-of-pearl and gleaming gold. It smacked of her own childhood, one where a housekeeper polished the furniture daily, according to Father's instructions, in a house ruled by decorum and not by love. Miranda's heart twisted. She did not regret for a moment her flight from home and all the privilege she'd left behind.

What she hated was leaving now.

"You take good care of Baby Beth." Miranda pressed her hand briefly against the side of Josie's cheek, the skin child-soft and precious. "Goodbye, dear heart."

"Where you goin'?" Josie tipped back her head as Miranda stood, her lower lip beginning to quiver.

"Remember my mother's locket." Miranda pressed the child's hand to where the gold winked in the lamplight. "Thank you for keeping watch over me, Trey."

He stood, scooping the child up easily in one arm. "There's no need for you to leave. Your ticket was for Missoula, which is a long way from here, on the other side of the Rockies."

She'd developed quite a skill for slipping off a train unnoticed while hired guns climbed on. "This is where I intend to get off."

"I don't think so. You're not going to leave like this." Trey towered over her, one-hundred-percent might, blocking her way. "From here on out, until this train reaches Willow Creek, I'll be your good-luck charm."

The ability to speak seemed to flee as Miranda tilted her head to get a thorough look at the man who stood between her and doing the right thing—getting off this train when violent men were after her. They might not care whom they hurt. But she did, she cared.

The door at the rear of the car banged open, propelled by a hard gust. Miranda jumped, her gaze darting around

Trey's well-hewn upper arm to the dark-jacketed man striding down the aisle. Two holsters hugged his denim thighs, and both beefy hands were poised above the handles of the battered revolvers.

A bounty hunter. There was no mistaking the determined, ruthless gait or the emotionless set to his eyes. She eased back, trapped between the window and Trey.

"I'm not only a dashing traveling partner—" he leaned close to murmur, his breath hot against the outer shell of her ear "—but did I mention I was a fantastic dinner companion?"

"No, you failed to list that as one of your many flaws," she whispered past a dry throat. Fear trembled through her, leaving her cold and shaking. "Fortunately for you, I have a sudden urge to leave this car."

"Me, too." Shielding her from sight with his body, he backed out into the aisle.

Miranda slipped ahead of him, pushed open the door. She knew the bounty hunter, still searching the faces of the seated passengers, was close, but he hadn't noticed her.

Yet.

She stepped into the next car, and Trey's hand settled against the small of her back, guiding her through the dining car and toward the table tucked away in the back.

"Wait." Trey's hand guided her to a stop. He stepped close so the hard curve of his shoulder and the plane of his chest pressed against her back.

Heat scorched her as they touched. Her skin felt ready to blister, but Trey didn't move aside. She heard the door behind them slam as the bounty hunter strolled into the car. She stiffened, but Trey held her steady.

"May I seat you?" a waiter appeared.

"Please." Trey's rum-smooth voice warmed her, gave her hope. "My wife would like a window table."

"This way."

Miranda held her breath as the bounty hunter prowled past. He barely even looked their way. Josie reached out for her, and she took the child into her arms. Trey's deception had worked. The hired gun was looking for a woman alone.

She breathed a sigh of relief when he left the car.

"Am I a genius or what?" Trey winked, his grin jaunty.

"I wouldn't go that far." She thanked the waiter, who pulled out a chair for her. "But you did good. Thank you."

"Why, anything for my wife."

She laughed and couldn't remember the last time she had. It had been before her father's betrayal, before she left a world she'd loved, never to return again.

Chapter Three

"Relax." Trey handed the menus to the waiter, who hurried away with their order. "The train's pulling out. That no-good hired gun could have scouted the cars and climbed right back onto that platform. He could be wiring ahead to his cohorts that you weren't on this train."

He'd meant to comfort her, but the worry lines slashed deep in her brow remained. "Or maybe he did see me. Maybe he's just biding his time—"

"No, men like that don't like to wait. He would have tried to get you off the train before it started to roll."

"Then I have a lot to be thankful for." Her voice wobbled, and above the tinkle of silverware and the clinking of china, her gratefulness rang like the sweetest vibrato, rich and rare. "You kept him from finding me. You kept me safe."

"It was nothing."

"It was everything." Her eyes darkened and she looked away, ready to change the subject.

Josie leaned close, asking Miranda to retie Baby Beth's bonnet strings. With a gentle smile, one that chased the anxiety from her eyes and softened the stark set to a face too beautiful to be so afraid, Miranda tied the tiny ribbons into a plump bow.

There was an innate kindness in her that shone like the first brush of dawn, like new light upon a dark land. Pure and true, she was the kind of woman a man prayed for.

Not that he was in the market for a wife, no sir, he was busy enough with his work. He'd given love a try once and it hadn't been to his liking. He didn't have the time for a woman's demands, no matter how fine the woman. But that didn't mean he couldn't appreciate one.

"He must be a real jackass." Trey thanked the waiter who returned with a hot pot of steeping tea.

"Who?" Miranda reached for the gleaming pot.

"Your fiancé." He scooped up the dainty gold-rimmed cup for her to fill. "You mentioned him, remember?"

"I hoped you might forget all about that." She poured, but the stream of fragrant tea that spilled into his china cup wasn't steady or even.

"Did I mention in addition to all my other attributes that I have an excellent memory?"

"You're also conceited. Another flaw." A hint of a smile tugged at the tight line of her mouth, but when she lifted the teapot, his cup full to the brim, she miscalculated and hot liquid plopped onto the back of his hand.

He jerked back, tea sloshing over the rim and onto his other hand. He cursed mildly, the burns hot and stinging. He set the cup in its saucer, already nearly full with spilled tea, and reached for his napkin.

She was faster. Heat stained her face as she dabbed at the mess. "I can't believe I was so clumsy. Are you hurt?"

"Not a bit. Nothing lasting, anyway."

"This time I didn't do it, Uncle Trey." Josie, pleased because she excelled at spilling drinks at the table, clapped her hands. For an instant she looked more like the little girl he remembered, eyes bright and sparkling, the smallest pleasure alight on her pixie face.

For a moment, it was as if the past had returned, that Madeline could be alive and well, and this child's heart whole. His chest tightened as the moment passed. The train rattled, shuddering against the steep slope as they climbed in elevation. The gladness drained from Josie's face and she climbed into his lap, quiet and subdued.

Miranda noticed as she added cream and sugar to her own cup, took Josie's vacant seat between them, and offered the girl a sip. Trey's heart squeezed a little tighter. He was grateful to this woman, a stranger, who'd taken the time to comfort a frightened little girl.

He wondered what road lay ahead for him and Josie. He didn't think he could keep her, despite his sister's wishes. There was so much he couldn't give a child, even though he wanted to.

The waiter arrived with their first course, steaming clam chowder garnished with bits of green onion and tiny oyster-shaped crackers. Their server had the foresight to bring a small bowl of those special crackers just for Josie.

"I hate to admit it, but you were right." Miranda dipped her spoon into the thick chowder. "He is a jack-ass."

Oh, yes, the fiancé. "He would have to be to let a pretty lady like you run off on him."

"I never said—"

"Did I mention I also read minds?" His dark eyes glimmered, full of mischief. "Just another one of my many talents—"

"Flaws, you mean." She startled when the door opened at the end of the elegant car.

A well-dressed man, distinguished in a black suit,

stepped inside, and she relaxed. "Lewis wasn't the man I thought he was."

"Ah, the real truth of love relationships." Trey scooted Josie closer to the table, so reaching the bowl of crackers wasn't such a long stretch for her. "One day the fantasy wears off, and you're left with reality—a plain man with flaws and failures, not some shining hero of your heart."

"Now you think you're an expert on a woman's love life, is that it?"

"Well, I have observed quite a few situations—"

"It's not like that." Irritation sliced through her, and she frowned at him. It was her experience in life that men took a very cynical view of love, and it bothered her to no end, as if women were made to love and care for others but did not deserve great affection and esteem in return. "Lewis is an awful man. He's charming and—"

"Debonair and dashing?" Trey cocked one brow, attempting to tease her away from her anger.

Well, she wasn't about to be cajoled out of anything. "Yes, that's right. He thinks he's handsome and intelligent and so very fine, but he's the worst sort of man."

"Just like me?" Trey's brow crooked higher.

Oh, she would not grin. She wouldn't. "As a matter of fact, he's exactly like you."

"Surely a man any beautiful woman ought to run screaming away from." He might be humoring her, but the light in his eyes was fading, as if he sensed what she was about to say.

She pushed aside her soup, no longer hungry. The man, who'd stepped into the car earlier, settled into the table behind her. Aware, she lowered her voice. "I did run away screaming."

Her palms prickled and every muscle in her body began to quake. The pleasant dining car faded away until memory dominated her senses. She saw again the parlor's drapes pulled tight against the midday sun and smelled the fragrance of freshly blooming roses.

She closed her eyes, hoping to stop the memory, but she still heard the click of the big double doors closing, locking her in with the man she'd given her heart to. She'd escaped him before he could rape her, but he'd blackened both her eyes, and when she'd leaped out the window running, she'd believed her father would protect her.

But Father only handed her back to Lewis, his words destroying every illusion she'd had about her life.

"I'm sorry he hurt you." Trey's words rumbled low like thunder, as powerful as a storm, more comforting than any man's voice had the right to be. "Is there—"

"No." She stopped him before he could offer more than she could endure. She didn't want to go back, she didn't want to dwell on what could never be changed. Or remember more of that day, of what she could not face again.

"I'm fine, really. I got away before he could take from me what no man should have by force. I—" Her voice wobbled, and she hated it. She hated that he could coax secrets and wounds from her heart with such ease.

"He's the one after you?" A muscle jumped in Trey's jaw, and there was no longer even a glimmer of humor. His gaze was as harsh as any bounty hunter's and twice as determined.

She shook her head. "My father. He's a powerful man. He's dead set on this marriage. Lewis is his protégé, a young doctor he's groomed in his own image. He wants him for a son-in-law."

"Your father thinks so little of you, his own daughter?" Trey's words came low, but his anger boomed.

"My father is a man just like you." She lifted one brow and waited. "Charming, debonair..."

"Aw, but he obviously lacks my kinder nature toward the fairer sex."

"Obviously." She almost smiled, their gazes latching together.

She felt it like light to her soul. She saw past the dark brown of his eyes into a deeper place, where his concern gathered with a quiet strength she'd known in no other man. A strength of character and heart, not of brawn and force. Her hand trembled, and she was glad she wasn't holding the spoon, because she would have dropped it.

The train jerked, breaking the motion, and the renewed howl of the storm slammed into the north side of the car with inhuman force. Josie cried out, tears rising, the trauma of the wreck and losing her parents stark against the other passengers' gasps of concern.

The brief smile was gone, the fears of an orphaned and injured girl returned. Trey wrapped his arms around the girl, holding her close, reassuring her. The door at the end of the car banged open and the bounty hunter strolled in.

Fear ran like ice water through her veins, and Miranda eased from her chair. She knew Trey was armed, but he was holding a child. There would be no confrontation, no risk to Josie or anyone else in the car. There would be no gunfight, no bullets firing wild.

The hired gun's gaze fastened on her and she felt the impact, cold and lethal, as cutting as a blizzard's wind. The train shuddered again, doubling the sound of Josie's cries. Trey, busy with the child, hadn't noticed the man behind him, and maybe it would stay that way.

She took a quick breath, gathered her courage and stood from the seat.

"I need to excuse myself," she whispered, so he would

think she was headed to the water closet. It was better to repay him this way for his kindness. She wanted him safe. After all, he had Josie to protect.

She'd never wanted her freedom to come at the price of anyone else coming to harm. Her days of dreaming dreams and wishing on first-stars-of-the-night were past. There was no sense in running. She would give herself up before the bounty hunter decided to fire his gun again.

As if reading her mind, the ruffian slipped one gun from his holster, the smooth glide of steel against leather lost in the noisy car. Cocked, then aimed.

Her chest felt so tight, it was impossible to breathe. She couldn't let Trey face down an armed man. She couldn't! Her knees wobbled and her throat was dry, but she managed to keep breathing and put one uncertain foot in front of the other.

"Hold on a minute." A man's voice—it wasn't Trey's—boomed with heated fury and cold threat. The well-dressed man seated at the adjacent table now towered behind her, gun drawn, his aim steady on the threatening man. "I'm a Pinkerton agent, and she is *my* quarry. Back down, bounty hunter, if you value your life."

Out of the corner of her eye, Miranda saw Trey set Josie in a vacant seat. He rose, a man of might who stole her breath and made her heart stammer. He wrapped his hand around the Colt's handle and drew, standing between her and the bounty hunter, as strong as legend, as powerful as myth.

She did not doubt that he would protect her. But it wasn't protection she needed.

It was her freedom.

It was all she wanted.

"Put down the gun, bounty hunter." Trey nodded toward a neighboring table, where diners turned with gasps and exclamations. This was not the kind of behavior they expected to see in their first-class dining car.

Miranda took one step toward the door, afraid to draw attention to herself but longing—how she longed—to escape.

"We're being robbed!" one woman cried, her hand flying to cover the flickering diamonds at her throat, more gemstones flashing on her fingers.

Cries of fear and outrage exploded like dynamite in a tunnel. Miranda ran. Chaos reigned as the men in the car banded together against the bounty hunter, whose shouts for her to stop were drowned by the cries of outraged women. Above it all Trey's voice lifted, in control, determined to keep his word.

At the threshold, Miranda risked one glance back. Josie sat at the table, hugging Baby Beth tight, tears glimmering like stars. There was no time to say goodbye, not if she wanted to escape. And it tore at her heart that all she could offer the girl now was a wink and a wave. Then she was gone, dashing through the door.

A flimsy roof overhead hardly protected her from the force of the blizzard as she pushed open the door that led into the first-class cars.

She hurried through them, not knowing if another Pinkerton agent could be watching. Heart pounding, she hurried down the aisle as the train bucked and groaned. The blizzard outside was worsening.

Where should she go? She couldn't jump. They were in the middle of the Rockies and there were no more stops, not with the way the train was creeping along, at least not for a long while.

As she pushed open the door at the front of the car, a man in the back stood, pulling his well-cut jacket over the gleaming handle of a revolver. Heavens, there were more of them.

She slammed the door shut and stood facing the sleeping cars. No, she wasn't likely to escape in here. Besides, she'd rather not be captured by an armed man within reach of an empty bed. Not after what she'd learned of human nature.

She faced the ice-cold wind that sliced right through her. Sandlike pellets of ice scoured her, stinging her face and unprotected hands as she gasped for breath. The bitter, vicious wind drove the air right out of her lungs. Lord, if she jumped she wouldn't survive ten minutes in this.

But the door behind her was kicked open and a man filled the threshold, dark and deadly, the nose of his gun swinging toward her. She would not go back, not on her life.

But what should she do? She wouldn't let him catch her. She *wouldn't*. She climbed up the waist-high steel barrier. The wind battered her face and the snowy banks whipped by at an alarming rate.

Jump? No, it was far too dangerous. But surely there was a way…

Inspiration struck. As fast as she could, she swept off her bonnet and, on a prayer, leaped out into the storm.

"Miranda! Come back." Josie's wail brought Trey around as he tried to stop the Pinkerton agent from taking off after Miranda.

"I'm in my perfect legal rights," the man bit out as he shoved past Trey.

"Did that young lady do something wrong?" the woman with the diamonds wondered, as the security guard barreled into the car and Trey scooped Josie out of her seat.

"Miranda left. And w-we d-didn't even get to f-finish the crackers." The girl buried her face in his neck, holding on with all her strength.

Trey could feel her need, and he knew all that Miranda had done for them, for no reason other than her caring heart. She loved children—it had shone in her eyes as bright as the apology when she'd fled the car.

She'd made the decision to leave his side, when he could have protected her, damn it. He kicked open the door and bounded down the aisle of the next car, the news of the supposed robber buzzing in the air. He didn't see Miranda, so he kept going. She wasn't in the next car, but up ahead, the door slammed shut. A bad, bad feeling curled around his spine, and he started to run.

"I'm scared, Uncle Trey," Josie whispered against his neck. "Where's Miranda?"

Alone and afraid and needing my help. He couldn't explain why, but he knew she had no one else. It was his job, he'd spent many years helping women who slipped into his clinic on the run from their husbands, unable to pay for the broken bones he set and splinted or the lacerations to their head and face he stitched.

Maybe it was because as a very small boy he'd seen his own mother treated this way during her second marriage. Finally his stepfather had had enough of Trey and sent him to an orphanage. The horror and shame still lived with him, that his mother had endured a hellish existence in order to provide a home and meals for her children. As if by helping a woman with fear in her eyes and a man on her trail, he could make a difference now.

No, it was more than that this time. Miranda wasn't a stranger who'd knocked at his office door. She'd shown him a part of her he'd forgotten existed in this world sometimes without hope and mercy. In a world where a little girl as sweet as Josie could lose her parents. In a world where people grew ill and died and he could do nothing to save them.

He wanted to know he could make a difference somehow, make a small piece of the world right again for a woman with gentle eyes and a smile as bright as an angel's. It didn't hurt that she'd been the first woman in a long time to make him feel every inch a man and forget his profession, to feel need and excitement and warmth.

He knocked the door open and nearly collided with a man in the small passageway between the first-class cars. The Pinkerton agent.

"She jumped. I saw her hit the snowbank." The same agent he'd overpowered in the dining car shouted to be heard above the howling wind. "That's why we were quietly following her. Why we didn't want a scene. Now she's dead, and there goes my damn bonus."

She'd jumped? She'd been so desperate that she'd choose death? *I failed her.* Trey's stomach turned, and he laid a hand on Josie's back, keeping her safe in the shelter beneath his chin.

Emotion twisted through him, a mix of fury and grief so sharp he didn't think he could control it. It quaked through him and he fisted his hands, gritted his teeth. Josie needed him. He couldn't go leaping out into that storm. Yet every part of him screamed to do it.

It killed him to turn around and seek the shelter of the snug passenger car, safe from harm and the weather. Conversations littered the air. He paid no attention as he slumped into the first seat he came to, no longer able to stand. His knees shook, his legs shook, even his arms were trembling. He couldn't believe she was gone. Just like that, she would choose death over relying on him—on anyone—for help.

He bowed his head as the storm outside the train worsened, forcing them to a slow crawl. There was speculation if they would have enough speed to crest the mountain peak, or if they were in danger of crashing, just as the train had done last month.

Josie's locket caught the light, and he lifted it from the front of her wool dress, felt the light weight and warmth in his hand. Filled with a mother's love, Miranda had said.

And he'd failed to protect her.

Chapter Four

The train jerked to a stop. Miranda sat up and pushed her way off the extra baggage piled in the corner. Was it safe? Had they reached a town?

Light splashed through the unsealed cracks in the car. She eased through the darkness, leaned against the uneven painted boards and squinted through the narrow slat.

Yes, it looked like a train platform. Relief shivered through her. If she slipped off now, the men after her might never know where she was. Maybe they still believed she'd jumped and given up their search. *Maybe*.

But memory of the bounty hunter's flat dark eyes frightened her. He was a ruthless one, the leader of determined men. She'd been eluding him for the last six months.

He was smart enough not to be fooled by a bonnet in the snow.

Lights glowed like faint beacons through the shroud of the storm, calling her out of the corner and toward the closed door. She caught her toe on an edge of a trunk and her shin slammed hard into another piece of luggage as she fell. Pain felt far away—she feared her feet were frostbitten.

Just as her hands were. She couldn't feel the edge of
the door as she tugged it free, but she could hear the creak
of steel as the opening widened. Driving snow fell like a
veil, obscuring even the platform from view.

Thank heavens for this storm. It folded around her as
she stepped out of the car, isolating her from the rest of
the world. Ice scoured her face as she hunched into the
wind. The wind beat against her, but she gritted her teeth
and stumbled forward. Pain shot up her too-cold legs in
fast, knifelike slashes.

The faint glow of light at the edge of the platform
seemed too far away.

Just keep going. She concentrated on that light, and it
guided her across the confusing world of wind and snow.
The world was one icy blur, and she felt alone even
though there had to be other travelers struggling against
the storm.

*You're safe, Miranda. Keep walking. You can't quit
now.* A gust of wind blew her backward.

When she turned around, the train was nothing but the
faint glow of lit windows in the dark cold night. *It looks
like you've escaped them. For now.*

Suddenly the wind eased, and she stumbled against the
protective wall of the ticket booth, closed tight for the
night. The snow thinned, and she leaned against the frozen
board, struggling to catch her breath.

The shrill train's whistle blasted apart the night. Heart
pounding, she waited to see if anyone was following her.
The wind died in a sudden gust, leaving the snow to fall
in graceful swirls to the ground and illuminating her to
anyone who stood on the icy platform.

Panicked, she stumbled deeper into the shadows. The
train shuddered, and the engines roared. The glow of
lighted windows shadowed both the falling snow and the

edge of the platform where a shadowed figure stood, surveying the night.

The whistle blasted again and he hopped back aboard, his predatory movements familiar. The bounty hunter.

Had he been fooled after all? She pressed deeper into the shadows and held her breath. The clackety-clack of the churning wheels made the whole platform rumble as the train slid into the dark, taking away her adversary.

For now. Relief sliced through her, hard as the blizzard's wind. She'd escaped him again.

"I'm awful cold, Uncle Trey," a thin voice belled above the howl of the tireless wind. "Where's your house?"

"Not far at all," Trey's whiskey-warm voice answered. "You hold on to me tight and before you know it, we'll be sitting in front of a hot fire and maybe, just maybe, I'll warm up a cup of hot chocolate."

The veil of snow hid all but the shape of the man and child from her sight. Her chest ached and she wished she could step out. But he'd met the Pinkerton agent face-to-face. He'd seen the bounty hunter. He must have heard she was an heiress and that her father had offered a small fortune for her return.

The sweetness she'd felt with him and Josie remained in her heart. She would not forget them. She would not forget the man who'd made her laugh.

"Miss Miranda? Miss Miranda, is that you?" Josie called out above the sounds of the storm.

What should she do now? Through the curtain of snow and darkness Miranda watched as Trey strode closer. Brushed by darkness, touched by a flicker of light, he held Josie in one steely arm. His Stetson kept both the shadows and the snow from his face.

She couldn't hide any longer. Miranda stepped out of the darkness. "Hello, Josie. Trey."

"It *is* you." He fought the urge to reach out and touch her, to see if the silk of her hair and the smooth angles of her face were real and not a dream. "The Pinkerton agent saw you jump from the train and—"

Miranda stepped farther out of the shadows, courage and grace. She was caked with ice and snow and shivering so that her teeth chattered. Her skirt was torn beneath the hem of her cloak and blood dotted her sleeve.

He still couldn't believe it. "We all thought you'd jumped to your death."

"No, I just made them think I did." She brushed the snow from her eyes with one mittened hand. She glanced over her shoulder where the train had disappeared, the platform now empty, sheened with thick ice. "Are you going to contact them?"

"Not on my life." His throat ached. "You're the woman who gave Josie her good-luck charm."

The wariness in Miranda's eyes changed, and she bit her bottom lip. She looked vulnerable, lost in the storm. She brushed a mittened fingertip beneath Josie's chin. "See? Didn't I tell you that locket was magic? You're safe and sound, just like I promised."

"Your locket sure worked real good."

Pleasure lit Miranda's face, and as the storm swirled around her, she looked like an angel, not a ghost, alive, not part of the shadows. "Every time you're afraid, you just make a wish on that locket, and everything will be fine. I promise."

She gazed up at him with eyes so wide, his heart stopped beating. "It was good seeing you again, Trey. You take good care of Josie."

She eased back into the unlit shadows, choosing the

darkness to the light. Again she glanced over her shoulder into the darkness, where the tracks stretched unseen for mile upon mile.

Snow tapped to the hard ground, veiling her as she vanished from his sight.

"Wait!" He hurried after her, but the platform felt empty. He couldn't see anything in the storm.

She was gone, just like that, just as she'd done on the train when he'd thought her dead and lost forever. His chest balled up tight.

"Miranda! Miranda, don't go." Josie's distress keened in the harsh night. "Uncle Trey, you gotta find her."

"Did you see where she went?"

The wind slammed hard, driving him back a few steps. The blizzard curled around them, dimming the already faint lights of town.

There. He caught a shifting shape and headed down the street, where the livery barn shadowed the wind. "Miranda."

Her shoulders stiffened. She kept walking. The wind tangled her skirts around her ankles, and she stumbled, but caught herself before he could reach her. "You're following me."

"Usually the pretty women chase after me, but in the dark it's hard to be swayed by my good looks and charm, so I have to chase you." He held out his free hand and the two bags—his medical bag and her satchel. "I have something of yours."

"My clothes. Thank you." She smiled sunshine as the blizzard howled around them. Her gloved fingers brushed his and heat snapped up his arm.

She took her satchel with a flourish. "I figured the Pinkerton men would confiscate this."

"I just didn't tell them I had your satchel. It didn't

seem right. We thought you were dead, and those agents were mourning the loss of a fat bonus. I just didn't have the heart to interrupt their grief.''

"So, I guess you know about the reward.''

She might shine like a rare diamond, but she was lost, alone and afraid. His heart tumbled. He'd always been a soft touch for anyone in need. "Is there a reward? For returning your satchel?''

"You know I meant something else.'' She brushed snow from her lashes.

"Right. You're afraid I'm going to turn you in. Now, I could hand you over to the sheriff, if you turn out to be a dangerous felon, but it's a bad storm. In another minute all three of us are going to be icicles. So why don't we just find a diner and have supper.''

Could it be true? Maybe some good luck finally was catching up with her. "Are you saying you'll forget I'm on the run if I buy you a meal?''

"No. I'm the man. I'll buy.''

Even in the dark, his grin dazzled. Though he was half frozen in the wind, humor sparkled in his eyes. The strong line of his shoulders and chest blocked the wind and most of the snow. He'd saved her on the train, just like he was doing now.

"Goody!'' Josie managed to say, despite her chattering teeth. "I'm real hungry, too. Miranda, do you like fried chicken when it's really crispy?''

"Absolutely. Trey, she's cold. You should get her inside.''

"Then come help me. There's an inn just a few steps from here.''

Miranda hesitated. What should she say? She needed to find a room and keep quiet. Make sure the bounty hunter hadn't sent one or two of his men to check out the town. "I can't."

"Not even for fried chicken?" Josie's teeth chattered again. "It's my very favorite."

Miranda hadn't wanted anything this much in a long time. "I am looking for a place to stay, and I don't know where to start. I suppose I could go with you."

"Then the locket you gave Josie is working." Trey leaned forward, his chin grazing her cheek, speaking so only she could hear. "Because it brought you to us."

A roaring fire crackled in the inn's dining room and drove the ice from her bones. Miranda shrugged out of her cloak, startled when Trey caught the garment by the collar and helped her out of it.

He hung her cloak on a peg by the hearth. Other jackets lined the wall, collecting heat for the other diners in the room.

I shouldn't be here. She could feel it. She should stay hidden. She may have fooled the bounty hunter, but he would be back. As Trey led them to a table near the hearth, every one of the six customers waved greetings.

This was a close-knit community where a stranger would be noticed.

"Let me." Trey pulled out her chair, towering over her, mountain-strong.

The breath stalled in her chest. Her skin tingled as she slipped past him. She sat down, knowing he was behind her. Having a meal with him was a very bad idea.

"Do they have mashed potatoes here, too?" Josie gazed up at her uncle, as if she had to make sure. "And not the lumpy kind?"

"The smoothest in the entire town." He tucked her into

the chair beside Miranda. "Does Baby Beth like potatoes, too?"

"She's a baby, Uncle Trey. She's got a bottle." Josie rolled her eyes.

Trey's grin flashed, sending shafts of heat straight through Miranda's heart.

The waitress appeared to take their order, on friendly terms with Trey. When she left, Trey leaned across the table, the candle flickering between them, and caught hold of her left hand.

He turned her palm over in his to study a gash, puffy and darkened by dried blood. "Let me bandage this for you. You could use a few stitches."

"It's not that deep." She slipped away from his touch. "I'll tend to it myself."

"You're the independent sort. I noticed that." He brushed his finger against the edge of her sleeve. "That's a bad bruise on your wrist. Let me look at it. Did you do that escaping from those agents?"

Fire scorched across her skin, and she hauled her injured hand beneath the table. Out of his reach. "I cut my hand on the rail when I pretended to jump."

"What did you really do?"

"I swung over to the ladder on the side of the car. It was within reach."

"Pretty dangerous." But judging by the light in her eyes, she'd taken pleasure outwitting those Pinkerton agents. "I've never met a woman who could climb up the side of a moving train."

"It wasn't moving very fast." She dipped her chin enough to hide the shadows in her eyes.

He wondered what injuries lay within, ones he couldn't see. "You stayed on the roof the entire train ride?"

"No, I climbed down into the baggage car and took shelter there."

"Did you hurt your wrist on the ladder, too?"

"You're relentless, do you know that?"

He pushed back his chair. "Just add it to my list of character attributes."

"Flaws, you mean. All right, I was crawling across the roof of one of the passenger cars and a gust of wind pushed me into the metal lip on the roof."

She shrugged, as if she'd done nothing unusual. She didn't fool him, she was a woman of courage and grit. A combination he admired.

He knelt beside her and cradled her injured hand in his. Her wrist was delicate, the skin like silk. She still felt cold, oh so cold.

"I don't need a doctor's help." She tried to wrestle her arm from him, but she lacked strength.

She *was* injured. "You could have a fracture, Miranda."

"I can move my fingers just fine."

He unbuttoned her sleeve and ran his fingertips across the inside of her wrist. Her skin was purple-tinged, but her wrist wasn't broken. "Remember what I said on the train?"

"You said a great deal on the train." Her skin seemed to burn beneath the gentle stroke of his finger.

"I'm your good-luck charm for as long as you need one. So relax and let me take care of this." He grabbed his medical bag from beneath the table, then worked with efficiency.

Swabbing the wound stung a little. Then he wrapped the white muslin around her palm and between her thumb and forefinger, then around again. His fingertips grazed her skin. She burned and tingled from the contact.

He was strength and gentleness. He was bold and caring. He deftly knotted the last bit of muslin into place and then moved away. It felt as if the heat drained from her body and she thirsted for more of his touch.

She'd never had this reaction to a man before. Why was she feeling this now?

Throughout the meal, Miranda watched the windows. The blizzard beat against the panes with inhuman force. Once, she saw a shadow against the glass but couldn't be sure.

She tried to relax and enjoy the meal while Trey teased smiles from Josie and tried to do the same to her. But her stomach was twisted so tight she could barely eat. She couldn't shake the feeling the bounty hunter was out there, even though she'd seen him reboard the train as it departed.

Any number of his men could have disembarked during the storm, as she had. The snow had been so thick, she never would have seen them. *What if they are out there looking for me?*

Earlier, she felt certain she'd evaded them. But instead of quietly finding a room and staying hidden, she was here in plain sight in the light and the warmth. Anyone could see her through the glass.

This was a bad idea. And growing worse every time Trey flashed her a charming grin. Had she ever seen a more handsome man? She couldn't think of one. The square cut of his jaw, the strongly chiseled face, the jaunty grin and sparkling eyes, that was just for starters. His shoulders looked sculpted from pure bronze, his personality glittered with humor and radiated compassion.

Every time he flashed that one-sided grin, she felt hotter. More aware of herself as a woman. Sure, she was lonely. But she would have to be in a coma not to respond to this mesmerizing man.

She didn't even get the chance to pay her share of the bill. The waitress didn't even bring it. Apparently Trey was a frequent patron because he was billed monthly.

"I never have time to cook," he explained, draining the last of his coffee cup. "I'm always working."

"A doctor's life." Miranda knew it well. "How long have you been practicing here?"

"Five years. A small-town doctor isn't a rich man, but I like what I do." His voice rumbled with affection. "Josie, you've got dark circles under your eyes. Time to get you home."

"Can Miranda come, too?"

"Well, she's certainly welcome." Trey quirked one brow.

"No." She saw right through that look of his. "I'm not staying in your house, Mr. Dashing and Debonair."

"I guess there's the small matter of your reputation."

"Exactly." Heat flushed her face and a flicker at the window caught her attention. Someone on the boardwalk? Or just her imagination?

Trey watched her carefully. "The wind is getting worse. If this keeps up, the whole town will shut down. It's almost there now. Look, there's the sheriff."

A definite shadow moved outside the window. The door swung open. Frigid wind drove through the dining room. The rugged lawman shouldered the door closed and crunched through the ice thick on the floor. The waitress hurried to speak with him.

Maybe it had been the sheriff outside, and not a bounty hunter.

Trey circled the table and wrapped one hand around the

back of her chair. She stood, and she tingled from head to toe. "Are you going to stay here? This is a good inn."

"I might." She gazed at the window, remembering the frigid walk from the train depot. "I don't want to go out again. I just got warm. Do you and Josie have a long walk home?"

"Not far at all." Trey scooped the little girl up into his arms.

She stifled a yawn. "We don't hafta go outside again."

"Sorry, Red." Trey's affection came light and gentle. He settled the girl on his hip. "That big yawn is a sign. I'd better get her home and in bed."

Now that it was time, she didn't want them to go. For a little while, the loneliness in her heart had fled. But it was creeping back again. And a long lonely night stretched ahead.

Miranda followed Trey through the empty dining room. The lawman left with a bang of the door, and the waitress announced they were locking up early. Sheriff Kelley was closing down the town.

"You'll be comfortable here. I know the innkeeper." Trey reached for his jacket. "Rest easy, Miranda. I'll come by tomorrow."

She almost told him not to bother but held back the words. Why complicate things? She had her life to fight for. He had Josie to protect.

Trey shrugged into his coat. "Let's get you wrapped up, Red."

"Baby Beth needs her cloak, too."

"She sure does."

Miranda watched as Trey patiently sorted through the bundle of wool, found the doll's matching cloak and handed it to Josie. He knelt down beside his niece and helped her into her heavy cloak. With care, he wrapped the scarf around her neck and worked the cap over her head.

His tenderness wasn't feigned, but came from the heart. As Josie snuggled in Trey's strong arms, sheltered and safe, Miranda's arms felt empty, and she couldn't help dreaming. Couldn't help wishing that one day there would be a child of her own she could hold and comfort and make the world right for.

"I didn't see any of those men following you get off the train. I thought you might like to know." Trey faced the door. "Do you want me to watch over you? I can stay."

"Not necessary." She was better off alone. "Good night, you two."

"'Night, Miranda." Josie peered over Trey's shoulder as he pushed out the door.

The night and storm enfolded him, stealing them away from her. The door clamored shut, snow drifted to melt on the floor, and once again she was alone.

"This is your house?" Josie stood in the dark, clutching her doll tight, her voice wobbly.

"It looks better if you can see it." He felt through the dark for the match tin and lit a lamp. Light danced to life, illuminating the log walls and sparse furniture.

Not a home for a child, that was sure. He'd have to do something about that. First thing tomorrow.

"For tonight, you're going to sleep in my room." He didn't mind the sofa. He swept the girl onto his hip, knowing her leg had to be hurting.

"Don't I get a room?"

"Sure. But we've got to get it all ready for you. I can take you shopping as soon as the storm breaks." He shouldered open the bedroom door. "You like to shop, right?"

Josie nodded, her fine red curls catching on his whiskered chin.

Already, he'd disappointed her. In truth, he hadn't been prepared when his sister's lawyer contacted him. His work occupied every spare moment of his life lately and he'd barely had time to make full-time arrangements with Mrs. Stoltz. Now he regretted not doing more.

He pulled back the dark green quilt. The clean flannel sheets smelled of soap and winter sunshine. "C'mon. Climb in."

"I'm still wearin' my clothes, Uncle Trey." Josie rubbed her eyes, tired and sleepy. "I need my nightie."

"We don't have it yet. Your trunks are still at the train station because it's too dangerous to have someone deliver them tonight. You can sleep in your long underwear. They'll keep you warm."

"Okay." Josie sounded weary, and he knelt to pluck at the row of buttons marching down her back.

In no time the dress and her shoes were off and laid on the seat of the nearby chair. He carried her and Baby Beth to the waiting bed, unlatched her brace and helped her settle between the sheets.

"I could read to you for a while, if you want." He reached for one of the books on the nearby shelf, looking for one appropriate for a little girl. "I know you like being read to."

"I'm tired." Josie rolled on her side, her arms wrapped tight around her doll. "G'night, Uncle Trey."

"Sleep tight, sweet one." He pulled the quilt up to Josie's chin. Wetness dampened his fingers.

"I miss my mama." Her words came muffled by the covers. "I miss her so much."

"Me, too, honey." Trey laid his hand on her back and felt the shake of her sobs. She didn't want to be held, but stayed huddled in a ball until sleep claimed her.

When he reached to turn down the crystal lamp's wick, Miranda's locket caught the light, burning steady and bright. When the wick sputtered and the flame died, the locket held a reflection for just a second longer, then darkness filled the room.

Chapter Five

The blizzard continued to howl between the buildings like a trapped wolf. Wrapped well against the early morning temperatures, Miranda kept her head bowed to the wind and tried not to slip on the boards.

Many merchants hadn't opened up yet, or were still out attempting to shovel off the boardwalk. Snow drove so hard it was impossible to see the street beside her.

It was her lucky day. The mercantile was open. A striped awning sheltered the front door, where a freshly shoveled path led into the store.

A bell jangled overhead, the scents of wood smoke, leather, the pickle barrel and a blend of hundreds of other scents welcomed her. A potbellied stove in the middle of the store glowed red, puffing out heat.

"'Mornin'." An older gentleman straightened from his chair near the warmth.

"Good morning." She slipped between rows of canned goods and tugged her shopping list out of her pocket.

"Miranda!" Josie limped toward her, locket sparkling against her blue wool dress. "Are you shoppin', too?"

"I firmly believe that shopping is a girl's duty." Warmth gathered behind her breastbone, and she knelt so she was eye-level with the child. "You've got an empty basket."

"I can't decide. I'm tryin', but it's hard." Josie's brow wrinkled. "Uncle Trey doesn't know anything about shoppin'."

"Men never do. It's one of their many flaws."

"I heard that." Trey's boots knelled on the floorboards. "My flaws are only good ones. And Josie, I can, too, shop."

Miranda gazed up the strong column of Trey's legs, encased in soft denim, past the breadth of his chest. Her heart kicked just from looking at him. Heavens, he was a handsome man.

"You can't, either, Uncle Trey." Josie shook her head. "I gotta have curtains and not plain white ones."

"White curtains?" Miranda lifted one brow. "Surely you can spring for a nice print."

Trey held up his hands. "What's wrong with white? It matches everything."

"I see your problem, Josie." Miranda tried hard not to look at Trey again. "It looks like you need help with that flawed uncle of yours."

"I may be the best doctor this side of the Badlands, but I'm confused. I don't know what's wrong with white. We can have white curtains, white quilts." Trey gestured toward the ready-made items spread out on a back counter. "Maybe blue?"

"But it's for *my* bedroom." Josie grabbed hold of Miranda's hand. "'Cept we don't got a bed yet, and I'm only five."

"You need help, Josie. You can't trust a man to do a woman's job." Miranda took a breath, heart pounding. "I could help you out this morning. I have a few hours to spare until the train comes."

"The train?" Josie's brow furrowed. "You can't leave. You just can't. You got off at my new town and everything."

Miranda gently brushed soft red curls away from the girl's sad eyes, feeling Trey's scrutiny like a physical touch. "This isn't my new home, Josie, not like it's yours. I have to go."

"Oh." Josie blinked, and tears gleamed there, honest and aching.

Trey's face darkened, the jaunty grin gone from his mouth, leaving only a stark strength. "Miranda, where do you plan on going? There won't be a train today."

"I have a schedule right here in my pocket."

"The passes are closed due to the storm."

"Closed?" That didn't sound like a good thing. Not good at all. Maybe for the train, but not for her. "The trains will run as soon as the storm's over, right?"

"It's not that simple. You're in Montana Territory now. The word is that there won't be a train for a few days after the storm or more. Maybe an entire week. We've got twelve-foot drifts out there."

"A week?" She couldn't stay here for a week. That would give the bounty hunters too much time to backtrack. Now what did she do? "I can't leave until the storm clears."

"No one leaves this town or enters it until then. We're rimmed by mountains on all four sides, and the teamsters' routes take as long to clear as the tracks."

"We'll see." She'd been in worse straits and figured her way out of them.

"Will you really help me, Miranda?" Josie clung tightly to Trey with one hand, and Baby Beth with the other. "Mama made my other bedroom, and now I only got Uncle Trey."

Trey gazed down at her, sizzling male power. "Yes, Miranda, help us. I'm woefully inadequate."

It had been so long since she'd felt like this, full and alive, as if she could make a difference. As if she had worth.

But what if one of the bounty hunter's men had spent the night here, too?

Either way, she was trapped in this town until the storm passed. "Okay, I'll help you out. Let's take a look at these quilts again. Tell me which ones you like."

"I like the dotted one." Josie ambled away from Trey's grip. "And the flowers. Do you like them?"

"Absolutely."

Miranda let Josie study the two patterns she liked for a long moment. Trey didn't leave. He stood behind them, his presence as hard to ignore as the blizzard outside. Every hair on the back of her neck tingled, as if his look were a touch.

Why did her skin sparkle, as if waiting for his caress? After how Lewis had tried to hurt her, the last thing she wanted was a man's affections.

Every time she looked up, Trey's gaze met hers. Every time Josie limped to him, eager to show her uncle every item she'd decided to buy, he grinned.

Why on earth did his smile make the emptiness in her chest fade away?

The door blew open with a bang. Miranda protected Josie from the wind as Trey gestured for them to enter his home. Snow drove past them onto the rag rug in the entry, and Miranda took Josie's hand, careful to keep her from slipping as she stepped with her bad leg on the slick wood floor.

"Let me tend to Josie." Miranda knelt down to unbutton the girl's ice-caked cloak. "It's too cold to leave the deliveryman outside."

Trey kicked the door closed, wrapped in snow. "Doesn't look like Mrs. Stoltz is here right now. I hate to ask—"

"Go help the deliveryman." Miranda nodded, peeling Josie out of her cloak. "I have a feeling they don't usually do this in the middle of a storm."

"Whoppler owes me a favor or two." He winked, knelt down to ruffle Josie's red hair. "I'm going to need a doorman."

"I can do it!" Josie lit up. "I know I can."

"The floor's awful slick."

"I can be careful."

Affection flickered in his eyes before he tugged open the door and struggled outside into the mighty storm.

"Are you excited to get your new furniture?" Miranda tugged off Josie's rubber boots.

"Uh-huh. It'll be like I have a home here now."

"I'm glad." Miranda hung the little cloak and scarf onto wall pegs to dry. "Can you go fetch me a towel? I'll get this floor cleaned up, so you won't slip."

Josie took off, her gait hurried but uneven. Miranda slipped out of her wraps, taking a moment to look around. The windows were dark, even for midday, casting the room in shadows.

Honeyed log walls and floors kept the bitter cold out. She knelt before the gray stone fireplace and stirred the banked embers. Exposed to air, they glowed. When she added kindling, they became fire.

She lit a lamp, and she could see the room better. A fine carpet softened the wood floor. The overstuffed sofa looked comfortable, the perfect place to relax after a long day. A book lay open on one of the cushions.

What would it be like to live in a home like this? Snug and cozy, safe from the bitter storm and all her troubles? To curl up on a sofa and read for hours?

"Here's a towel." Josie, breathless with excitement, walked as fast as her injured leg would allow.

"We'd better hurry." Miranda set aside her daydreaming.

She barely finished drying the floor for Josie when a bump sounded at the door. Miranda opened it and let the little girl hold it open for the men.

Trey backed into the room, carrying a heavy piece of furniture. Whoppler's youngest son held up the other end, and the men plowed through the room.

"That's my bureau!" Josie's eyes shone.

An hour passed before the delivery sleigh was unloaded. Each time Josie's happiness grew a notch, her sadness faded away. Each time Miranda felt a little brighter.

"That's it." Trey burst through the door alone and dropped a bundle on the ground. "The blizzard looks like it's blowing out. It's hard to tell, though. It feels like a three-day-er."

"A what?"

"A three-day blizzard. We get them all the time."

"Uncle Trey, you look like a great big snowman!" Josie clapped her hands.

"Watch out, or I'm going to melt all over the floor. Who would treat Mrs. Watts's rash then?" Trey swiped at his jacket, but the driven snow was so thick, it didn't crumble. "I can't find my buttons."

"Lucky for you, I'm here." Heart full, Miranda swept the broom's bristles across his chest. "I've always wanted to take a broom to a man."

"I bet you have." A slow smile crooked his lips and his gaze. Why, it looked as if he was staring at her mouth.

Heat flushed her face. She didn't lift her gaze from the broom as she swatted the stubborn snow. It wouldn't break apart. Like a miniglacier, it remained on his chest, immovable, while she could feel his gaze on her face, soft like a touch.

She knew that touch. She'd felt it before. It was the way Lewis had looked at her when she'd thought... *There.* The snow cracked. One more determined swipe sent the whole of it smashing to the floor.

"Miranda, come see!" Josie pulled aside the oilcloth protecting her purchases. "Oh, the flowers look so pretty."

"Pink roses are my favorite, too." Miranda set the broom aside, but Trey caught her hand.

It was impossible not to look at him. Not to feel a spark of attraction, a spark she didn't want to feel, when his gaze fell to her mouth. "Have I thanked you today?"

"You don't need to."

"I saw the men after you. I saw how badly they wanted you. I just want you to know—" His voice dipped, so only she could hear. "I appreciate what you're doing for Josie. Look how happy she is. Because of you."

"I'm sure it's because of her dashing, debonair uncle with the big billfold."

"Yeah, but I couldn't have picked out the curtains to match the quilt. Or the ten other things you helped her choose. You did a good job with her."

"Hurry up, Uncle Trey." Josie, the shades of grief gone from her face, hugged a lace pillow in one arm and Baby Beth in the other. She limped toward her bedroom door. "I wanna see it all perfect."

"Then we'd better get busy." Trey's lips brushed Miranda's cheek, quick and light, but the contact left a snap of sensation on her flushed skin. "That's for Josie's smile."

Even though she knew what all men were beneath the polish and charm, she liked him. Heaven help her, she *really* liked him.

Mrs. Stoltz returned in time to hem the curtains while the soup warmed. By the time the noon meal was ready, the new curtains, tiny rosebuds printed on creamy white cotton, were, too. Mrs. Stoltz promised to add ruffles later.

Trey hung the curtains across the wide window after the meal, according to his niece's careful instructions.

The rose-and-green braided rug graced the gleaming wood floors in the room's center. Josie's white four-poster bed was tucked in the corner, next to the warmer inside wall. The thick quilt sported appliquéd roses against rose-bud-print calico blocks, a match to the curtains at the window.

"Oh, Miranda." Josie clasped her hands, swirling awkwardly on her injured leg. "It's so pretty!"

"You really like it?"

"I do! It's not like my old room at all, so it won't make me sad."

Miranda felt a mix of emotions, shades of sadness for the girl's loss.

"It's a good thing we had Miranda to help." Trey laid his hammer on the brand-new bureau. "I might have talked you into the polka dots. We'd have had a disaster on our hands. Guess what?"

"What?" Josie gazed up at her uncle. "You got me a surprise?"

"You're too smart. I can't get nothing past you." Trey gently tweaked her nose. "This should keep you and Miranda busy for the rest of the afternoon. Unless you two have designs on the rest of Mrs. Stoltz's chocolate cake.'' He cast his gaze to her.

''The offer of cake is mighty tempting.'' Miranda's heart was warm, filled with the sweetness of the day.

''I'm glad we've tempted you, Miranda.'' Tiny lines crinkled in the corners of Trey's eyes, laugh lines carved there over time. ''Wait until you see my surprise. I'll be right back.''

She tried not to watch him, but her gaze followed him across the room. He looked strong from the back, too, she realized, her breath catching. Wide shoulders, muscled back, lean and powerful thighs.

What was she doing? She should head back to her hotel, study the map she'd bought and figure out the best way to keep ahead of the bounty hunters. This storm wouldn't last forever.

But she didn't want to go. She didn't want this happy feeling to end.

Trey returned with a trunk.

''That's no surprise. Those're my clothes.'' Josie tugged at the clasp.

''That's what you think.'' Trey snapped the lock and lifted the top. ''These are things I saved from your house.''

''Mama's afghan.'' Josie trembled as she pulled the length of wool into her arms.

''And look, things she made.'' Trey lifted delicately crocheted doilies by lacy edges. ''I thought you'd want to have them here with you.''

Josie nodded, tears gleaming.

''Wait, there's something else.'' He fished a brass frame from inside the brimming trunk. ''A likeness of your parents.''

Josie added the daguerreotype to the bundle in her arms and hugged it tight, looking not quite so lost.

Without words, he pressed a kiss against her cheek, his love for her so true.

I don't belong here. Miranda felt it like a punch. She backed out of the room, her step made quiet by the howling storm outside.

Regret filled her, and she could not look away as the big man and little girl fished through the treasures in the chest. Treasures Trey was probably hoping she would help Josie find places for.

She wanted to stay, but it wasn't her right. She tried to keep her step quiet on the parlor's polished wood floors, heading for the door.

"Where do you think you're going?" Trey strode through the parlor as she cinched her sash tight. "What about my chocolate cake bribe?"

"Tempting, but Josie needs you." She reached for her cloak. "Thanks for including me this morning. I'll keep the memories in my heart for a long time."

She stepped out into the cold and closed the door before the honest plea in Trey's eyes changed her mind.

The cold blizzard battered her, isolating her until she felt alone in a world of wind and white. She struggled through the deep snow toward the street. At least, she thought it was the street.

Now she wasn't certain of the direction. Snow pummeled her from every angle. Town was left, right? She turned around. A shadow hazed through the snow.

Fear licked through her, and then she recognized the jaunty angle of a Stetson. Trey broke through the veil of snow.

"Miranda." He leaned close, cheek to hers, to be heard above the wind. "Let me see you home."

"But Josie—"

"Is fine. Mrs. Stoltz is with her." Trey offered his arm. "It's time to let me take care of you."

Take care of you. Lewis's favorite phrase. Miranda couldn't shake the uneasy feeling as Trey tucked her hand against his elbow.

It was too hard to talk. Trey led her the few blocks to town, where the boardwalk provided scant shelter from the storm. Storefront windows gleamed with light. The boardwalk was nearly empty.

With every step she took, he was beside her, towering over her, protecting her from the wind and snow. His arm felt iron-dependable hooked in hers.

Trey pushed open the inn's front door, but her hand caught the wooden frame, too. She would hold her own door. She would take care of herself from here on out. She wasn't looking for someone to shoulder her problems.

Trey swept off his snowy hat. "This doesn't have to be goodbye."

"Yes, it does." She couldn't forget the sight of him and Josie kneeling before the trunk, haloed by lamplight, surrounded by love. She was glad they had each other.

"Thank you for joining us." Trey turned to her in the foyer, where the dining room stretched behind him, empty and bright with lamplight. "You don't know it, but you made my first day as Josie's guardian a good one."

"That's what you are, a guardian?"

"According to the lawyer." He unbuttoned his icy coat, ambling toward the potbellied stove in the lobby. "But truly, I'm not sure what I am. I just know that she's my sister's daughter, and I love her."

"Believe me, love is enough." She heard the ghosts of the past in her voice, and she bit her lip. Those ghosts were best left behind and forgotten. But this day would linger in her heart a long while. "You'll do just fine, a dashing and charming man like you."

He nodded once, slightly, his smile slow as he faced her. "What about you, Miranda? The train will be running by the end of the week, and you'll be short one good-luck charm."

"I'll manage. Josie needs it more than I do." Miranda paused. "Will her leg improve?"

"According to the specialist? No, but then, I'm an optimistic man. There's no telling what the future holds." But his eyes said it all, shadowed with quiet grief. Josie might never walk without a brace again.

Miranda's throat ached. She wished…no, she'd given up wishing on first stars of the night, in believing there could be fairy-tale endings in this cold world. "Maybe her new good-luck charm will help."

"Maybe."

"And if not, then she has you."

"Me?" He shrugged one brawny shoulder. "I'm not sure she got a good bargain in gaining me for a parent. But I'm going to try to do right by her."

"Try? You're going to do fine." What was this man, with the saucy humor and charm, who'd stood up to an armed bounty hunter on the train, that he sounded uncertain now? "You're wonderful with her."

"I'm a good uncle. I don't know how good a father I'm going to be."

"Probably the best one in the territory." She waited until a grin tugged at the corner of his mouth. "Be careful heading back. The wind's rising."

"I'm an old hand at handling blizzards." He caught her gaze, intimate as a touch, as tangible as a breeze to her face. "Josie and I won't forget your kindness. Remember, you have a friend if you ever need one."

His words rang in her heart. She couldn't speak as he stepped out into the storm. The wind roared, fierce and brutal, and the darkness stole him from her sight.

The staircase curled up into the dark, the polished banisters gleaming in the parlor's light. The boards squeaked beneath her step. Her stomach felt tight, her chest fluttery. She'd find another inn. Just in case. It never hurt to be careful.

She packed her satchel and checked out. She'd noticed a quiet hotel just a block away. Lucky for her, they had an available corner room with two big windows and a fireplace to chase away the winter's cold. It would be her home for the duration of the storm, and she was grateful for it.

Alone, she pulled the book out of the mercantile's brown wrapping and settled down beside the fire to read. Alone, the minutes passed slowly. The hour hand on the clock crept across the small etched face.

She ate in her room and went to bed early, reading until her eyes were heavy. But the minute she closed her book, Trey materialized in her mind. His saucy grin, his twinkling eyes, the tender way he'd given Josie her parents' picture.

She lay in the dark a long time, listening to the howl of the storm, hearing its loneliness.

"Uncle Trey?" It was the faintest whisper.

He looked up from his medical journal, blinking. The lamp at his elbow cast only enough light to read by; he couldn't see anything else but darkness in the room. Then a ghostly wisp of pink flannel shivered through the deep shadows.

He rubbed his tired eyes and pushed back his chair. "Josie? What are you doing up?"

"Nothin'."

She sniffed once, and his heart broke. It simply broke. How was he going to make her world right again?

Determined, he pressed a kiss to her brow. "You've got to be awake for a reason. Don't tell me you've developed a bad rash on your big toe and it itched so much it woke you up."

"Nope. No rash." She sounded so sad.

"Maybe you've got a big boil on your nose."

"Oh, Uncle Trey. That's not it at all."

"I bet you can't sleep because you missed me." He knelt down to gather her into his arms.

With a sob she flew against him, a fragile waif of a thing. Her arms wrapped around his neck and felt so tiny. She felt incredibly small cradled to his chest.

Tenderness crept into his lonely bachelor's heart. "Did you have another bad dream?"

Josie pressed her face hard against his neck, and her tears were hot and wet. She trembled in his arms. "I dreamed about the train wreck."

She'd been sleeping in the room next door. He would have heard her if she'd cried out. But she hadn't, her terror had been silent. He held her tighter and listened to her racking sobs, silent and draining, hard with grief.

He carried Josie back to her pretty new bed, holding her tight, not knowing what to say. How could he hush away her hurts? They were so huge and he was no expert. He only knew about physical wounds—how to stitch up cuts and bind broken bones—not emotional ones.

"Do you want me to read you a story?"

She shook her head, her baby-fine curls catching on his unshaven chin.

"I could make you a cup of hot chocolate?"

"Pa used to do that."

"I could sing to you."

"Mama did that, too." Grief ached in those words. Her little arms tightened around his neck. She burrowed hard against him.

He sat on the edge of the bed and held her. He didn't know what else to do. He pressed a few kisses into her hair and wished to heaven and back there was a way to heal this little girl's grief.

The winds strengthened and ebbed, a last fight for life. It succeeded and the storm regained its strength. The scouring sound of ice hitting the north wall drummed through the house, silent but for Josie's sobs.

Chapter Six

*T*he brutal wind battered her like a dozen fists. The blizzard roared, beating bits of ice against her with enough force to tear her from the ladder. Miranda clung tighter, her bare hands screaming in protest. The rung she gripped was caked with snow, but she refused to let go. She couldn't.

Were they following her? She turned her face into the wind, grimacing against the blade-sharp bits of ice. The wind tore away the air and she struggled, unable to breathe, unable to see anything in the gray-white swirl of the storm.

Already she couldn't feel her hands. She struggled against the wind and the rocking speed of the train, like living things trying to tear her from the side of the car. Miranda gritted her teeth and pulled with all her strength. She collapsed on a slick layer of ice sheeting the roof.

No one followed, but she could feel him out there, past the powerful storm, a dark force waiting. Just waiting.

Driving snow held the faint taste of coal smoke. Shivering hard against the cold and fear, Miranda eased carefully along the roof. But it was too icy. Her hands scraped on the hard-packed snow and she slid backward.

She was falling, skidding along the ice, driven by the wind. She dug in her heels as icy pellets beat against her and drove the warmth from her body.

The edge of the roof rose up to meet her and she was falling, falling through the storm and the darkness.

A scream tore from her throat. Miranda sat up in bed, the muslin sheets rustling. Without a candle, the room was too dark for her to see.

It's all right. She breathed deeply until the terror of her dream faded. Only the howling wind remained, battering the windows and scouring the outside walls. It was only a dream. Just a dream.

But the helplessness she'd felt alone in the storm remained.

She slipped from beneath the warm covers and hurried across the cold floor. Frigid air blasted through the well-battened walls and the window glass. She felt it as she pulled aside the ruffled curtains to gaze out at the storm.

The hair on the back of her neck prickled. Was it the bounty hunter out there? Or just a lingering fear from the dream?

She could see nothing of the street below, nothing beyond the black storm. Panic rekindled, and she leaned her forehead against the cold glass.

Maybe reading would get her mind off the dream.... A floorboard squeaked down the hall, a faint sound that could barely be heard over the storm. The back of her neck prickled.

It could be one of the lodgers. The inn was nearly full. But if it wasn't—

Miranda grabbed her shoes from the hearth and struggled into them. The blizzard howled against the windows with renewed fury, masking all sound.

Maybe she just imagined it. Maybe—

Her doorknob jiggled. A key scraped into the lock.

One of the bounty hunter's men. It had to be. Miranda grabbed her cloak from the peg by the cold hearth and her reticule from the mantel, shoving it deep into her pocket.

The lock clicked.

Hurry. She unlocked the closest window and shoved it open. Arctic wind needled snow against her face and hands as she grabbed hold of the frame. The blizzard raged at her as she hauled one leg, then the other over the sill.

Two hands grabbed her around the waist from behind. She braced her feet and fought with all her strength, but her fingers slipped on the snowy window frame. *"No."*

Then she was falling backward and into his arms. He pulled her against his chest and pinned her there with one arm.

"I've been chasing you a long time, missy. Six long months of false leads, dead-end trails and misery." His voice rang as cold and lethal as the revolver he pressed to her jaw. "I'm going to make you pay for every goddamned minute. Starting now."

He hauled her toward the bed and she screamed. She kicked hard. Her heel caught him in the knee.

"Let her go. Right now." The sound of a rifle being cocked echoed in the room.

The bounty hunter spun around, dragging her with him.

Mrs. Howell, the innkeeper's wife, stood in the hallway. Her rifle was cradled in hands that were trembling with fear. "I said, let her go."

"Drop the gun and scram, old lady." He thumbed back the hammer, swinging his revolver toward the trembling woman.

"Don't hurt her." Miranda swung but couldn't break his hold. She kicked, but he only laughed.

"Don't annoy me, missy. Old lady, drop the gun or I'll drop you. I don't give a damn which."

"Please go, Mrs. Howell." Miranda didn't have time to thank the woman who was no match for a ruthless gunman. Apology shone, and then the woman laid the rifle on the floor.

"I guess that changes my plans, but not much." Cruel triumph flickered in his downturned smile. "Grab your clothes and come with me."

"But the blizzard is still—"

"Do as I say." He raised his arm and cuffed her with the back of his hand.

Pain exploded along her cheekbone, radiated up into her eye and into her ear. He shoved her toward the hearth. Scant light from the hallway illuminated her clothes piled neatly on the chair.

Keeping her back to him, she grabbed her wool petticoats and tugged them on over the long underwear. Her hands shook, and her cheekbone throbbed harder every time she moved.

"My boss figured if you managed to live, you'd show up here. I thought he was crazy, but it looks like I've struck pay dirt. Ten thousand dollars' worth."

Miranda tugged her wool dress over her head, fighting to keep quiet. He reminded her of Lewis. They had the same downturned grin and love of money.

His gloved hand shot out, bruising as it curled around her upper arm. "Don't give me a reason to kill that old lady. She's still in the hallway. Too chicken to use that gun, the fool. Fight me, and I'll shoot her. Understand?"

Miranda nodded, crying out as he jerked her toward the

door. He smelled of cigar smoke and old sweat, and the scent of him turned her stomach.

"Move your feet," he bit out, shaking her hard.

Pain shot through her shoulder socket. Her cheekbone pounded. She bit her lip, refusing to cry out. His chest rubbed against the upper curve of her back. His groin and hip pressed hard against her backside.

The stairs squeaked beneath her step. She heard Mrs. Howell's rapid breathing and the bong of the foyer clock as it struck one. His sour breath blew hot and moist against the back of her neck. Thick and raspy, betraying his excitement.

Panic skidded down her spine, icy like freezing water. Her whole body went numb. She had to stop him, she had to find a way...

"Move it, missy, before the law shows up." His teeth nipped her ear and laughed. "I'm not about to lose you now. I've waited too damn long."

The foyer was empty and unlit, and there was nowhere to go, even if she could escape. The rage of wind and ice beat at the door. She dragged her feet. How was she going to stop him?

"I told you to keep moving." His grip felt unyielding. He had to be twice her strength.

She fought, but he pushed her easily across the polished floor. The door was getting closer and closer. She wasn't strong enough to stop him. "I have money. More than my father's offering you. If you let me go—"

"I know about your money, High Society Miss."

"Then let go of me, and I'll—"

He cut her off with a teeth-rattling shake. "I know your inheritance is tied up in trust and you can't touch it."

"But I know how to get it."

He tore open the door, refusing to believe her. She

fought, but he pushed her through the threshold. She saw only darkness. A thousand grains of ice bit her face and drove through her clothes. Wind tore the heat from her body in one blow.

"Damn, it's miserable out here." He pulled her hard against his groin so she would understand his meaning. "Lucky for you, my bed's warm and waiting."

Fury beat through her. She hadn't fought off Lewis to suffer a worse fate with this criminal. She had to keep calm and think. There was a way out. She just had to find it.

He forced her out onto the boardwalk, and the inn was lost to the storm. Her shoe skidded on an ice patch, but he caught her before she could hit the ground.

She kicked hard, her heel connecting flesh. He shouted, and she fell headlong into the storm. She couldn't break his hold on her arm. He hauled her against his chest and trapped her there with one massive arm.

She had to keep trying. She had to win. She wasn't going back home, not like this, not ever.

A wind gust slammed against them, and her shoe hit ice again. This was her last chance. She threw her weight into the fall, twisting away from him. Her knees hit the boardwalk with bruising force, and the wind caught her full-force, snatching her away.

She was free. Miranda dropped and rolled, knowing she couldn't climb to her feet fast enough to run. Through the veils of driving snow, she saw fury spark in his eyes as he reached for his gun. He wasn't going to let her go— at any cost. Ice shot up into her face, and she rolled off the boardwalk into the street.

Cold pain cracked through the outside of her left arm. Had he shot her? She scrambled to her feet, stumbling into the wind. She ran, but the wind rammed her back toward the boardwalk, toward him.

She threw herself into the blizzard with all her might, but the storm spun her around. Which way was the street? She dove into the wind again, and a gust knocked her feet out from under her. She hit the ground hard. Pain shot through her knees and the heels of her hands.

The wind rammed her along the ice. She dug into the snow with her fingers, struggling to hold on, but something hard bit into the small of her back. The boardwalk.

Horror pounded through her as she felt steely hands clamp around the curve of her sore shoulder, trapping her. The icy nose of a revolver nudged her spine.

"Don't think I won't shoot," he growled into her ear, as heartless as the storm. "I'm going to take this out of your flesh."

He jerked her to her feet, but she couldn't feel it. Her body felt numb and useless. She had no strength left, half-frozen and bleeding. How could she fight him now?

A dark shadow moved ahead. A man? Someone who could help? No, it was just the storm.

He tugged her along an ice-crusted storefront. Then Miranda saw the shadow again, taller this time and broader. The intangible shadow became substance. Trey emerged from the veil of the storm, and she had to blink her eyes to believe it.

"I've got a gun on you, bounty hunter, and I didn't come alone." He looked undefeatable, untouched by the storm raging around them.

"Put down your gun, bounty hunter." Another voice ordered from behind. "My deputies are well-armed."

Miranda felt the gun wobble against her neck. She could feel the bounty hunter's body stiffen as he realized there was no way out. She felt the slight jostle as he cocked the gun. *He was going to shoot.*

She twisted away, a gun fired, and the bounty hunter lay motionless at her feet. Trey's arms folded around her, safe and sheltering. The flat expanse of his chest felt cold against her cheek, but she didn't care. She held on tight, seeking his comfort, accepting his protection. She breathed in the winter-and-leather scent of him and never wanted to let go.

"You're safe, Miranda." His words were welcome and his breath tender against the shell of her ear. "Come, let's get you out of this storm."

Whatever trouble she was in, she was a good woman. Trey stood in the threshold to his clinic office and watched her drowse on the floor in front of the fire.

Flames tossed orange-tinted light across her dark curls, shimmering like the rarest silk. She felt his presence and twisted from her slender waist. Her smile wobbled. "Is that tea?"

"With a touch of honey." He stepped from the shadows, into the light. "Looks like the ice has melted off you. Feeling warmer?"

"The tea will help."

He knelt beside her. "How are those hands?"

"They hurt." She took the cup, wrapped in a towel to protect her sensitive hands. Her fingers brushed his, soft as silk, as dazzling as fire.

"That's a good sign." He could still see the gun pressed to her jaw and the cold flat hatred in the bounty hunter's eyes. He'd wanted to hurt her.

Trey felt sick inside, glad Mr. Howell had gone to the sheriff for help. Damn glad. "We need to warm you up slowly. How are your feet? Can you feel them yet?"

"No, and I'm afraid to." She was shaking, sloshing the tea she cupped in both hands. "Where's Josie?"

"Probably still asleep." He peeled back the blanket and worked the ice off her shoe buttons. "She talked all evening about you. She loves her new room."

"You didn't leave her alone?"

"No, I had Mrs. Stoltz bring her over from the house. Josie has nightmares and I wanted to be close to her." Her left shoe slid off in his hands. Bits of snow tinkled against the hearthstones.

Her stocking was riddled with ice. He worked on the other shoe. Her right shoe slipped from his fingers, thudding to the floor. Her ankle felt delicate in his hands.

"The sheriff usually asks a doctor to help him confront an armed criminal, does he?" She gazed up at him over the rim of the cup, her eyes pinching with what looked like admiration.

Admiration? He shook his head. "The sheriff's been known to need the services of a doctor now and then. Besides, he remembered seeing us together in the dining room. Did you know there was a bounty hunter in this town? Is that why you changed inns?"

"I didn't know. It was just habit." Miranda sipped her tea, drinking in the warmth. She closed her eyes briefly, enjoying the sweet drink. She looked so beautiful, the air caught in his lungs.

No woman made of kindness should be treated like this. She didn't deserve to be hunted. She deserved to be safe.

"It's twice now you've saved me."

"Pure luck. I was in the right place at the right time." His chest ached with tenderness. "I'm glad I was able to help."

"I can't believe what I'm hearing." Her lower lip wobbled, even as she fought to tease. "You're actually sounding modest."

"A moment of weakness."

"I don't think so. There were a lot of other people on that train who didn't step forward and help me. There've been a lot of people over the last six months who—"

"Six months? You've been on your own that long?"

"Since summer."

She held her chin firm, as if she were tough enough to live forever on the run, forever alone. He tugged off one stocking, then the other.

Her skin was bright pink, not a sign of frostbite, but other than that her feet were perfect. Slender ankles, a delicate arch and the curve of slim toes.

He reached for the pail of snow and hated rubbing the small handful against her icy skin, knowing it would bring her pain. Her heart-shaped face pinched. She closed her eyes and didn't say a word.

The fire crackled, but he could barely hear it over the beat of his own heart. He cradled her feet on his knees, and the gentle weight of them seemed to add fuel to that warmth in his chest, to that growing admiration for her.

"Here." He measured a fistful of snow into a cloth and pressed it to her sore cheekbone. "This will take away some of the swelling. You look like you tangled with a bounty hunter."

She'd drained her cup and now carefully set it aside, gathering courage. Her chest felt tight, her nerves on edge. "When you were on the train, after I ran away, what did the bounty hunter tell you? I need to know everything."

"I already told you. He didn't say a thing." Trey toweled the melted snow from her skin, trying to stimulate her circulation. "You aren't very trusting, are you?"

He felt her muscles tense beneath his fingers. She took a shaky breath. "It's kept me safe so far."

"You're safe here." Trey filled his hand with snow and rubbed it across the bottom of her left foot. "You don't believe me?"

She winced, pain furrowing across her brow, settling into her face.

"You aren't the first woman I've taken into my clinic, no questions asked. I've seen a lot over the years being a doctor, things I wouldn't believe a human being capable of."

He looked so sad, his shoulders burdened as if the weight of the world rested there. Brushed by light and hardened by shadow, he was more than the dashing and handsome doctor she'd met on the train.

He was a hero.

The snow thawed her feet a little more, and blade-sharp pain knifed through her heels. Trey reached for the towel with infinite care, his healing hands brushing her skin with an archangel's softness.

"You said there were other women?" she asked. She had to know for sure.

"Mostly women battered by their husbands, afraid for their lives." He set aside the towel. "Some with children, some without. Some beaten so badly it's a wonder they were able to leave at all."

It was there in his eyes, the truth so stark and severe she believed him. She could feel his sadness, feel the weight of it, heavy and dark and unrequited. A man of his word, a man of honor.

"Like I said, I'll be your good-luck charm for as long as you need it." He set her feet on the floor with care. "You're almost thawed enough for a warm bath. I'm go-

ing to heat the water. Can you manage the bath by yourself?''

''I think I can handle it.''

He gathered the towel, the pail, the empty teacup and
left the room. His step drummed solemnly against the
floor, the sound knelling above the popping fire and the
howling storm.

''Trey?''

He hesitated in the threshold, lost in shadow, distant
and yet substantial.

''Thank you.''

''Any time, Miranda.'' She couldn't see it, but she
could hear the smile in his voice, and maybe a little wink.

Then he was gone, leaving her alone with the storm.

The tepid bathwater thawed her, and Miranda hurt like
she'd never known before. Flashes of pain told her at least
her feet were going to be just fine, but her hands, they
were the worst. They'd been bared to the minus-twenty-
degree temperatures.

Alone in the patient room, where a neatly made bed
waited, washed in lamplight, she managed to climb into
her comfortable long underwear. The flannel felt soft on
her tender skin.

The blizzard raged against the outside wall, forcing
back memories of the battle she'd fought tonight. Now
that it was over, she started shaking. Images of the night
assaulted her—his arm clamping her to his chest, the
sound of the gun, the heat of his breath against her ear.

But she was safe now. Thanks to Trey and his six-
shooter. A man who'd kept his word, who'd protected her.
Now she was safe, but was it right to involve him?

There had been one bounty hunter. There could be a
second.

She added sticks of wood to the fire, shivering hard, but not from the cold. She feared she would never be warm again.

"Are you thawing out?" Trey asked from the other side of the door. "I can give you something for the pain."

"It will pass." She tried to lower her aching body to the edge of the bed without moaning, but one slipped past her clenched teeth. "You can come in, Trey."

The door whispered open, and he filled the threshold. His dark locks were tousled and exhaustion bruised the skin beneath his eyes. He set a blue-speckled enamel mug, steaming and fragrant, on the nightstand.

"Willow bark tea." The heat from the cup scorched her sensitive hands.

"Let me." Trey lifted the mug. As if she were a small child, he touched the rim of the cup to her lips and gently tilted it. Just enough so she could sip.

His unbelievable tenderness brought tears to her eyes, and she struggled to swallow past the unyielding tightness in her throat. She couldn't remember the last time when anyone had taken care of her.

The tea warmed her from the inside out. She felt less shaky, and less feverish.

"Let me take a look at your hands."

She jerked back. "They're better."

"You don't have to pull away from me." He flashed her a wider grin, lopsided and far too confident, and a contrast to the steady understanding in his eyes. "I've been told I have a fantastic bedside manner."

Laughter bubbled up past the wedge of uncertainty lodged in her chest. "The last thing I need is a doctor, trust me."

"Your arm is injured. I was hoping you'd lower that

fierce independence of yours for two minutes so I can take a look at the bullet wound.''

"It just grazed me. Took a little skin, that's all."

"A gunshot isn't anything to gamble with." He flicked open the button at her wrist. "An infection would stop you pretty fast. You'd be easier prey for those bounty hunters."

"You're right. That's why I'm going to take care of it myself."

"But I'm the doctor here."

"And I'm not helpless." She tried to pull her hand away.

"I never said you were." His fingers held her, both determined and gentle. "Contrary to what you think, I'm pretty good at my job."

"Too bad I don't need a doctor."

"You do." No anger. He didn't even sound irritated. He simply flashed her a wink and tugged on the button at her cuff.

Saving her from the bounty hunter was one thing, bringing her tea another, running her bath and providing his protection, it could all be written off easily. He helped other women like this.

But this, the way he carefully rolled up her sleeve, exposing inch after inch of her forearm, this terrified her. It was too personal. He felt too close. She felt too vulnerable.

She could feel the heat radiating from his body, smell the faint scent of tea, wood smoke and tobacco on his shirt, feel the tender brush of his skin that felt like satin and steel.

"That's going to need a couple of stitches. Let me get my things." He left her, taking the warmth of his presence with him, leaving the air cold at her side.

It wasn't only protection and medical care he offered her, but his comfort. And *that* frightened her.

He returned, the flame flickering dark, then bright as he strode past. "I'm going to bandage this other gash, the one you wouldn't let me look at last time. The one I bet you got trying to climb around on top of the train."

"Climbing down, actually."

"In the middle of a blizzard. You've influenced Josie, you know."

"Judging by the way you say that, it's not a good thing?"

"Very bad." He winked. "She believes what you said about the locket. She let me exercise her leg tonight, before she went to bed. I know it hurt her, but she was brave. By your example."

"I'm sure it had nothing to do with her wonderful uncle."

"Not a thing." He cleaned her lacerations with care. "Like I said, she believes the story about the locket."

"That it's filled with a mother's love?"

He nodded, intent on his work. "She doesn't want to open it. I think she knows it's just a story, but every child needs magic to cling to."

"Who said it was just a story?" She tried not to wince as he finished the last stitch. "So, am I going to live, Doc?"

"As far as I can tell. Next time you're abducted by an armed man, make sure you grab some mittens."

"I'll try to remember."

What she wouldn't forget was how it felt to be this close to him. Close enough to see the texture of his unshaven jaw, the dimple carved into his chin, and something else, something infinitely comforting and exciting.

"There." His fingers swept heat and sparkle along the

outside curve of her arm. "The sheriff sent a deputy to keep watch over you tonight."

"Why would he?"

"Because he's a good lawman. And because I asked him to." Trey uncapped a vial.

She recognized that label. Laudanum. "I don't want any drugs."

"You're fighting a fever, Miranda. Take it. Just this once. Give your body the rest it needs."

"I can sleep just fine without it."

"I think you're in too much pain." He brushed the curls from her brow as if she were a child, but his touch was meant for a woman. She could feel the heat of it and the tenderness, like kindling sparking.

"Drink this." He stirred the powder into the tea, metal scraping enamel. He seemed sure and in control, so undaunted by the tension snapping between them. "There will be other days to run, but for now, you're safe. I swear to it."

Heaven help her, she believed him. She trembled, touched by his strength. Every instinct shouted for her to look away, move away, anything to escape this unbearable closeness.

But her heart made her stay.

The fire snapped, radiating heat against her, but it wasn't as hot as the keen, bright awareness flickering between them.

His gaze darkened, then he closed the distance, slanting his lips over hers.

Sensation telegraphed along every surface of her mouth. His kiss felt like heated silk and tasted like home. Fiery sparks brushed everywhere their lips met. *He was kissing her.* She couldn't believe it. She couldn't believe a kiss could feel like this.

Then he pulled away, leaving her shaking and confused. Her body felt alive, her mouth tingling, but he moved away, silently studying her.

"You're my patient." His eyes pinched with regret but shone like starlight. "I shouldn't have kissed you."

"Is this a reward for suffering through your stitches?" Teasing was easier than speaking her fears. Is this what he did with other women? Kissed them when they were confused and grateful? Was she foolish because she liked it? Because it felt personal?

"You're the first patient I've ever kissed." His brows furrowed. "Damn. I acted on impulse, and I apologize."

"I only hope you won't put charges for that kiss on my bill." Because it hurt to look at him, she stared hard at her hand, thick from the new bandage.

"Is it truly all right?" His fingertip brushed her chin, tilting her head back. "I didn't mean to hurt you."

"I'm fine." Why was he looking at her mouth again? She watched his eyes grow black. The air between them stretched taut, thrumming with awareness. *I want him to kiss me like that again.*

His mouth covered hers with a moan that made her melt. Heat spiraled through her chest, and she couldn't deny the attraction for this man whose kiss left her defenseless, left her reeling.

She couldn't move away. Her fingers curled into his shirt, and she moved against him, feeling the hard curve of his arm against her shoulder. Their breaths mingled. Their tongues entwined. Pleasure and comfort pounded in her chest until it hurt.

He broke away, breathless. She uncurled her fingers from his shirt. With a dazzling brush of his hands to hers, Trey gave her the laudanum-dosed tea. The sweet taste of peppermint tickled her nose as she inhaled. The medicine was bitter against her tongue.

The memory of the bounty hunter faded with Trey at her side. To her surprise, he pulled back the comforter and sheet for her.

She stretched out, strangely vulnerable. She couldn't remember the last time anyone had tucked her in, safe and sound. Breathless, she waited as he turned down the wick. Light died, leaving them in complete darkness.

But he didn't leave. He sat in the chair by her bed. The night, the darkness, and the sounds of the storm surrounded them. But she was not alone.

Chapter Seven

Pain woke her. Her hands throbbed as she pushed back the covers and sat up to face the new day. Silence met her ears. The howling storm was gone, replaced by peace and sunshine teasing at the edges of the drawn curtains.

The floor was cold against her aching feet. She found her clothes, dried and folded on a chair by the bed where Trey had been last night.

How long had he stayed, watching over her? And why, when he had nothing to gain? Now that the storm was over, she had to leave. Now, while the good weather lasted.

She pulled on her dress, wincing. How was she going to manage the buttons? She knelt to fasten her shoes, enduring the discomfort.

"Miranda?" Josie's knock rattled the door. "Uncle Trey says I gotta check on you."

"Tell him I'm almost dressed."

Josie limped in wearing a grin and a pretty dark green flannel dress. "That's good, 'cuz Mrs. Stoltz brought lunch and she says it's gonna get cold."

Miranda forced her thumb to push a button through the

fabric, gritting her teeth to keep from crying out. "Are you any good with buttons?"

"I'm pretty darn good."

"Then come and help me." Miranda managed to kneel so the girl could reach.

"It snowed lots and lots." Josie tugged on the dress as she worked. "It's almost up to the windows."

"The windows?"

"A bunch of children are already outside playin'." Her heavy sigh wasn't self-pitying, just sad. "I can't walk on the snow yet 'cuz of my leg. There, I'm done. C'mon."

Small fingers curled around hers and pulled with surprising strength. Cheery sparkles glittered in those emerald-green eyes as the girl tugged her the length of the hallway and into a front room where a stove radiated heat and sunlight beamed through welcoming windows.

"Look!" Josie splayed both hands on the glass and pressed her nose to it. "It reaches all the way to the door. Uncle Trey got up early to shovel it away. He said folks would need to come see him and he wanted them to be able to find the door."

She could just hear Trey saying that, with his saucy drawl and a flash of charm. "Where is he now?"

"Seein' people." Josie gestured with one hand.

Only then did Miranda notice they weren't alone. An older man and woman were seated quietly in the corner, watching her.

"Mr. Shay, Mrs. Shay. Good morning to you both." Trey strode into the room, catching her attention, changing everything.

He appeared every inch a competent doctor, although he hadn't cast off his gunfighter image. A holstered revolver hugged his right thigh, and somehow his blue shirt and trousers made him look ready to ride the range instead of calling on his next patient.

Her mouth tingled as she remembered the heated brush of his kiss.

"Miranda." His gaze fastened on her, closing the distance between them. "What are you doing out of bed?"

"I felt adventurous."

"Yes, but how's that fever?"

"Fine." In truth, her skin felt hot and her chest achy, but the night was over.

"You look flushed." He smelled like coffee and felt like comfort. He towered over her, both iron-strong and gentle, and the combination dazzled her. His hand covered her brow.

Heat flamed across her skin. Her lips buzzed as she remembered his kiss. Her face felt hotter. Lights danced across her eyes, and she felt dizzy.

His hand curled around her waist, holding her up. "Mr. Shay, why don't you go on back to the treatment room. I'll be right with you. I need to check on Miranda first."

"I'm fine, Trey."

"Sure, for having a fever and a bullet wound." His grip remained, steadfast and supportive. The steel band of his arm fit into the small of her back and guided her down the hall.

She tried not to think about how safe she felt in his arms. How good he smelled. Or how much she'd liked his kiss. "I just need something to eat."

"You need bed rest or you'll wind up with a serious illness. A bad case of pneumonia will stop you real fast."

"The storm's over."

"And the town is still digging out." He navigated the door and eased her onto the edge of the bed. "Head still spinning?"

"Not as much."

"I'll have Josie bring the lunch basket in here." He warmed his stethoscope in his hands. "Let me listen to your lungs."

There was no way she was going to unbutton her dress for him, sore hands or not. "I'm not ill."

"Good. I want to keep you that way." He tugged at her top buttons. The silver disk skidded across her skin.

She breathed according to his instructions. "I'm fine."

"You've got a fever. Enough to keep you here for a day."

A day. It was so much time just to spend in bed. She had so much to do. She needed to stock up on a few necessities, in case she had to leave town in a hurry. She needed a map, to figure out where to go next. "What if there was a second bounty hunter nearby?"

"The sheriff's having his men keep an eye on the clinic. They're out searching the town." Trey knelt to slip off her shoes. "If there's a gunman anywhere, they'll find him."

Trey sounded so certain. "Just rest, and I'll be back."

Her heart flip-flopped. Why on earth would it do that? And why did her gaze keep following him as he walked away? Maybe because she couldn't stop feeling the ghost of his kiss on her mouth.

Just don't think about it. It seemed a simple enough solution. Except her lips kept buzzing with the memory.

"Miranda! Miranda! Mrs. Stoltz made chicken sandwiches for lunch." Josie limped into the room, followed by a sturdy middle-aged woman carrying a basket. "Uncle Trey said I could eat in here with you, if you want. Is that okay?"

"Perfect. Come sit on the bed with me. We'll have a bed picnic." Miranda thanked Mrs. Stoltz, who set the basket on the mattress beside her, then moved toward the stove to add fuel. "I hear a lot of children playing on the street outside."

Josie crawled awkwardly onto the bed. "They're sledding off the livery stable roof."

Miranda tugged back the curtain to gaze out on the street. "I've never lived in a place where I could use a sled on a roof."

"My pa said I could have a sled when I turn six." Only a little sadness showed, and Josie didn't seem able to tear her attention from the bigger kids climbing up the huge snowdrift, then up the roof, to slide right back down again.

A man, probably the livery stable owner, stalked into sight, arms raised, his voice carrying. The kids raced off skidding and sliding every which way on the icy streets, which were almost window level.

No one else was out yet, and the whole downtown, which she could see from the windows, gleamed white, dazzled by the winter's sun.

Josie dug a sandwich out of the basket. "Do you like to play in the snow?"

"Me?" Miranda laughed as she opened a pickle jar. "I'm a city girl, I'm afraid. The streets were too busy to sled in, and my father didn't like the snow disturbed on his front lawn."

Those memories and more, so long buried, teased at her heart. Memories of wanting to be held tight and wishing for a voice gentle enough to make everything right. "A lot of my friends went sleighing with their beaus, but I didn't have much time for boys. My father didn't approve."

A floorboard squeaked as Trey strode into the room. "I can see why. You probably had hundreds of men flocking to your door just to admire your beauty. It probably created traffic jams for the neighbors, and horses were panicking right and left, causing all sorts of trouble.''

''Are you speaking from experience?''

''Women are always flocking to admire me. Right, Josie?''

''They don't even notice you, Uncle Trey.''

Humor danced in his eyes, and he chuckled, laying a black notebook down on his desk. ''I can see it's going to be hard on my pride to have two females in my life.''

''Just one.'' Miranda finished her sandwich. ''I'm going to head over to the inn. I've got to get my satchel before Mrs. Howell decides I'm not coming back for it, and then I'm skipping town.''

''You're feeling up to that, huh?'' Trey quirked one brow. ''Of course, there's always the weather to stop you. Those drifts are pretty deep. No one's going in or out of this town.''

''For today. But what about tomorrow?''

''I'm only worried about today.'' He pressed a cup of water into her hands and handed her a waxed paper packet of white powder. ''You need rest, Miranda. Besides, it's not even above zero out there.''

''I can handle the cold. I feel better.''

''Probably because of my expert medical care.'' He laid a hand to her brow. ''Did you know that I'm the best doctor in this town?''

''I bet you're the *only* doctor in this town.''

''That still makes me the best.''

''And the worst.'' She drew him like stars to the moon, and he felt breathless as he pulled his hand away. His skin tingled where he'd touched her and kept tingling.

He'd never known a woman's touch to sparkle like that.

''Let me see your hands.'' His fingertips brushed the

sides of her palms, sensation exploding through him. "They look a little swollen."

"They aren't sore."

He didn't believe her. "It can't hurt for me to look."

It had last time. He'd kissed her. Her chest felt fluttery at the memory. She had to stop thinking about that kiss. "See? My hands are fine."

"It would be best not to get chilled for a couple of days." His gaze latched onto her mouth, and his throat worked. "You might as well stay inside until it warms up a bit."

"I can't wait that long. I bet it doesn't warm up around here until June." A smile shaped her mouth, and he couldn't look away.

Damn. Hadn't he resolved not to think about those kisses? She was his patient, even if she was a pretty woman. Surely he could manage a little self-control.

"Josie, I'm making Miranda your patient." He headed toward the door. "You tell me if she tries to get out of that bed."

"Okay, Uncle Trey." Josie set her chin. She looked as if she wasn't about to let Miranda leave.

"Trey." Miranda called him back, sitting up in bed, the window behind her. "You aren't playing fair. You know I have a soft spot for Josie."

"I take what advantage I can."

Sunlight sparkled on the snow behind her and haloed her soft face.

All he could think about was last night's kiss. She might be his patient, and he couldn't dream of kissing her again. But his lips remembered the taste and texture of hers.

He left to take a look at Mr. Shay's back injury caused from shoveling too much snow.

When he passed by Miranda's room thirty minutes later, Josie was still with her. The little girl was in Miranda's arms, both sleeping quietly in the sunshine.

The twist of wind and the scour of snow tilted the world upside down. Confused, she stumbled and hit the ice. Pain shot through the heels of her hands. She fought hard against the inhuman power of the storm.

She could feel him, even if she couldn't see him. He was out there, just a step away…. The wind scooted her backward and the icy nose of a revolver bit into the small of her back. Defeat pounded through her. Steely hands spun her around. Lewis stared down at her, triumph glinting in his cold eyes….

She woke, stifling a scream. Lamplight slanted through the half-open door and into the room, casting long shadows across the floor. A fire crackled merrily in the pot-bellied stove, and the low murmur of voices droned through the walls.

She was safe from Lewis, safe from the bounty hunters. But not if she stayed in one place for long.

She pushed aside the blanket and sat up. Twilight grayed the world outside the window. Her headache was gone. She felt better, stronger, but it was too late to try to leave today.

Footsteps tapped against hardwood somewhere in the clinic. Was it Trey? She crept to the door and peered out. A single light glowed through the darkness, beckoning her to the room at the end of the hall.

Trey's office. Thick bound books were crowded into dusty oak bookcases, which lined three of the four walls. The lamp stood on Trey's desk in the corner, splashing light across his face and onto another man sitting in a chair, his back to her.

Then the sheriff turned. "You look pretty bruised, miss. I'll have you know the man after you is dead."

"I figured." She didn't know what she felt, her stomach tied up so tight that the knots were impossible to unravel. "What are you going to do with me?"

Trey stepped forward, somehow filling the room. Maybe it was just his presence or maybe her growing awareness of him. "He's going to protect you, Miranda."

"That's right." The sheriff stood, tall and steely. "This is a free country. No one has the right to print up a bunch of wanted posters and turn you into a fugitive."

"My father does." And Lewis. That night returned in scraps of memory, and she squeezed her eyes shut, driving away the images.

"No one does." Trey's certainty cut through those images. "No one."

The sheriff held out a folded piece of paper. She could only stare at it. Her father's reward notice. Had the lawman come to take her in?

"Received this about a month ago. It's the reason you haven't tried to find help, isn't it?" The sheriff gestured toward the folded poster. "You haven't broken the law, and so it's my duty to keep you safe."

How could she trust him? How could she believe a stranger would turn down the chance for easy wealth just like that?

"I've got my men out searching for more of those varmints." The lawman scooped his hat off a wall peg. "If you can identify the men after you, it'd make my job easier."

"Your job?"

"Arresting criminals trying to kidnap an innocent woman." He, too, seemed to operate by the same code as Trey did. He headed toward the door, and he looked honest. He sounded honest. He met her gaze and she could read him clear as day.

He was a man of his word, and it was as simple as that. "I'll do what I can. My deputies will keep an eye on you, just in case. Women are safe in my town, and that's the way it is."

He tipped his hat, nodded to Trey and closed the door behind him.

Miranda sank into a hard-backed chair. "Will he—"

"No." Trey wouldn't let her finish the question. "Mac Kelley is as good as they come. I mean it when I say you're safe in this town with handsome men like us watching out for you."

"Well, *he's* handsome...."

"And you don't think I am? I'd better check your eyesight." A dimple carved into his left cheek as he teased.

"I can see just fine, believe me."

"So, you think the sheriff is more charming than I am?" He turned her toward the light when she wanted to stay part of the shadows. Darkness was safer.

His fingers brushed tousled hair off her brow and settled there. The heat of his palm eased sparks across her skin. She tried not to notice he was so close she could see the flecks of black and cinnamon in his brown eyes and the smooth texture of his jaw where he'd recently shaved.

"Your fever was short-lived." He stepped away intentionally, avoiding her gaze. "You're lucky."

"Thanks to you. If you hadn't gone out in the storm to find me—" She hated to think what could have happened. She would have fought that bounty hunter, but that didn't mean she would have won. "Well, let's just say I'd be needing more medical treatment."

"Then I'm glad I could help. I like my patients healthy." He laid one hand over the revolver holstered to his hip, leaving no doubt. "I know that you have to be worried. But you're safe here. This isn't the first time I've done this, and it won't be the last."

"I don't think I've ever met a man quite like you."

"Is that a compliment or a complaint?" He stepped into the shadows, away from the flick of lemony lamplight and the darker glow from the crackling fire.

"Definitely a compliment."

"So, you're starting to notice a few of my attributes." His humor filled the emptiness as he placed a small basket of food on the little table beside her. "The handy Mrs. Stoltz left this for you."

She wasn't hungry but needed to step away from him. Maybe it was the dark, maybe it was her own fears, maybe it was because he was tall and captivating, but her heart skipped a beat, then two. She couldn't bear it if he kissed her again.

Shadows grabbed at her as the single flame danced on its wick. She took the small basket to the hearth. She heard Trey's chair scrape the wood floor as he settled into it. The *scratch, scratch* of his writing seemed to fill the room.

She would take his advice. She didn't want to come down with pneumonia if she went back out into the cold. She'd rest tonight and leave first thing in the morning. But with the way her skin tingled from being in the same room with Trey, maybe tomorrow wasn't soon enough.

She slept like an angel. The light from Trey's candle caressed her with gentle force. Her face was like porcelain, creamy and flawless, and in sleep, her features were more relaxed, softer. She was like starlight, a perfect brightness against unending darkness.

Her forehead was cool when he brushed his fingers

against her skin. She smelled of moonlight and pepper-mint and woman, rare and sweet. Candlelight danced over her face and stroked her like a lover's touch, lingering on those full lips, bow-shaped and perfectly made for kissing.

His mouth tingled, remembering. What had he been thinking to kiss a patient like that? She was a woman, vulnerable, alone and disillusioned.

He had no right kissing her. Or wanting to taste her again.

Timothea Kelley moaned across the hall. He peeked in on her, but she was fast asleep. She'd taken a bad fall on the ice today and would be bedridden for a while. He checked on the old woman, careful not to wake her.

A knock rattled the back door. He wasn't expecting anyone. A patient would use the front door. He'd locked up early tonight, to keep Miranda safe. He unsnapped his holster, just in case.

It was Mrs. Stoltz, Josie sobbing in her arms. "She had another bad dream."

"Uncle Trey." The little girl reached out.

He pulled her against his chest, the cold night air shivering around them. He thanked the housekeeper, who didn't look happy to be hauled out of a warm bed in the middle of the night.

His chest tightened, and he vowed to figure out a better solution for Josie. She was all that mattered. "How did you know I was lonesome for you?"

She shook her head. "You ain't l-lonesome."

"Sure I am. A dashing man like me. I always appreciate the company of a pretty girl."

Josie hugged Baby Beth tight. "I don't wanna go back to sleep, Uncle Trey. I don't wanna dream."

"Lucky for you I'm a darn good doctor." Trey locked

the door and carried his niece to the hearth, where a toasty fire raged. ''I know a surefire cure for that.''

''For being afraid to sleep?''

''Sure. I've got the medicine right here.'' He fetched a jar of candy from his desk. He uncapped the lid.

''Those are gumdrops. Not real medicine.'' But she dug into the jar, anyway, filling her fist.

He did the same, settling down on the floor next to her. ''The red ones are the best at chasing away bad dreams. Make sure you eat lots of those.''

''Can Baby Beth have some?''

''I imagine she wants good dreams, too.''

Josie's cheeks sheened with shed tears, but at least they'd stopped falling.

A step brushed outside the door. He turned, his chest warming when he saw Miranda standing in the threshold. He couldn't stop his gaze from traveling up the willowy length of her body to the cut of her mouth, so lush and tempting.

Fear darkened her eyes, and he could read the relief on her face. She'd heard the knock at the door, too, and expected the worst.

He held up the jar. ''For medicinal purposes.''

''Of course.'' Miranda swept toward them. She'd changed for bed and wrapped herself up in one of the clinic robes.

She smelled fresh as roses as she knelt beside him. Her slender fingers curled around a few pieces of candy. Her dark hair tumbled over her shoulder, the satin-richness brushing his cheek.

Fire shot through his spine. His gaze fastened on her lush lips. She opened her mouth, and the gumdrop she ate left a trail of sugar on her bottom lip.

He ached to lick away that sweetness. His blood pounded with the need.

"Did you have a bad dream, too, Miranda?" Josie pushed the candy jar closer. "Better have lots of red ones."

Miranda snared a red gumdrop. "I thought you and your uncle might have gone home by now. It's late."

"Nope. He's workin'."

"I've got a couple patients to look after." Trey inched closer because she moved back into the shadows, just out of reach of the light. "Not just you, so don't give me that look."

"You work nights, too?"

"It doesn't happen too often. I really miss having a nurse. No, two nurses. Believe it or not, I'm having a hard time employing nurses. They either keep getting married off or after one winter here, head south."

"Your dash and charm can't win everyone, I guess."

"Pity." He winked, and because he saw admiration light her eyes, he looked away. "I need to find a nurse, because I have Josie to take care of now. Don't I, Red?"

She nodded. "I'm pretty little."

Trey's throat ached, emotions so tight he couldn't name them. He loved his niece, but he wasn't father material. He didn't want to fail her.

Just as he didn't want to fail this woman by his side, who needed a friend more than she needed a confirmed bachelor's kiss.

"C'mon, Red. My clinic beds are full. But my sofa is as comfortable as they get." He swept her off the floor, tucking her beneath his chin and against his heart. "I think it's the best sofa this side of the Missouri."

"Oh, Uncle Trey." Josie wasn't about to be fooled. "I don't wanna go to sleep."

"What? Are you telling me that you doubt my medical knowledge? Gumdrops always work against bad dreams, I swear. And if they don't, I'll be right here."

"Promise?"

"Absolutely." He pressed a kiss to her brow, her gossamer curls tickling his nose. He grabbed the blanket off the back of the sofa and shook it open. He rolled both Josie and Baby Beth in snugly, and pressed a pillow beneath their heads.

"Sweet dreams." Miranda brushed past his shoulder to tuck the blanket beneath Josie's chin. "I'll see you in the morning."

"Do we get to play in the snow then?" Josie brightened, studying him with an ardent plea.

"We'll see." He listened to Miranda pad from the room without another word for him, leaving them alone.

"Uncle Trey, are you gonna get married some day?"

"Now, why would you ask me a scary question like that?" He grabbed another blanket and swept it across her.

"'Cuz you don't gotta wife. That's why you had to hire Mrs. Stoltz to take care of me. Families always have a mother."

"I work so much, I'm not looking for a wife, Josie." He turned down the wick until there was only darkness. "Are you afraid I might get a wife? A little girl who lost her ma might not want a stepmother right away."

"I just want her to be nice." Josie sighed. "And someone who can braid hair. Mrs. Stoltz ain't very good at it."

"If I'm suddenly overcome with the notion to marry, I'll let you know." Trey heard what the little girl couldn't say. "Get some sleep, Red. I'll be here if you need me."

Josie hugged her doll tight. The fire in the grate crackled, tossing a dark orange glow over the child's face. The tracks of her tears still showed.

He kissed her brow and left the room.

Chapter Eight

Miranda looked like summer against the windows glazed with winter's touch. Her dark hair shimmered as if caressed by a full sun, and her smile was gentle like the warmest breeze. "How's Josie this morning?"

"She's still sleeping." Trey nodded toward the hallway, where his office door was closed.

"I guess those gumdrops worked."

"Hey, I'm a doctor. I know what I'm doing. I've got a hot pot of coffee. Figured I'd need it to get through the day. I know you prefer tea."

"I'd love anything hot." She didn't look at him as she knelt down before the fire, holding out her hands to warm them. "How much do I owe you? I've probably worked up a huge doctor bill by now."

He grabbed a hot pad and lifted the rumbling coffeepot from the stove. "You don't owe me a thing."

"This is how you make your living, Trey." Her footstep brushed on the wood floor behind him.

His skin tingled. "It's my prerogative to charge a patient or not. And you're not just any patient, Miranda."

"You stitched up my arm and I slept in your bed, like many patients before me. I still owe you."

"Then how much do I owe you for the locket? How much for spending time with Josie?" He filled a blue speckled cup and handed it to her. "I owe you."

She was like sunlight on this gray, chilly morning. And the sight of her warmed him. "Are you headed to the inn? I can give you a ride in a few minutes. Sheriff Kelley is coming to take his aunt home, and then I've got a few house calls to make."

"I can manage on my own. I need to get going."

"Where?" He offered her the sugar bowl, and she spooned in a liberal amount, betraying her sweet tooth.

"Somewhere far away, where those bounty hunters can't find me. Where no reward notice is going to end up in the local sheriff's office."

"You're safe here."

"For now. Because of you and the sheriff." She turned away, gazing out the window where snow fell from sky to earth in gently dizzying waves. "But I'm not truly safe. There could be a man hiding somewhere in town, waiting to grab me. Or that bounty hunter could be riding back here to capture me."

"Believe me, no one's going to be riding into this town."

"How do you know? Those mountains look rugged, but so are bounty hunters."

"There's no way in or out of town, not with these drifts. No one much braves the mountains this time of year. No stage lines are running. The trains are stuck in the passes until they are shoveled out. And the roads are closed."

"And I should believe this because you say so?"

"Absolutely. You're safe here. I promise it."

He could make her believe anything. He felt as reliable and solid as those mountains in the distance. He towered over her, a powerfully built man, but his strength ran deeper, truer.

"When the first train comes, it could bring the bounty hunters. Are you sure there isn't someone I can hire to take me over the pass?"

"No. Like I said, there's no safe way over those mountains in the winter. Storms strike with a minute's notice. You know what a Montana blizzard feels like."

"I can't just sit around and wait for the train."

"You could get a job."

"What?"

"It's still snowing. Who knows how long it will be until the railroad is running again? Find a temporary job, put some money back in your pocket and rest up. I'd hire you." He flashed her that one-sided smile that made her resistance melt. "Even without references."

"If I help you, then I'm not letting you pay me. I'll work off my doctor bill."

"That doesn't sit right with me."

"Well, too bad. I don't like being a charity case."

"Then it's a deal."

A deal. Just like that she had a job. With him. What was she thinking? A part of her found him highly attractive. Anyone would. He'd tended her wounds, rescued her from danger and kept watch over her last night. And she'd trusted him.

It had been a long time since she'd been able to trust anyone. A long time since she'd seen goodness in a man.

But now she couldn't afford to mix admiration with desire. And how could she relax, when a bounty hunter could be hiding in this town, waiting and watching?

She gazed out through the frosty glass at the falling snow, blanketed town and shrouded peaks. She was a city girl. She couldn't tackle those mountains. She had no choice but to stay here.

"I'm no nurse. Father wouldn't allow me to attend college, but I am an experienced hospital volunteer." Determined to keep her heart steady, she looked anywhere but at him.

"You don't say. Miranda, I'm doubly lucky to have you work for me."

It had been a long time since she'd been needed, and it lightened her heart. She would make something of her stay here. Pay back her debt to Trey.

The memory of their kiss burned like a firestorm. The memory of his touches seared like flame to skin. Trey had tended her like any good doctor would, checking her wounds, worrying about a possible fever.

No one had taken care of her like that since her mother's death. She was grateful, that's all, nothing more. She couldn't afford to be attracted to Trey Gatlin.

Not when the world glittered before her like paradise, fresh, new and full of promise.

"When Miranda comes back, can she really come outside and play with me?"

"As long as the clinic doesn't get too busy this afternoon." Trey knelt in the kitchen, Josie's wraps in hand. "Let's get you and Baby Beth ready to go. It's cold enough out there to turn you into an icicle."

"Miranda's nice, don't you think? Just like Ma was."

Madeline… Trey hurt to remember. "Yeah, she's pretty nice. This doesn't have anything to do with last night's conversation, does it? About me finding a nice wife?"

"You don't want a mean one, Uncle Trey."

He held her cloak as she struggled into it. "Don't forget your hat."

"You think Miranda's pretty, don't you?"

"She's real pretty," he confessed, although *pretty* was too small of a word to describe the woman's beauty.

"Good."

Hope. He saw that in Josie's eyes. The hope for someone to cling to. Could she feel his doubts? Could she sense this was scaring the heck out of him? His guts squeezed tight with old memories and even older wounds.

"Are you all wrapped up good and tight?"

"Yep."

Trey opened the door and took Josie's hand. "Mrs. Stoltz will keep an eye on you. You go in when she tells you, understand?"

A vigorous nod.

"Have fun, Red." He tugged on her strawberry locks as she limped outside, like a tiny cardinal against a world of white. He grabbed his jacket and hurried out after her.

"I'm gonna make a snowman right here." Josie bent and filled her mittens with snow. "The biggest ever."

"Good. I need something to decorate my front lawn. Look how dull it is."

Josie rolled her eyes, and he knelt beside her. A plan was beginning to formulate in his head, and that was always a bad thing. But he couldn't help it. Kissing Miranda had opened his eyes. She mattered to him and to Josie.

He was going to make certain she knew it. "Miranda seems pretty sad, don't you think?"

Josie nodded. "Those mean men were chasing her."

"That's why I thought we should try to make Miranda happier. Do you like that idea? Will you help out your poor old uncle?"

"Are we gonna give her presents? That's what my pa always did to make me happy."

"That's exactly what we're going to do, but I don't know what Miranda likes. That's why I need your help. Will you ask her a lot of questions for me?"

"Do we getta go shoppin'?"

He wasn't fooled by the gleam in those eyes, not one bit. "Yes, we get to go shopping. Someone has to buy all those presents."

"Goody. I love to shop." Josie lit up like a flame.

That's when he knew his plan was a good one.

"Goodness, don't mention it." The innkeeper's wife, Mrs. Howell, unlocked the door to Miranda's room. "To think that horrible ruffian thought he could break into my peaceful establishment. Why, it makes my blood boil, how he could scare decent people. Why, I'm glad my husband thought to run for the sheriff the way he did."

"I'm very grateful. If you and your husband hadn't helped me, I would be—" Fear vise-gripped her chest.

"I know, dear. But you mustn't worry about this happening again. That was the first problem we've ever had in the five years we've been here, and my husband is installing bigger locks on the outside doors this very day."

"I brought trouble to your home, I—"

"Heavens, no, dear. I swear, there is trouble everywhere a woman looks in this world. I hope you won't hold this incident against us and move out. We'd love to have you stay, at least until the train is running again."

"I hear it could be up to a week's wait."

Mrs. Howell sorted through her key ring. "Who knows when the train will run again. Those fancy engineers from back east didn't take our winter storms seriously. The train gets caught in the pass on and off all winter. Sometimes it's a few days, usually it takes a week, sometimes even more for them to dig the engines out. Here you go.''

Miranda took the offered key. She looked around the room, made tidy by Mrs. Howell. The bed was made, fresh wood was stacked in the cold fireplace. The floors and furniture gleamed with new polish.

Could she stay here? Memories of that night flashed before her eyes, but what was the point in moving?

"I'm going to stay." The Howells had been good to her, and if there was another bounty hunter in this small town, he'd find her wherever she went.

"I'm so glad, dear." Mrs. Howell touched her arm. "There are a lot of bad men in this world who take instead of give, who don't know what tenderness is even if it hit them upside the head. But our Doc Gatlin, he's a good man. I'm glad he patched you up. That bruise on your cheekbone should be gone in a few days. Let me heat up a poultice that will take care of it.''

Since Mrs. Howell wouldn't take no for an answer, Miranda agreed, and the innkeeper hurried off to whip up her home remedy. A stranger's kindness could hurt, too, and Miranda had seen the understanding in Mrs. Howell's eyes.

Her stomach felt as hard as stone. She didn't want to remember the bounty hunter. She didn't want to remember Lewis. But the six-month-old memory of her fiancé's hand at her throat, holding her to take his kisses, remained after all this time.

She sat down on the window seat and leaned her forehead against the cold glass.

A scream erupted outside, ringing down the street. Miranda jumped, squinting through the shafts of sunshine to the dazzling street below. Where were they? Where were the bounty hunters?

The scream sounded again. This time she realized there were no bounty hunters and no danger. Just three little girls playing in the snow, their sled delightfully out of control on the wind-swept snow. Relief lashed through her, leaving her weak.

Just children playing. That was all. The three little girls wore homemade cloaks and handknit mittens and hats. They screamed again, their glee unmistakable.

A boy grabbed the sled's rope and ran down the street. They giggled, clinging together as the sled tipped over, spilling them into the snow. Merry laughter rang like bells, crisp and clear.

The snow dazzled beneath the kiss of the gentle sun, and the town stretched for blocks, veiled white from the storm. Smoke rose from chimneys where families huddled, trying to stay warm.

On the street below, the little girls climbed back up on the sled, and the older boy pulled them back down the street, faster and faster.

A sense of peace filled her. She was lucky to find this slice of paradise, hidden high in the Montana Rockies. If she had to be trapped by a snowstorm, she couldn't have picked a better place.

Boots knelled in the hall. It sounded like men, striding confident and bold. Was she safe? Habit forced Miranda to the door. She peered around the frame, and relief felt as welcome as spring. It was the sheriff, and Trey was at his side.

Her heart flip-flopped. How could she help it? She liked this man far too much for her own good.

"Miss." The sheriff tipped his hat.

Something was wrong, she could tell by the pinch

around Trey's eyes. He wore his gun, snug against his muscled thigh. His mouth was drawn into a hard line. "The sheriff wants you to take a look at a man. Could be a bounty hunter."

"Sure." She'd meant to change clothes, but she could see it in Trey's eyes. This couldn't wait. "I thought you were on your morning rounds."

"The sheriff caught up to me. He owes me a favor." Trey was all uncompromising steel.

They hurried down the boardwalk and across the street to a dilapidated saloon near the railroad tracks. Four men were in the smoke-scented room, including the bartender. A deputy looked up from his plate of uneaten bacon and eggs, and nodded to the sheriff.

"He's right there." It was Trey who laid a hand on her shoulder and guided her along. "Don't worry, we're not going to let him hurt you."

She knew that. Gratitude tore through her, making her knees tremble. She'd been alone for so long, afraid and running. How good it felt to know someone cared, someone as fine and extraordinary as Trey.

"Come with me, miss." The sheriff motioned to her as he paced the room. He halted in front of a scruffy man, face weathered and mean. "I've had a talk with this man, but he swears he isn't a hired gun."

"I'm a drifter, just passing through." The guns strapped to his thighs contradicted him.

No recognition flickered in the man's feral eyes.

"I've never seen him before." She'd had opportunity to come face-to-face with many of the men hunting her. Especially the bounty hunter and his hired men trailing her now.

"Sheriff..." The barkeep spoke up. "He came in on the last stage through the pass last week."

The sheriff considered, then faced Miranda. "Do you want me to lock him up?"

"He's not a bounty hunter." She would have seen it in his eyes, the greed for her father's exorbitant reward.

"My men will keep an eye on him." The sheriff nodded, and Trey propelled her to the door.

"You're shaking," he said once they were outside. "Kelley didn't want to make a scene bringing him in. He thought this was better."

She nodded. She wasn't sure now, but she could feel it. Here, among the saloons, where not even the falling snow felt clean. Every paradise had its serpent, and he was here. She couldn't see him, but she could sense him.

Was he watching her?

"Don't worry, Kelley will find him, if he's here." As if Trey felt it, too, he held her a little tighter. She leaned into his heat and strength, stealing this moment of comfort.

Then the wind tousled his hair, making her see his strength. His black wool coat stretched across the broad line of his powerful shoulders. He looked as dangerous as any outlaw and as handsome as any hero.

Her mouth tingled as she remembered his forbidden kiss. A kiss that had been tender and amazing, that had warmed every inch of her.

Trey walked her back to her room and gave her a key to his clinic. He didn't touch her again.

The exhaustion of a tough day weighed like an anvil on his back. On his way home through the poorer part of town, a woman called out to him in broken English, begging his help. She couldn't pay him all at once, she struggled to say, but her baby was desperately sick.

He'd assured the woman he was more worried about

the health of her son than the fee, but she'd still fretted. Her home had been clean and lovingly decorated, but the insufficiently sealed walls did little to keep out the bitter cold.

He'd stayed until the baby's fever eased a bit, gave strict instructions to the mother to come to his home tonight if the baby worsened. The woman, still afraid he would charge her more than she could pay, nodded her appreciation.

The thought of any child going without treatment tore him up. He headed home, vowing not to forget to return and check on the infant.

He walked through the snow, freezing and weary. But he knew Miranda would be waiting, and that made his step a little lighter.

No lights were on in the clinic. He'd started down the alley when he heard Josie's voice, bright and merry, sounding like she had before the accident.

"Miranda, you have to make the head bigger!"

"Bigger? Are you sure?"

The sound of laughter rang like a distant bell and grew louder as he strolled down the street. There were two figures in his front yard, one elegant and tall, the other girlish and bundled in bright red. Both were a welcome sight to his heavy heart.

"Look. It's all wrong." Josie patted the middle of the halfway-constructed snowman. "He's lopsided. Uncle Trey, Uncle Trey! Come see what we did."

"Trey." Miranda spun, her dark curls brushing the curve of her face, her breath rising in great clouds.

"Any trouble while I was gone?"

"Mrs. Watts came for more cream for her rash, and she was the only one all afternoon." Miranda bent to push a growing snowball. "I fed the fire in the stove and left a note on the door. Someone, I can't imagine who, charmed me into making a snowman with her.''

"Gee, I wonder who that could be.''

"It was me, Uncle Trey.''

Miranda's eyes sparkled with mirth and kindness. He liked her weakness for Josie. There was something about Miranda that drew him. Something he couldn't explain.

"Uncle Trey! Look!'' Joy danced in her emerald eyes and made her sparkle. "Miranda and me found buttons from Mrs. Stoltz's sewing basket for the eyes, and we got lots of stuff. I'm making the biggest snowman ever.''

"It sure looks that way. He's the biggest I've seen, and I've been walking through town all afternoon.''

"Really?''

"Honest. To tell you the truth, the Steiner girls made one, but theirs is ready to topple over.''

Josie's halting step had a little bounce to it as she checked on Miranda's progress making the biggest-snowman-ever's head.

"Bigger!'' Josie proclaimed.

"Bigger?'' Miranda shone, too, like sunlight on snow, pure and true and so beautiful it hurt to look. "If this gets any heavier, I'm not going to be able to lift this. Your snowman is going to look funny with his head on the ground next to him instead of on his shoulders.''

"That would scare all my patients away.'' He was a wise man and saw his opportunity to be closer to Miranda. "Let me take over.''

"Should we trust him, Josie?'' She straightened away from the large globe of packed snow. The hem of her cloak swirled with the movement, showing off her shapely ankles. "Exactly how much experience do you have with snowmen, Doctor?''

Trey bent to roll the bulky snowball. "I'm the best

snowman maker in this whole territory. I bet you didn't know that about me.''

"Self-appointed, I'll bet."

"Hey, I've got proof." He gave Josie a wink. "Right, Josie?"

"I dunno, Uncle Trey. You aren't doin' that head right."

"What?" Sure, it was a little lopsided. "It's hard to roll and charm the ladies at the same time."

"Then just roll the snowball, because I have to tell you that you're not that charming." Miranda was brightness and light.

He wanted to take her mouth one more time. To take those lips between his and suck and taste, lave and nibble. To savor the flavor of snow and the winter's wind on her skin. She looked like heaven in her dark wool coat, cinched at the waist and stretched just right over the curves of her breasts and hips. She was shapely everywhere. And he couldn't stop imagining...

"Uncle Trey." Josie intervened, certain the snowball was big enough. "Lift it up!"

"Will do, boss lady." Trey hefted the head and placed it dead center on the portly snowman's body. "Look at that. Perfection."

"His head's shaped like an egg, Uncle Trey."

"Well, now, I meant for it to look like that."

"Sure." Miranda brushed close to wrap a scarf around the snowman's neck.

"Hey, that's my scarf."

"Really? I found it in the closet."

"And that's my hat." He couldn't believe it as Josie handed his old bowler to Miranda. "What else did you two robbers take from me?"

"Just your pipe." Miranda peered at him over her

shoulder and the light in her eyes, as tempting as choco-late, nearly undid him. "That's all."

"That's all? What am I going to smoke tonight?" He heard Miranda's laughter, light as snow. He flashed a wink at her, drinking in her beauty. She'd done this for Josie. And look what she'd done to him. "You know, this could be a good opportunity for me to take up chewing tobacco."

"Chewing tobacco? You mean, like in your mouth?" Josie wrinkled her nose. "That sounds icky."

"Yeah, but then I get to spit. That's always fun for a man."

"That ain't fun."

"A man's got to have a bad habit. Didn't you know that? If I give up one, then I have to go find another."

"Trey, you're deluding yourself if you think you only have one bad habit." Miranda produced two black buttons for the snowman's eyes. "Right, Josie?"

"Right." The girl's laughter rang true and pure.

Trey hugged her tight, grateful. His chest hurt with emotion. Miranda had done this, spinning magic with snow and love.

"I think Mr. Snowman looks lonely." Warmth snapped in Miranda's cinnamon-warm eyes, refusing to let the hap-piness end.

Josie sighed, contemplating their very big and solitary snowman. "He needs a wife. Let me down, Uncle Trey."

He set her feet on the slick snow, and she was off, absorbed in her play. Beside her, Miranda listened pa-tiently, then set out to roll a new snowball.

Her skirts swirled around her willowy woman's body. He couldn't help watching, couldn't help noticing. A strange fluttery feeling wedged in his heart and expanded until he couldn't breathe.

* * *

"Let me walk you home."

Miranda looked up from buttoning her cloak. "There's a deputy outside. I imagine he'll make sure I reach the inn. Thank you for asking the sheriff to help me. I know he's doing this because of you."

"He's a good lawman. Whatever he read on that poster made him angry."

"Did you read it?"

"No." He cut her off before she could finish. Truth held him up, making him taller, better. "That's your business, Miranda. I admit, I'm curious. But only because I want to help you, maybe know you better."

"You hardly know me at all."

"I know what counts." He closed the damper and straightened from banking the coals. He put out the lamp, leaving them in darkness. "You may come from a comfortable way of life, but it didn't make you happy."

He opened the door for her, letting in the icy wind. "The real you, the part that matters, is your beautiful, caring heart. I'm glad to know you."

"I thought the privilege was mine. After all, you are the best doctor in the territory." She tried hard to deny his words, they weren't real. She knew firsthand she wasn't beautiful.

How many times had Father made a point to tell her? Lewis, thought to be one of the finest catches in all of Philadelphia, wasn't attracted to her but to her sizable trust fund. He'd said to her face that he didn't think she was pretty. So why did Trey?

Wood smoke scented the evening air. Already it was dark, men hurrying from a long day's work to the lighted warmth of their homes. Horses clomped by on the street, drawing sleds whose runners squeaked on the snow. A cold wind blew straight through her.

She'd held so much inside for so long, and it ached in her throat, needing to be said. "The truth is that I'm an heiress. My grandfather died a year ago and left me his fortune."

"To you? Not to your father?"

She tried to squeeze the ghosts of memory from her mind, but they beat at her. Father's rage, Lewis's sudden interest. "He was my maternal grandfather and I hardly knew him, but he willed all his money to me. I wasn't of age then, so it was placed in trust. And now…"

"Now you're of age," Trey guessed.

She nodded. She said nothing more, but he knew there was more to the story.

At least now he knew why the bounty hunters had proved so ruthless. A sizable reward must be awaiting the man who returned an heiress to her family.

"Some families hurt. It's just the way of things. I see it all the time. That doesn't always mean that they aren't good people. Families are tricky things."

She looked up at him with such wonder in her eyes, a sparkling glow that lit her from the inside. "How did you ever become a doctor?"

"I was smart enough to get into medical school." He said it just to tease a smile across her amazing mouth. And it worked. "I got this crazy notion somewhere that I could make a difference."

"That *is* a crazy notion."

"Don't I know it. I was living in an orphanage at the time. I was miserable there, but lucky, too. Because one of the teachers said she saw something in me. I was pretty good at math and science, and she helped me get into college. Can you believe it? I was a scholar."

"Not a serious one, I bet." She peered up at him through the sheen of light spilling onto the boardwalk, and he could see a sparkle of the deeper, more authentic Miranda. The one she protected so carefully.

"I've always been trouble." He winked. It was easier than the truth. He'd been a country boy at heart, and he missed the territories. The big-city college fed his intellectual curiosity, but those tall buildings and stone streets stifled his soul. "I did well enough and came back to Montana as a certified medical doctor."

"And you stayed, despite the weather."

"All this snow is good for business. Strained backs from shoveling, twisted ankles from slipping on the ice."

She laughed, chasing away the shadows of the past, bringing back the light to her face. "Here you had me almost believing that you were a rare doctor with unending integrity."

"I'll try harder." He wanted to keep her laughing so that her fears would never again haunt her. He wanted to hold her, so that she wouldn't feel alone. He wanted to treasure her so she would never feel without value.

But those feelings felt too new, too uncomfortable. He was used to being alone. He had to hold back, protect his heart and maybe hers, too.

He held the door for her, seeing her safely home. He resisted the urge to wrap her in his arms and kiss her. He knew this kindling desire would haunt him tonight.

She loosened her scarf and headed up the dark staircase. He watched until she disappeared from his sight, but not from his thoughts.

Chapter Nine

"*M*iranda, you're looking lovely tonight." Lewis broke through the crowd, another one of Stepmother's dinner parties, in a handsome black suit. "I've been looking for you."

He said it as if he expected her to apologize. But she wouldn't. The only reason she'd come tonight was because her father made her. After the way Lewis had treated her, only Father's threats could have brought her here. "There are guests to attend to. Stepmother is unwell tonight."

"You mean drunk." Scorn laced his words. Confidence shaped his face, making it hawklike and shiny. He imprisoned her wrist, his fingers bruising. "Come to the garden with me."

"No, Lewis. I must—"

"Shh." His lips grazed her cheekbone, not a pleasant sensation. He used his greater strength to spin her into his arms, and she looked around, silently hoping for rescue.

If she made a scene, her father would be furious.

"It grows harder by the day to keep from making you mine." Lewis's mouth covered hers, both hands tight at *her throat. His tongue surged into her mouth, wet and cold.*

Miranda tore awake. The dream faded, but the sick feeling in her stomach remained. Wind whipped at the eaves. She eased the curtains back to the gray light of early morning. Dawn could not penetrate a thick mantle of clouds and falling snow.

A shadow shifted on the street below, lost in the storm. One of the bounty hunter's men? She couldn't shake the feeling that it could be.

She didn't feel safe here, and she couldn't leave. All she could do was tell the sheriff, and what would she say? That she had a feeling?

I'll be your good-luck charm for as long as you need it. Trey's words rang warm in her mind.

What was she going to do about her feelings for Trey?

He found Josie already at the table, dressed for the day, changing Baby Beth out of her nightgown. He dropped into the chair next to her. "'Morning, gorgeous. We've got a busy day ahead."

"Are we goin' shoppin'?"

"We'll have to sneak away when Miranda isn't looking. She's coming today to help me out."

"She likes fried chicken." Josie plopped the nightgown on the table and contemplated poor naked Baby Beth. "We better have that tonight if we wanna make her happy."

"Did you hear that, Mrs. Stoltz? I guess we've got a request for supper. How do you feel about making dessert?"

"You name it, and I'll bake it." The capable woman set a platter of scrambled eggs on the table and the steaming coffeepot on a trivet.

"Chocolate cake!" Josie tugged a warm wool dress over Baby Beth's head. "With lots of chocolate frosting."

Was that Miranda's favorite or Josie's? Trey hid his chuckle as he poured a steaming cup of coffee.

A tap at the door drew his attention. Miranda smiled through the small panes of glass, snow clinging to her dark cinnamon-brown curls.

Josie launched off the chair, going as fast as her brace would allow. She flung open the door. "Miranda! You came."

"I did." She pushed the door shut. "I was up, so I came over. Trey, I wasn't sure how early you started your rounds."

"It depends on the morning." He stood to take her wraps and hang them near the crackling stove. Her rose scent tickled his nose. "Some patients can't make it in, especially in this weather, so I try to go to them. I've got a full day ahead. Did you want to accompany me this morning, get to know some of my patients?"

"I'd like that." She shook out her hair, scattering fragile bits of snow onto the hearth.

The blood kicked in his veins. He stepped away, trying to hide his reaction.

"Miranda, could you help me, please?" Josie grabbed Miranda by the hand and dragged her to the table. "I can't get Baby Beth's hair fixed right."

"Then it's a good thing I came by."

Trey watched, blood hot, chest tight, as she sat down next to Josie and took the doll into her lap.

The gentle play of Miranda's fingers made his blood even hotter. She was only braiding the doll's hair, but what would it feel like to have her fingers touch him like that?

That was the last thing he should be thinking. Trey

turned away and put more wood on the fire. The heat blazed against his face, and he tried to remember Miranda worked for him now. Well, sort of worked for him. No matter what he felt, he was determined to treat her with respect.

Woman and child huddled together, bent over the important job of making Baby Beth presentable. As if she felt his gaze, Miranda glanced up, her smile all for him.

"Look what I found." Sweet bells chimed as Trey drove up to the back porch in his sleigh. Music trilled in the snowy air.

"Jingle bells!" Josie clapped her gloved hands. "They sound so pretty."

"I thought you'd like them, Red."

Miranda watched the little girl amble carefully over the snowy ground, hindered by her injured leg. Snow clung to her gray wool cap and to the golden shade of her strawberry locks. She caught hold of a bell and jangled it. More music rang in the air.

"Are you gonna take me sleigh riding, Uncle Trey?"

"Not now, I've got my rounds to do, but this afternoon I will, if you're good."

"But I'm always good."

"That's what you think." The devil gleamed in his eyes, dark and nothing but trouble. Miranda felt mesmerized.

He waited until they were together speeding away from the house, waving goodbye to Josie and Mrs. Stoltz, before he leaned close to rumble in her ear. "After we finish the rounds, I'm going to take Josie for a ride. I'm thinking that the jingle bells might make her forget how afraid she is of any moving vehicle."

"Another of your doctor's remedies? Like red gum-drops?"

"We'll see if it works before I claim any credit."

Dulcet chimes rang through the air, merry and sweet. Miranda leaned back in the little seat, her thigh danger-ously close to Trey's beneath the cozy fur. She could feel his body's heat and smell the wood smoke clinging to his jacket. Snow danced in front of her eyes and clung to the brim of her hat.

Speeding so close along the top of the snow, she felt free. Happiness warmed her, despite the cold air stinging her face and hands. The merry bells jingled as the store-fronts zipped by in a blur.

A teamster unloading his wagon called out a good morning. The grocer sweeping snow off his awning did the same. Trey tipped his hat, a casual and masculine gesture that emphasized the broad cut of his shoulders and the iron strength in his arm.

Miranda couldn't help admiring that arm. A strange heat felt like liquid silk in her veins.

Too soon, Trey halted the horse in front of a house on the far side of town. The buckskin gave a toss of her head, sending a final jingle of music through the peaceful morn-ing.

Always a gentleman, Trey held the fur aside and as-sisted her from the sleigh.

As she followed him up the walk, she noticed the paint peeling over the door. Gaps in the doorframe were filled with newspaper and straw. Trey didn't seem to notice, something her father surely would have commented on, as he knocked.

"Oh, Doc-tor." A woman with blond hair and dark eyes looked almost panicked when she saw them standing on her crooked porch. "I did not ask—"

"I know. I wanted to come see your son." Miranda knew, by the respect in Trey's voice, that he was a kind of doctor different from her father and Lewis. Different from any she'd known.

He lowered his voice so that Miranda couldn't exactly hear, but the woman nodded and allowed them in.

No charge, he'd said, she was sure of it.

He led the way through a tidy parlor where an infant drowsed in a roomy basket, set close to the stove. The air was chilly, but when Miranda knelt to look at the baby, it was warm enough.

"He's a handsome boy," she told the mother, who beamed with pride and love. She ached to hold him. She missed caring for the children in her ward.

Trey swept the baby up in his arms, cradling the infant with an easy experience. His gentle hands tugged back the collar of the handknit sleeper and the neck of a little undershirt. He warmed his stethoscope before setting it on the baby's chest.

Trey listened a moment, gazing down into the boy's round face. Miranda stared in fascination. Such tenderness. She felt touched with the power of it, touched clear down to her soul. Trey cradled the boy against his chest, briefly, then laid him back into his warm, cozy bed.

Trey rooted through his black bag and produced a jar of menthol. Available at any mercantile, Miranda knew, but Trey gave it to the woman.

Miranda knew without asking there would be no charge for that, either. Trey opened the jar, dipped his fingers, and knelt down to apply it. His touch was so gentle against the baby's chest that the little cherub gave a big toothless grin.

"My husband and I, we thank you," Mrs. Vincetti

painfully articulated in her foreign English as she held the door. "We will not forget."

Trey wished her well. He ambled back to the sleigh as if he'd done nothing spectacular. But she knew. She'd worked for years in her father's hospital, tending children whose parents could pay.

An elderly woman crossing the street waved hello, and Trey waved back as he climbed into the sleigh.

As they sped away, Miranda felt a great shining light in her chest, made of respect and admiration. Honesty layered him, made him seem stronger, bigger than the entire world. And she couldn't look away.

"Dr. Gatlin, I heard there was a young lady who spent the night in your clinic. Unchaperoned." Mrs. Cavendish tsked, shaking her perfectly coifed gray head as she led the way down the curving staircase to the grand foyer below.

"She was a patient," he said, already knowing what the wealthy woman, who had too much time on her hands, was going to say.

Good thing Miranda had volunteered to help the sheriff's aunt for a while this afternoon so she wasn't here to be insulted.

"There's nothing unusual about that, Mrs. Cavendish. Injured or ill patients sometimes spend the night in my clinic."

"I'd heard she was in some kind of trouble with the law. I'm sure you're careful when it comes to your reputation."

"She was a patient, Mrs. Cavendish. And she's done nothing wrong, believe me." Trey loped off the last carpeted stair and marched across the imported marble that marked the path to the ornately carved door. "Keep your husband resting. If his chest pains resume, fetch me immediately.''

"Yes, yes." The refined woman waved one hand, diamonds and sapphires flashing. "I knew the rumors weren't true."

Trey headed his horse home. News traveled fast in a small town, and it always amazed him. Maybe Mrs. Cavendish would add her new tidbits of information and the gossips would move on to new subjects.

"Quite a get-up you got yourself there, Doc," Roy Danes called out from the hardware's back door.

"I thought the bells might catch me the attention of some beautiful woman." He slowed the mare. "How's that knee of yours?"

"Still a bit swollen. Gettin' better, though. Take care, Doc."

Trey tipped his hat. He liked living in a small town, where neighbors knew neighbors, where the air was clean and the mountains within reach.

He pulled up to Timothea Kelley's house, and Miranda was tapping down the shoveled steps as soon as the last bell chimed. It was good to see her. "You've been busy, I see."

"I tried." She slid into the cozy seat, her slim shoulder brushing his.

Her rose scent, light and sweet, filled his senses. "You shoveled the walk, swept off the porch. What else did you do?"

"I put warm compresses on Mrs. Kelley's back. I think it helped her pain."

"Should I run up and check on her?"

"She's finally sleeping soundly."

He tucked the fur against her chin, so close he could see the satin texture of her skin and smell the snow in her hair. She bit her bottom lip, worrying that lush softness and drawing his gaze.

Heat pounded through him, and he wanted to kiss her again. Shaking with need, he stared hard at the road ahead, vowing to keep this unusual reaction under control.

"Trey." Sheriff Kelley wheeled his mount out of a side street and drew the animal to a halt. "How's my aunt?"

"Miranda says she's feeling better."

"Good day, ma'am." The sheriff tipped his hat. "I've got some news for you. My deputies and I just finished a sweep of the town. There's no bounty hunter holed up anywhere, not that we could find. Now, those scoundrels are like rats, they can hide in the cracks. But we haven't found any. Chances are, you're safe. My deputies and I will still keep an eye out, but I'd breathe easy if I were you."

The sheriff was such a capable-looking man. Anyone could see he did his job well. And Trey trusted him. She just wasn't sure she'd finally escaped those dangerous men. She wanted to believe it. She really did. Slow hope lit like new embers in her heart.

Yet she still didn't feel safe.

"Thanks for letting us know, Sheriff." Trey's shoulders eased a fraction, as if he'd been worried, too.

"I'm keepin' an eye on the telegraph office and on the drifter we uncovered. Just so you don't worry, ma'am." He tipped his hat and rode on, guiding his big black horse up the drive.

"That's a piece of good news." Trey headed his mare down the street. Fences and houses streaked past. "Now do you believe me?"

"I'm starting to." She'd been running too long to feel completely at ease. Maybe it was because she'd never really been safe, never at peace. Living in her father's home hadn't been easy. "Where are you taking Josie today?"

"Wherever she wants. I just want to get her into this sleigh. She's got a mountain of fears to overcome."

"She's had quite a trauma. She lost her parents and her entire life."

"True. And now I'm trying to build her a new one." Wind tousled thick dark locks over his brow, hiding his eyes. "I'm going to start with her fears. I want to get rid of them one by one, so she can sleep through the night."

"With gumdrops and jingle bells?"

"If I can get her to sleep through the night and ride in a vehicle again, then it's a start." The forthright clench to his square jaw, his fisted, capable hands, and the conviction that stiffened his spine told of Trey's deep love for his niece.

"I'll do anything to help," she offered, her voice shaky.

"Then watch the clinic for me today. That would give me time to take her out shopping."

"I can change bedding and bandages, but I'm not a nurse. I don't want to mislead you."

"I just need someone to wait for disaster and then direct it to me." He winked.

He was funny, all right. "I'm not doing very much to pay you back."

"You'd be surprised." He stopped the sleigh in front of the clinic. "I can send Mrs. Stoltz over if you don't want to stay alone. But if Kelley gave you the okay, then you're safe as you can be, given the situation."

"I'll be fine alone." Hope. It glowed within her, a meager, precious light.

Trey covered her hand with his. "We won't be long." He held the fur coverlet, and she climbed out into the cold. He dashed away, bells ringing melody and harmony, fading into silence.

Snow fell, the wind whispered, the wind carried the scents of wood smoke and winter. But her heart felt like spring, newly touched by a light great enough to warm anything.

"Uncle Trey!" Josie waved from the bottom step where she sat alone, ready to shop. "I've been waiting and waiting."

"Me, too. Do you know what we're going to get?"

"Candy, first." Josie limped toward him, that bounce new in her step, Baby Beth clutched in one arm.

"Hop in. You should hear how pretty the bells sound."

"I've heard 'em before, Uncle Trey. I sure like 'em, but I'm starting to get scared."

He held out his hand and she stepped into the low-slung sleigh. "Miranda told me she likes the bells."

"Miranda?" Josie's eyes lit, distracted from some of her fear. "Boy, we're really gonna make her happy, aren't we?"

"Sure. The chocolate cake alone will do that for most people." Trey tucked the fur around the fragile little girl, then gathered the reins. "I prescribe a lot of chocolate."

"That's even better than gumdrops."

"Did you know chocolate's good for making scared feelings go away? Maybe we'll have to pick some up at the mercantile."

"Oh, Uncle Trey." Josie rolled her eyes. "That's what peppermint is for."

"Oh, I get that wrong sometimes." He winked, keeping the mare to a walk.

Josie's eyes widened as the sleigh shot forward. "I th-think I c-could use some peppermint right now."

"All I've got is gumdrops." He pulled the paper bag out of his jacket pocket. He always kept candy handy for his littler patients. "Maybe the yellow ones will help."

Josie looked skeptical but picked out several yellow candies from the bag.

"What song does this remind you of?" Trey tucked the bag back into his pocket.

"Jingle bells."

"Sing the words to me."

Josie's thin soprano carried the melody, and the bells chimed an off-rhythm harmony. Main Street stretched ahead of them. The snow was tapering off, and the child beside him began to relax as she belted out the chorus.

He tucked her safe against his side and joined Josie's wobbling second verse.

Miranda helped an old lady home, who'd come to the clinic for a minor cut and was afraid to walk back as twilight fell.

It was dark by the time she returned to the clinic. The black windows told her that Trey hadn't returned yet. She wondered how Josie managed the sleigh ride.

She turned the doorknob and stepped into the darkness. A shadow stirred. A footstep drummed on the floor.

She took a step back, fear sluicing through her veins like ice water. A bounty hunter? Maybe he'd hidden from the sheriff. Maybe—

"Miranda, is that you? Goodness, I didn't hear you come in." The shadow moved, and a blaze of orange light speared the darkness as someone opened the stove's door. Mrs. Stoltz.

Relief left her shaking hard.

"I heard when I stopped by the mercantile how you were helping Timothea. Word travels fast in a small town.'' The brisk woman managed a tight smile as she unloaded the wood she held into the snapping fire. "I can't tell you how we've missed having a nurse around here."

"I'm not a real nurse."

"No? Well, a good deed is a good deed. Come sit by the stove and thaw out. Goodness, you look half frozen. Dr. Gatlin isn't back yet." Mrs. Stoltz slammed the iron door shut. "It's good of him to take over the job of raising that poor orphan, but he's a busy man. I suppose that's the reason he brought you in."

Miranda bristled at the veiled censor. "He didn't bring me in. I—"

"Always looking out for others, that's our doc." Mrs. Stoltz's mouth thinned, and she strode toward the hallway with force. "Make sure you remember that."

Miranda sensed the housekeeper only meant to protect Trey. She wasn't the only woman he'd patched up, sheltered, protected. But there was a hint of judgment there, too, as if Mrs. Stoltz had guessed Miranda's true feelings.

Was she that obvious? Embarrassment heated her face. Had Trey noticed it, too?

Miranda lit a lamp so the shadows didn't feel so heavy. But the brightness only cast back her reflection in the windows and made her visible to the street. Horses clomped by on Main, the noise faint and muffled. Like the voices of schoolboys who called out, running for home.

She didn't like being visible from the street. Old habits died hard, and she'd kept one step ahead of the bounty hunters because of it. Her stomach tightened, and she tried to tell herself she was safe here. The sheriff said there was no danger.

Or any that he could find.

She drew the drapes, and even in the privacy of the waiting room, she felt exposed. As if a threat lurked out there in the dark on those pleasant streets.

She wouldn't stay here. Not for long. As the fire crackled, radiating a welcome heat, she took the greenbacks from her cloak pocket, given to her by the woman she'd helped home as payment on account.

She turned down the wick, preferring the anonymity of the darkness. But as the light faded, it felt suffocating. She headed down the hall to Trey's office. The sound of her shoes striking the wood floor boomed in her ears, unnaturally loud.

This didn't feel right. She didn't feel safe. She kept walking, breathing carefully, trying to keep panic from mounting. Fear fluttered in her chest and she fought to control it.

The sheriff said it was safe. Trey believed him. Then why was she panicking? Why—

A careful squeak split the air. It was the front door. Someone was opening it. Miranda froze against the shadowed wall, melding with the dark. She had to think. She had to figure out what to do.

The door clinked closed, and heavy footsteps thudded on the floor. "Hello? Anyone home?"

She wasn't about to answer. If she could just make it to the back door quietly…then a board squeaked beneath her foot, giving away her location in the dark.

Boots drummed in her direction.

Miranda raced through the dark, smacking her knee into the back of a chair. It skidded across wood, making a horrible racket.

The footsteps were right outside the threshold. She fumbled with the back door's knob, and it wouldn't turn. Darn it, she couldn't be trapped in here. She just couldn't.

"Doc-tor, is that you?" a man's voice asked, confusion heavy in his baritone.

A match flared to illuminate a stranger's face, not a gunman's. He wore a heavy fur coat and workman's boots, flecked from the hard-falling snow outside.

"Oh, pardon me, ma'am. I come to pay what I owe."

Miranda could have melted to the floor in embarrassment. "I, uh…Dr. Gatlin isn't here."

"You are alone here and I frightened you. I must apologize." He reached into his pocket and pulled out his billfold. "Will the doctor soon return?"

"I-I'm not sure."

"He showed us kindness in treating our son with no worry of the bill first, and I intend to pay him. To show him we are good Americans."

Miranda saw the respect in this man's eyes. And knew then that Trey, in his own way, was a richer man than Lewis or her father could ever dream of being. "You can leave a payment and I'll make sure Dr. Gatlin receives it."

"It is all I can afford now, but my word is good. I will pay him what I owe." Mr. Vincetti laid three one-dollar bills on the corner of Trey's messy desk. "Good evening, ma'am."

Miranda's knees felt so weak, she couldn't see him out. Instead she collapsed into Trey's chair until the shaking subsided.

This time when the front door flew open on a gust of wind, she didn't startle. She recognized Trey's powerful, jaunty gait.

"Miranda? What are you doing there in the dark? Trying to hide from me?"

"Yes, but you were too smart for me."

"It's a gift, being smart." He winked, but he was serious, too, as he dropped his hat on the paper-piled desk. "Of course, in the dark like this, it's harder to admire all my attributes."

"Like your humility."

"Exactly." He noticed the money and the notes. "Thanks for seeing to this. I'm not likely to get rich in a small-town practice. Not like your father probably is. Or your fiancé."

Lewis. She didn't want to think about him. "What's money when a man has your dash and charm?"

"That's what I say." He held out his hand. "Mrs. Stoltz said I could find you here. Josie's waiting at the house. Supper is almost ready, and we need a beautiful woman at our table to make it complete."

"Too bad there aren't any beautiful women around here."

"Then you'll just have to do." He took her hand in his and helped her out of the chair.

Her heart skidded, and she felt lit up from the inside out. She shouldn't be reacting to him like this. But not even a hundred bounty hunters on her trail could frighten her away from this moment as Trey laid his hand across her back, a touch of comfort and friendship.

She felt engulfed by heat. By sensation. And no longer alone.

"Did I happen to tell you that tonight is a special evening?" His words vibrated through her like the resonant strings of a cello. "Josie needs some cheering up. I want to show her I'm her family now. That she can be happy with a dull old bachelor like me."

"What? Did I hear you right?" Miranda rebuttoned her cloak as Trey shouldered open the door. "Did you just admit you aren't always dashing and charming?"

"Shh. It's a secret I don't want to get around. This town

is a gossip mill.'' Darkness enveloped him, but his voice
smiled. ''It's draining on a man to be debonair *all* the
time.''

''Just what is it you want me to do for Josie?''

''Besides being your usual wonderful self?'' Trey led
the way through the shadowed snow, touched by silver
and gold wherever light brushed it. ''We're going to have
fun tonight. No work. No worry. It's all Josie's idea.''

Little tingles sped up and down her spine. His hand in
hers felt hot as flame. The bitter cold felt like spring simply walking beside him.

You aren't the only woman he's helped. She tried to
remember that. Tried to remember Mrs. Stoltz's sensible
warning.

''There you are!'' The front door flew open to reveal
Josie, fists planted on her hips. ''I've been waitin' and
waitin'. Guess what we're havin'?''

''Fried chicken, your favorite?'' Miranda stomped the
snow from her boots and shook flakes from her hat and
cloak.

''Nope. *Your* favorite.''

She studied Trey's innocent expression and Josie's excited one. ''That explains all the questions you've been
asking.''

''Yep. Come in. Hurry!'' Oh, she looked happy. Her
gait was faster, and her voice buoyant. Her dress swirled
around her as she fetched Baby Beth from the sofa. ''And
guess what? We're havin' chocolate cake for dessert.''

''And that's not all.'' Trey's hand lighted on her shoulder, his touch claiming.

Miranda froze at the bouquet of pearl-pink roses lying
across the extra place setting at the table. Her favorite
flower. ''How on earth—''

''Dashing, debonair men have our ways.'' His voice

sluiced across her nape. ''This is for you, Miranda. To remind you that sometimes anything is possible.''

''A prescription from the good doctor?''

''Absolutely.''

His lips grazed her neck in a molten, leisurely kiss. She felt the shock quake all the way down her spine.

He moved away, but the feel of his breath and his kiss on her skin remained.

Chapter Ten

"*The Adventures of Huckleberry Finn* is going to have to wait until tomorrow night." Trey closed the leather-bound book, drumming with growing need for the woman just across the hearth from him.

He'd been trying not to look at her all evening, but his rebellious gaze kept flickering over her, noticing every softness and every curve.

He focused on his niece, slumped on the sofa, feet up, doll tucked in one arm. "It's nearly ten o'clock and, Red, you're yawning."

"Nope. I was stretching my mouth."

"That was definitely a yawn." Miranda laughed, her voice lullaby-rich. "Baby Beth looks pretty tired, too."

"But I wanna stay up some more. Please, Uncle Trey? I wanna know if Huck and Jim get caught."

"Red, I may be the most fun-seeking uncle this side of the Badlands, but it's bedtime. March."

Josie let out a long-suffering sigh and hopped off the sofa. She clomped across the cozy parlor to her bedroom door. "Can Miranda come help me?"

"I'd love to." Miranda rose from the forest-green wing chair, all fluid grace and style. Her dress shivered around her slim form, the satiny material hinting at curved hips and slender thighs.

She left him near the window, so dazed he stared like a fish out of water, gaping without air or a sense of direction in this brave new world where her rose-colored skirts swirled around her ankles and her breasts stirred slightly with her gait.

Heat spilled through his groin, and he felt heavy. Very heavy. His denims were suddenly way too snug. *This is just lust.* He tried to find comfort in that thought. Lust not love.

Lust was dangerous enough, but it didn't carry with it the greater hazards of love. Lust was easier to control; after all, it was just a physical response. He could imagine cold Arctic winds, icicles hanging on the eaves, being caught in a raging blizzard, and control this physical and intense desire for her.

Except it wasn't working.

It had been building all evening, from the insane moment he'd brushed his lips across the back of her neck. He'd tasted satin heat. He'd breathed in her rose scent. And every major system in his body overreacted.

"Trey?" Miranda swept into sight. Backlit by the lamps in Josie's room she was beauty enough to fill his senses.

Thoughts of blizzards and icicles melted and he was left with a stuttering heartbeat and an ache in his chest he couldn't deny. Not any longer.

He wanted Miranda in his arms, to kiss her, to hold her, to give her as much pleasure as she would allow.

And, damn it, it wasn't his right. It wasn't his place. He couldn't take advantage of her like that.

He realized she was waiting for a response, and he cleared his throat. When he spoke, he could hear the strain in his voice, raw with need for her. "Does Josie want more hot chocolate? She's bribed me with two cups, saying it would help her sleep."

"Not that you denied her. Her little body is practically shaking with too much sugar." There was no censure. "She's far too wound up to sleep. I thought maybe you could read to her."

"She doesn't want—"

Josie's voice murmured in the background, and Trey fell silent, already knowing what she'd told Miranda. Her parents used to read her to sleep every night. She didn't want to be read to in bed. She didn't want to snuggle beneath the warm quilt, safe for the night, and remember her loss.

"Really?" Miranda listened intently to Josie, then turned to face him. Mischief shaped her kissable mouth. "Trey, I didn't know you play the guitar."

"*No*. No concert." Not tonight. He needed to stay as far away as he could from Miranda. Considering that his need to touch her still raged, it was the best option.

"Please, Uncle Trey?" Josie called from inside the bedroom.

"Yes, please?" Miranda's mouth moved over those two words.

That's exactly how her mouth moves when she kisses. His heartbeat kicked harder.

"It's late. Both of you are probably tired, and, Miranda, if you hear my singing voice you'll probably have nightmares for the next month straight. Not even red gumdrops will help."

"I'd be willing to risk it." She crossed her arms over her middle, drawing her dress snug across her breasts.

Those beautifully shaped breasts looked full and soft.

He ached to weigh them in his palms and draw their dark tips into his mouth one at a time....

She's a vulnerable woman in need of protection. If he repeated that enough times to himself, maybe his body would behave.

Now, if he could just sound casual when he answered, as if he hadn't been dreaming of her. He cleared his throat again. "I'm out of practice. Besides, I don't want to strain my fingers. I might need them in prime condition for surgery."

"Your schedule's clear for tomorrow. I looked." She crossed the room, her breasts slightly swaying.

"I've got to be ready for every emergency."

"I can't believe this. The dashing, debonair doctor is actually being modest." She knelt before him.

So close all he had to do was lean forward and cover those tantalizing lips with his.

"Come on, Trey. Do it." She was talking about him playing. "Josie's really counting on it."

He fought the urge to haul her across his lap and kiss her until neither of them could breathe.

"Just one song." She glittered like starlight on a dark ocean, silvered and bright and rare. Gone was the worry drawn tight around her eyes, the quiet distance, the need to run from anyone and everything.

She was here now, gentleness and grace. And she was all his.

"Let me step outside and bring in some firewood first." Maybe standing in the freezing temperatures would take care of his condition.

A condition that only, impossibly, grew harder as she leaned to press a kiss to his cheek. A brush of her silken lips, the satiny rasp of her hair and the soft burst of her rose fragrance filled his senses, left him breathless, left him reeling.

Then she smiled, and his whole heart tumbled.

Miranda couldn't even blink as Trey laid the flat of his right palm against the vibrating guitar strings, silencing the quiet vibrato of the ballad's last chord.

"I think she's finally asleep," he whispered.

"No, I'm not." Josie stirred, so sleepy she could barely open her eyes. "Don't stop the song, Uncle Trey. Please? I don't wanna go to sleep."

"Why not? That's how little girls grow." Affection harmonized his voice. "You don't want to be short all your life, do you? When you're thirty years old and the shortest woman in town, you'll be sorry you didn't listen to me."

Josie managed a sleepy smile.

"You don't believe me?" The guitar strings squeaked as he positioned his fingers on the bar. "That very thing happened to my stepsister, Rachel. She'd stay up reading when she was supposed to be sleeping, and today she's the shortest lady this side of Canada."

Miranda couldn't take her gaze from him. Low lamplight flickered shyly across his face, leaving him mostly in shadow. There was magic in this man of strength and might. It shone in his eyes and left no doubt.

Trey Gatlin was the greatest man she'd ever met. Strong enough to be gentle, mighty enough to love a child, and courageous enough to find happiness in a winter-cold world.

"Pledge to me only with your eyes," he sang. His voice was low as a lullaby, cello-rich, and lured her farther out from shore, away from the solid ground beneath her feet to feelings uncharted and new.

His guitar silenced. "There. Now she's asleep."

"She's not protesting."

"I think I might have found a way to lull her to sleep at night. Finally." He looked satisfied, as if a great burden had eased from his wide shoulders. "I'm glad Josie told me how much you like music."

"I'm not fooled, Trey. I know you were behind her questions and this wonderful evening."

He followed her to the door. "I wanted to give you something to remember us by. A moment of peace to a woman who looks as if she needs one."

She stepped into the warm parlor, keeping her back firmly turned. She wouldn't let her pillow-soft heart believe in a fairy-tale love that didn't exist. She was just being practical. "Do you do this for all the women you help?"

"Only for you." He laid the guitar into its case, the strings making an echo of melody and harmony that faded into silence.

Her heart melted. Just like that. She didn't want it to, but she felt lost at sea without the shoreline to guide her.

"I'm not sure what you thought of this evening." He stared hard at the floor between them, his throat worked. "You're used to a much fancier style of life. When I got the notion to do this, I didn't know you were an heiress."

"It was a beautiful evening. I can't hear music like that back home."

"Now you're teasing me." The distance between them seemed too far, and yet wasn't. He was just a touch away.

When he looked up, his eyes were dark, his mouth unsmiling. "I might as well come out and say it. I'm embarrassed about offering to pay you. I thought you might need the money, a woman on the run. I'm sure I can't pay the going wages for a beautiful heiress."

"Lately those wages have been pretty low." She still felt adrift, feeling the tug and ebb of emotions she couldn't name. "It was thoughtful of you, offering me work. It isn't like I can head back home and withdraw funds from my big trust fund."

He nodded, and a shock of dark hair tumbled over his brow. "I'm not used to being around big-city heiresses. I'll have to brush up on my manners."

"Not on my account. If you become any more wonderful, I'm going to be in big trouble."

"Why's that?"

"I just might start believing in this, this happiness. And then where will I be?"

"You should believe in happiness, Miranda. I do."

"And what's your secret, Dr. Gatlin? Is there a special medicine I don't know about?"

"Nothing I can prescribe." Moments ticked by as snowflakes pounded against the window and the wind gusted, puffing up ashes in the grate, feeding the fire. He reached for the edge of her collar, thumbing the lace trim, standing so close behind her she could feel his body's heat.

Her skin prickled, as if electrified. A strange, exhilarating tingle telegraphed through every part of her.

"You've made a difference being here for Josie." His lips brushed the outer shell of her ear, brief and light, the faintest of touches.

She felt it like a punch to her soul. Fire tore through her.

Desire warmed the chocolate flecks in his eyes. "I just wanted you to know we're grateful. You've made this transition an easier one for Josie and me."

"I'm the grateful one." Her throat felt raw and dry. "You're a good man, Trey. I never thought I'd say that any man, but just when I'd given up hope you came along."

"I thought the same about you." He stared so hard at her lips, her mouth burned.

He's going to kiss me. Tingling in anticipation, she leaned forward just a fraction. Aching for him, she waited. Her whole body hungered for his touch.

He moved a fraction of an inch closer, their breaths mingling.

His mouth softened, his lips ready to slant over hers. Her mouth opened, too, hungry for the velvet heat of his kiss.

He pulled away. Leaving her soft-mouthed and aching. Embarrassment swept over her.

A gust of wind slammed against the house, enough to rattle the front door in its frame. Snow drove through the minuscule crack beneath the door, and the temperature dropped in the room, leaving Miranda shivering.

"Looks like another blizzard." He pulled back the edge of the curtain. There was nothing but dark and storm. "Those winds are fierce."

"I'd better head home before it gets any worse."

"There are blizzards you can go out in and there are those you shouldn't. This is one of them." He squinted into the dark. "I can barely see the tree next to the house. It's nearly bent double."

"You can't mean I'm stuck here."

"You absolutely can't go out in this. Maybe the winds will die down in a bit—"

"I can't believe this." She shouldn't be alone with him tonight. Her soul ached for him. And he probably thought... She shook her head, remembering Mrs. Stoltz's warning. She shouldn't confuse Trey's warmth for, well, an affection that could never exist. "Maybe I can head over to the clinic."

"You'll stay right here where I know you're safe." A muscle in his jaw ticked. "Stay here where it's warm and I know you won't wind up with another case of frostbite. I'll sleep on the sofa."

"I'm not sleeping in your bed, Trey Gatlin."

"But—"

"*I'm* taking the sofa."

"It doesn't feel right."

"And what would?" There was no way she was going to lie on the same mattress where he rested every night. "If I stay, it's the sofa."

He raked one hand through his dark hair, leaving it tousled and rakish. Desire captured her like a crosscurrent, pulling her where she didn't want to go.

He disappeared into the dark, his step echoing in the necessary room. The closet door squeaked open, and she took a moment to take a deep breath and try to orient herself.

He's a friend, nothing more. She moved the guitar case from the edge of the sofa. Trey was a compassionate man. He helped those in need. He was helping her, that's all.

He knew you wanted him to kiss you. Heat crept across her face. How could she be feeling this way? She'd given up on wanting to love a man. Given up on thinking it was possible.

Now here she was, yearning for Trey's touch. This man who took time from his work to make a snowman with his niece, who adjusted his life to make room for an orphaned child, who helped whomever he could, without motive.

He was like no man she'd ever known before. Part hero, part dream, he made her begin to believe…

"For you, miss." He presented her a set of flannel sheets, crisply folded and smelling of soap and winter sunshine. He winked. "The finest pair in the house."

"You, sir, are too kind." She tried not to breathe in the wood, man and leather scent of him. Tried not to meet his gaze as she took the soft sheets from his strong, gentle hands.

"Let me help." His steely shoulder brushed her arm as he took the bottom sheet and shook it.

She caught the end, tingling from head to toe, and tucked it neatly into the cushions. They worked together, adding the top sheet and a couple of warm blankets.

All the while her nerves zinged with sensation. Heat built deep in her stomach and gathered. Why had a blizzard chosen tonight to hit?

She should be locked safe in her room alone and away from this temptation. Away from making a fool of herself.

"That wind's still howling. Sounds even worse." Trey turned down one lamp.

Flame flickered and died, giving way to darkness. Only one light burned on the table near the sofa, casting a sepia glow across the pillow Trey had found for her.

"Good night, Miranda." His step knelled through the shadowed room, tugging at her heart. "If you need anything, you know where I am."

She couldn't force a thank you from her too-tight throat. So much swirled inside her, from aching passion to old fears.

She'd loved this evening, loved spending time with Trey. From his thoughtful flowers to the rumbling power of his voice as he'd read aloud and then sang old love songs, she'd been spellbound. Every breath she took wrung her heart tighter. She wanted to love him.

She couldn't love him.

She pulled aside the curtain and leaned her forehead against the frosted glass. Ice cooled her skin. She rubbed her fingertips through the glaze until she could see the faint reflection of the room behind her superimposed over the black world outside.

Black ice slammed against the glass with gale force. The night was impenetrable and dangerous, and she could see only the faint outline of the tree right outside the window, shaking like a mop in the wind.

Then something moved. She could have sworn it was a man. She looked again and saw only darkness and only shadows. Her stomach constricted tightly. Was someone out there?

She saw the curved length of a fir bough, one shadow against a thousand others, undulate in the wind. A tree branch, not a man. Not a bounty hunter.

"Looking for trouble?" He was back, strolling across the floor with a masculine confidence that made the air rush from her lungs.

"Trouble? I think I found it."

"You sure have, lady." With the way his dark hair was tousled, he looked more like a pirate, untamed and dangerous. "That wind isn't going to quit blowing just because you want it to."

"You're spoiling my hopes, Trey." She turned away before he looked in her eyes, before he got too close. "I thought I saw someone."

"In this storm?" Trey shook his head. "Look at the ice being driven through the walls. No one's out there, Miranda. Trust me."

"I do." Her whole heart twisted. "I just can't…" She sighed. Her whole life was at stake.

"A man could go out in this, sure, but not for long. Not just to stand outside in the cold looking in. The doors are bolted and the windows are locked. It's a worse storm tonight than the one you were kidnapped in.''

''I know. I can tell the difference in the wind.'' She stepped back. Tonight she'd almost forgotten who she was and who was following her.

But what if there *had* been a man outside, gun drawn?

''You can't run forever, Miranda.''

''I'm not running from, I'm running to. If I can get far enough away, I'll be free. I can make a life for myself, my own life. I can have a home like this one, comfortable and peaceful.''

''You want a sanctuary. We all want that.'' He raked one hand through his hair, grimacing. ''Something tells me you wouldn't be happy in a place like this.''

''In Montana? Why not? It has everything that matters.'' *It has you.* The word caught on the edge of her tongue.

''It's not the world you're used to. You must miss home.''

''Sometimes.'' His words tugged at something deep within her, a lonely hurt wrapped up in fear. ''But it's one of the reasons why I'm running away.''

''For now, this night, you don't have to watch for trouble outside the window.'' His lips grazed her ear.

Miranda closed her eyes. She couldn't let herself act. She couldn't let herself feel—

''For tonight, there are no bounty hunters. No Pinkerton agents. No gunmen watching. No fiancé.'' His words brushed across the side of her face, coffee-sweet and male-rich. ''There are no more villains to flee, Miranda.''

She ached to turn to him, to lay her cheek against his chest and find sanctuary in his arms. *Remember what you are to him.* He helped women on the run, children whose families couldn't pay in full and anyone who needed him.

Her throat felt too full, her heart too raw. "Since the day I ran out of my father's study, I knew I could never trust anyone again. Not anyone. Until you."

"And look where that's gotten you." His kindness rumbled, his voice cello-deep.

"Yes, look where it's gotten me. This is the first time in forever that I don't feel alone." Even if it was just for this night, it felt like heaven. Like paradise had drifted down from the skies and landed at her feet.

"You don't deserve to be alone." He splayed his hand against the curve of her jaw.

She felt like rare silk and warm woman. He wanted to love her until the fear faded from her eyes. Until the disbelief vanished. But he didn't have the right.

She was an heiress, made of gentleness and grace. She didn't belong in a modest log cabin in the middle of Montana Territory. With a man like him.

He knew it. But that didn't slow the beat of his heart or the desire spinning magic in his blood.

It took all his willpower to step back when he wanted to hold her. To let her know she would always be cherished with him at her side.

"You're shaking." He couldn't help caring.

"I'm tired, and I don't want to stay the night with you."

"Are you afraid of me?"

"No." She squeezed her eyes shut, lamplight flickering like kisses over her fragile cheekbones. "It's been a long time since I believed in this."

"Me, too." The tenderness in his heart welled deeper every time he touched her. "For once, let someone take care of you."

"That's what Lewis always said. He just wanted to take

care of me." Her sweet mouth wobbled. "I don't think that's what you mean."

"No." He smoothed his hand across her brow. "Let me show you what I mean."

He fit her slim fingers between his, and palm-to-palm led her to the sofa. She brushed against his chest as he eased her down on the cushions, facing the hearth. The orange glow of flame worshiped her with gentle light.

A brighter flame sizzled through his veins and settled in his heart.

He tossed mossy logs in the grate, and the fire greedily sizzled and snapped. His desire for her was hotter, but he could control it. He eased beside her and tenderly drew her to him.

She was magic and starlight, angel and wonder, and she leaned against his chest with a sigh. Her hair smelled of roses and winter and the faintest hint of chocolate that made him ache to taste her. Her body was willowy and feminine-soft, and he gritted his teeth.

She needed comfort. She needed holding. She didn't need him to lay her back and explore her sweet woman's curves.

Light flickered across her face and burnished her hair. His heart drummed from wanting her. His blood sang with desire, but he continued to cradle her, safe and warm. The sweetness of holding her dazzled him.

The blizzard raged. He cradled her until she stopped trembling, and still she didn't move from his arms. She remained, snuggled against his chest as the hours ticked by and her breathing slowed.

Finally, her eyes drifted shut.

Something greater than desire sparkled to life in his heart. A long-forgotten emotion that filled him up until he couldn't breathe.

Love. A love he had no right to express. For a woman he had no right to claim.

Coppery blood filled her mouth. She could smell it in her nose, where pain split a sharp line from cheekbone to cheekbone. She wiped her face with her torn sleeve, and the fabric came away red.

Head wounds bleed a lot. It was nothing serious. *That was what Father had said. How could he say something like that?*

The carriage jostled hard, and her teeth clacked together. The right-side molars hurt when they touched. Hurt from the blow Lewis had given her.

Lewis is the greatest man I've ever known. *Father's words, too. Once she'd believed them. Now she didn't know how to make him see the truth.*

She only knew that she couldn't marry Lewis. Not even if the wedding date was already set, the gown measured and the church reserved.

She heard the clip-clop *of an approaching horse, faster than the others on the road. She twisted around, careful of her injured shoulder, and peered out the window.*

Miranda fought her way out of the dream. She woke up struggling for breath, but the fear didn't seem to overwhelm her. She was warm and not afraid. She struggled to open her eyes.

Bam. Bam. A hard bang rattled the front door in its frame. It wasn't the wind.

"Let me up, please." Trey moved, his hard male body scooting out from beneath hers.

No wonder she felt safe. She'd fallen asleep in his arms, lying on his chest. Heat lingered in her body, strange and tingling. Confused, she listened to Trey's step as he crossed the room, the howling blizzard and the rhythmic pounding at the door.

Fear sluiced over her like a hard rain. Was it a bounty hunter? Had the sheriff been wrong?

Trey threw open the door. A big man's frame shadowed the threshold, eerily silhouetted by the pitch blackness behind him.

Light flickered as he lit a lantern. Flame illuminated the carved wonder of Trey's shoulder and the sheriff's lean, hard face. Snow covered his fur coat, and his voice sounded grim. The lawman stumbled inside, half frozen.

Trey struggled to close the door. "Miranda, I'm heading out. The sheriff says a little girl wandered out of her bed and managed to get outside."

"In this cold? A small child could freeze to death in minutes." She slipped out from beneath the warm blanket, worry coiled tight. This time the fear wasn't for herself. "I'm going with you."

"It's too cold. Josie can't be alone—"

"Sheriff, how is the child?"

"Bad enough." The lawman shrugged out of his coat and knelt before the fire. He added wood, shivering so hard his teeth rattled.

"Then I'm going, too. Trey, you'll need all the help you can get." She climbed to her feet and tried to avoid the sheriff's curious gaze. "What about Josie?"

"She can't be left alone." Trey looked as if he was figuring out how to keep her here and safe.

"I'll stay with the girl." The sheriff chattered from the hearth. "It's going to take me a while to warm up enough to head back home. By then, one of you will be back."

"Thanks, Mac." Trey wrapped a scarf around his neck, dressing warmly but fast.

She slipped into her cloak. "What exactly did you plan on doing with Josie when you got a night call?"

"I haven't solved that problem yet." He pulled on a pair of gloves. "I'm figuring this out as I go."

Trey donned a wool cap, then reached for the knob. "Wrap up warm. It's only two blocks to the Steiners' house, but it will feel like a mile. Can you make it?"

"If you can." She tucked her scarf into place.

Trey's hand caught hers and he led her out into the brutal cold. The fury of the storm knocked her back against the wall. Trey tucked her against his chest and blocked the brunt of the wind with his body.

Protecting her. Always protecting her.

Chapter Eleven

The storm beat at the window in the bedroom where little Nellie Steiner lay shivering, tears of pain staining her cheeks. He'd given her as much laudanum as he dared, and hated those tears.

"She was supposed to be asleep in her bed." Mrs. Steiner's guilt and fear didn't relent. "I heard the door slam open from the wind, and I ran straight out of bed in my nightclothes. I should have been faster. No, I should have had a chain put on the door, one out of her reach. What was she doing?"

"I was looking for Santa Claus, Mama." Nellie cried out as Trey wrapped a warm cloth around her frostbitten hand. "I just wanted to see him. He checks on girls and boys when they're sleepin'. That's what the story said."

"The story I read to you tonight?" Kayla Steiner rubbed her face wearily, her shoulders slumping. Certain now her daughter's condition was her fault, she couldn't hold back the tears.

"I'm more sympathetic to all parents, now that I have a five-year-old of my own," Trey told her quietly, hoping to at least coax the mother out of her guilt. "I have learned more about dressing dolls than I ever wanted to know.''

Mrs. Steiner almost smiled. ''That kind of experience is good for a doctor.''

''Here. Hold her hand in yours, like this.'' Trey let Kayla take her daughter's frostbitten fingertips. ''Keep this pressed to her skin. Not too hard, just enough. We want to warm her up slowly. In a little bit, we'll try a warmer bath.''

He heard a thud and turned around.

Miranda knelt in the shadowed corridor, retrieving a fallen stick of wood. She leaned sideways to accommodate the heavy load she carried. Snow clung to her dark curls.

''You've got quite an armful here. Let me help.'' He reached out and lifted away more than half the wood.

''Thank you.'' She didn't meet his gaze. ''I had to go outside and get more wood. Nellie's bathwater is almost ready.''

''I didn't expect you to go back out in the storm. Not even to bring in fuel.'' He led the way into the heated kitchen. ''I don't want to have to treat you for frostbite, too.''

''I'm just fine.'' She wouldn't even smile. Keeping her back to him, she knelt to empty her load of wood on the hearth.

He caught hold of her wrist. His fingers covered hers, and he knew, even though she'd worn gloves, she wasn't telling the truth. ''Carrying wood isn't good for those stitches in your arm.''

''They're fine, too.'' She pulled her hand away. Wood clacked as she stacked it. ''How often do you have to do this?''

''Do what?''

"Charge out into dangerous storms to help children?"

"It's my job." He emptied the last stick of wood from his share of the load and helped her with hers. "A job that isn't compatible with raising a child."

"You're worried about Josie."

"I always figured I'd be able to stop by Mrs. Stoltz's and have her run over and watch Josie for as long as it took." He grabbed a hot pad and opened the oven door. "But tonight, when I didn't know how badly Nellie was frostbitten, I didn't want to take the time."

"I'm glad the sheriff could stay."

"He's a good friend. That's what a person needs to get by in life, the help of a friend. And a friend to help." He loaded the stove full. "I hear water boiling."

She moved away without a word. She grabbed two towels, as if to lift the heavy basin from the stove.

"Miranda." He closed the door with a bang. "You're still injured. You're not going to be lifting heavy pots while I'm around."

"I'm not helpless, Trey."

"I never said you were." She looked vulnerable, a lifetime of hurt echoing in her eyes. He resisted the urge to haul her against his chest and hold her until he figured out a way to drive the pain from her heart. "You have to take better care of yourself."

"I won't tear my stitches. They're almost healed."

"Now, listen here." His chest felt as though it was cracking, but he tried to toss her a grin. "I'm the best doctor in all of Montana Territory. Are you doubting my medical opinion?"

She tried to smile and failed, the pain in her eyes dark as a starless night. "I've lost all faith in doctors, Trey, but not in you. Let go of my wrist, so I can do my job."

"This isn't a job, Miranda. I'm not even paying you."

"There's a child who needs help. How can I turn away?" Her face crumpled when he lifted the heavy basin, refusing to let her do it.

Steaming water sloshed at the rim as he carried it to the tub. He emptied it, the splashing sound sharp against the howling wind, the crackling stove, and Miranda's silent heartache.

"Helping people is important to me, too." Trey filled the basin at the pump. "It's why I became a doctor."

"I thought it was because you got into medical school."

"Well, if I'd failed, I would've had to find another line of work."

"Something noble, I'm sure." She turned away, her voice strained. She piled towels on the table. "A lawman or a prince."

He set the heavy basin on the red-hot stove. "What about you? Why do you carry in wood and look after other people's children?"

"What else do I have?"

"Most women your age have found a poor man to capture in the chains of holy matrimony." Her back was to him, her slender shoulders slack, her head bowed forward, showing the vulnerable column of her slim neck. "Why haven't you?"

"Father wanted me to marry a man good enough to be associated with the family. Someone who would do him proud, the way I couldn't."

"You mean a daughter who spends her days volunteering in a hospital wouldn't make him proud?" He laid a hand on her shoulder, her trembling, delicate shoulder. "What kind of man is he? I've worked in a hospital. You didn't have the easiest job."

"No, but it was important to me. Just like being here tonight."

"You've made a difference, Miranda." But he knew she couldn't see it. She'd warmed water and prepared linens and bandages, allowing Mrs. Steiner to stay at her daughter's side. "You don't have to work so hard to be of value. You're something special all by yourself."

"You're saying that because you're my employer and the water's bubbling."

"I'm saying that because it's true."

She dipped her chin, maybe embarrassed by his compliment. Dark, shimmering tresses brushed her cheek and spilled over her shoulder.

He wished he knew how to help her, how to erase the hurt in her heart. To make her see what he saw. He dared to brush his hand along the curve of her neck. He felt the fast flutter of her heartbeat and the heated wonder of her skin.

Then she moved away, and he didn't know if she wanted his touch. He grabbed the basin from the stove.

"I'll tell Mrs. Steiner Nellie's bath is ready." Miranda whisked away before he could stop her.

He listened to her step tap down the narrow hall. He'd wanted to make it better between them, to be the man she could trust.

He couldn't fight the feeling he'd made everything worse.

While Trey made sure Kayla Steiner understood his instructions, Miranda wiped out the tub and left it to dry near the stove. The floor was mopped dry, the towels piled in the laundry, the basins washed and put away.

A sense of satisfaction filled her. They'd been lucky tonight. Nellie was going to be fine.

And, as dawn broke apart the wailing blizzard, she let herself hope for good things for all of them. For herself. Just a little.

"Ready to go?" Exhaustion shadowed his handsome face, but he looked iron-strong as he laid her cloak across her shoulders, holding the garment while she slipped into it.

How could such a simple, polite act make her heart ache? Make her throat knot with emotion? She turned away, snatching her scarf from the wall peg, trying hard to appear unaffected as she wrapped her head and throat well against the cold.

They headed out into the dying storm, and still she couldn't look at him. The night stood between them, the knowledge that she'd let down her guard enough to sleep in his arms.

"It's a long, cold walk across town," he said, his lips brushing her cheek, speaking to be heard over the wind. "You might as well head back home with me. Josie will be devastated if you don't."

"Using Josie to bribe me again, huh?"

"If that's what it takes. It's worked so far."

She should say no. Head home. Put as much distance between them as she could. The sweet life he'd shown her last night had awakened all the dreams in her heart. How could she stay? How could she reach out and find disillusionment again?

Lewis had done that. Charming and courteous, he'd made her feel alive. She'd fallen in love, foolishly giving away her heart. Look how that had ended.

Fear drummed in her veins as Trey's hand caught hers, drawing her against him, protecting her from the wind. Always protecting her. Always taking care of her.

He scared her more than Lewis did. Frightened her because he made her vulnerable. He made her want and wish and dream.

When they reached the intersection, she turned her back on town and went home with him. Was she making a mistake?

"Miranda! Uncle Trey!" Josie clattered across the kitchen. "Mrs. Stoltz isn't here yet. I'm gettin' hungry waitin'."

Sheriff Kelley ambled into the room. "I tried to convince her I make pretty good eggs, but she didn't believe me."

"Wise choice. I've had your eggs, Mac." Trey winked.

Miranda loved the warm, happy feeling in this kitchen. She gasped in surprise when Trey's fingers curled around her cloak collar. He held it for her as she slipped out of the snow-caked garment. Warmth sparkled through her from head to toe.

The sheriff shrugged into his jacket. "One of my deputies ran next door to fetch Mrs. Stoltz. I just got a report at the pass."

Another deputy strode into the room. "The blizzard came up fast last night, before the train crew could make it back to town."

"Mrs. Steiner's husband didn't make it home last night." Trey's throat worked, and Miranda could read the sad fear on his face. "Are you gathering up a search party?"

"Starting to. Looks like the storm's tame enough to risk it." Kelley tipped his hat to Josie. "Take care, little lady. Ma'am."

He pushed past her, lifting one brow at Trey. The doctor nodded, still in his wraps. "Miranda, will you check on Nellie sometime today for me? Mrs. Steiner might appreciate the visit.''

She nodded, unable to find the words. Trey headed out into the storm alongside the lawmen. Snow swirled around them and then they were gone, headed up to the dangerous mountains to save more lives.

''Uncle Trey sure works a lot.'' Josie hugged Baby Beth tight against her chest. ''He isn't gonna stay for breakfast.''

''No, but maybe he'll be back soon.'' Miranda tugged off her mittens and laid them on the stone hearth to dry. ''Were you worried when you woke up this morning and he was gone?''

Josie nodded, red locks bobbing. ''Maybe he won't come back, either.''

''He'll be careful up on that mountain. He'll come back to you.''

''It makes me real scared.''

''I know what you mean. I lost my mother three days before my tenth birthday.'' She lit the lamp on the table, the flame jumping and twisting to life, but the light couldn't reach the dark places in her heart. ''It was the saddest thing that ever happened to me. Is that the way you feel?''

Josie nodded. ''I miss my ma and pa. They can't never come back.''

''No, they can't.'' Miranda held out her arms and Josie burrowed against her. ''Things will get easier, I promise.''

Josie clung to her, her fine hair silken-soft against Miranda's chin. It was sweetness that filled her, maybe the old ache for a child of her own. For a family made from love.

Such dreams had only been that—fantasies woven by a little girl growing up in a house without love. Yearning for what she didn't know but could feel was missing in her life. Not until Miranda stepped foot inside this beautiful log home, did she know those dreams were real and lived by people every day.

Every single day.

She held Josie tight, cradling her with all the love she had in her heart.

It was late when the lock turned in the back door.

"Uncle Trey! You're back!" Josie jumped up, a stack of checkers tumbling across the table as she ran through the kitchen.

He came in with a burst of cold air. His breath rose in great clouds as he shut the door against the frigid night. Ice frosted his hat, scarf and jacket, and his face was pale from the temperature. Dark circles bruised his eyes, but his smile was warm as he knelt stiffly to accept Josie's hug.

"You're all crackly." Josie fondly played with his frozen collar. "Just like an icicle."

"I think I'm frozen clean through. It was cold up on that mountain." He unbuttoned his jacket, careful of a package he carried against his shirt. "Why don't you give this to Miranda?"

"Another present?" Josie stepped away, intrigued, even by the plain-wrapped package. Her gait rapped quick and steady along the wood floor. "Look what Uncle Trey got."

"I see." Miranda gazed over Josie's red locks. "Trey, what's this?"

"The baker's son was one of the men we brought in. He did me a favor and opened up his shop so I could pick out a few treats for my two favorite ladies."

"How are the men?"

"Cold and hungry, but alive." Free from his frozen wraps, he splayed his hands in front of the oven. "They huddled around a stove in a passenger car. Lucky for them, there was enough coal to see them through the night. I wasn't needed for more than a few stitches."

"That's good news."

"Absolutely. I like it when I don't have enough business. Means everyone's healthy." His teeth chattered.

Miranda set the package on the table and snared the teakettle from the stove. She poured, letting the tea steep. "Mrs. Stoltz went home after she cleaned up the supper dishes. There's a plate in the warmer."

"Good. When I thaw out, I'm going to be starving." How cold he looked, how weary.

She grabbed a hot pad and opened the warmer's little door.

"Hold it right there. I don't want you to wait on me." He took the pad from her hand and rescued the plate.

"I don't mind." She checked the tea. "After all, I can't do enough for the man who found roses in winter."

He caught sight of the dozen pink buds in a pitcher of water on the table. The petals of those flowers had the same pearled luster of her skin and the color was the exact hue of her lips.

He felt cold to the marrow of his bones, but the thought of holding her again as he did last night enflamed him. Her back to his chest, soft fanny cradled against his thighs...

His heart rate doubled. He cleared his throat and carried his plate to the table. There was a checkerboard spread out next to the vase of roses. "So, Red, you talked Miranda into playing with you?"

"And I'm beatin' her, too." Josie climbed into her chair.

"I think you've got to be the best checker player I know." He ruffled her fine curls. "You beat me every time, and I'm the best checker player this side of the Yellowstone."

"You still owe me two bucks from losing." Josie ran her finger over the package's white string. "When are you gonna open this, Miranda?"

"When I finish here." She spooned two generous helpings of honey into the tea, a home remedy for chasing off a sore throat.

All day he'd worried about Miranda. He hadn't been here to watch over her, even though Kelley left a deputy to keep an eye on things. It was good to see she was well, and relief gathered in his chest. He'd promised to watch over her, and he meant it. He wanted to be the one man she could trust.

She set the cup near his plate. "I stopped by to check on Nellie. She's feverish and her hands are tender. I think she's developing a cough."

"I'll head over first thing tomorrow." His gaze fastened on hers, and he felt the impact rock his soul. "Go ahead and see what I begged the baker for."

"Hurry, Miranda." Josie's eyes shone with anticipation.

Miranda left his side, leaving him cold. Lamplight stroked the soft contour of her cheek and glowed like midnight in her lustrous curls. "Want to help me?"

Josie eagerly tugged on the string. The bow glided away, and the string fell to the tabletop. At Miranda's nod, Josie tore back the paper to reveal a white baker's box. The little girl peered inside and squealed.

"Let me guess. Chocolate puff pastries." Miranda shook her head, delight warming the cinnamon flecks in her eyes. "You are going to spoil me so much, I won't want to leave when the train comes."

"Maybe that's the idea." Had he really said it? Been that bold?

"You have to stop tempting me like this." She shone like moonlight, a brilliant luster that brightened his night. "You're exploiting my chocolate dependency."

"Exactly. First chocolate cake, now this. Wait and see what I tempt you with tomorrow."

Miranda spun away, retrieving dessert plates from the cabinet. She didn't answer. Was she remembering last night, too?

"Can I have one now?" Josie asked, nearly bursting with anticipation.

Miranda handed her a plate. The little girl dug into the box, retrieving a chocolate-covered pastry with her fingers.

Miranda did the same. Chocolate clung to her forefinger and she licked it off with her tongue.

His blood heated. She sat down beside him, and he tingled as if they'd touched. She bit into the pastry, rapture marking her face, and she moaned.

Desire sparked through him with inferno force. She licked the chocolate off her lips, her eyes drifting shut as the delicate tastes of chocolate, cream and pastry blended on her tongue.

That was what she would look like in his bed. Her hair tumbling across her shoulders, her head tilting back to expose the column of her throat. Ecstasy would mark her face, pleasure would burn in her eyes.

Need beat hard in his blood, and he fought the urge to pull her against him. He knew how she'd feel, warm woman and soft curves.

"You're not touching your pot roast." Miranda licked the last speck of chocolate from her bottom lip.

"It looks boring next to those pastries."

"Uncle Trey, you can't have dessert until you finish your supper."

"Those aren't the rules in my house." Trey reached for his cup of honeyed tea to ease his scratchy throat. "I say, sometimes you've got to give in to the temptation."

Miranda's pulse leaped when she realized that Trey wasn't looking at the pastry box. He was looking at her.

She stared hard at her napkin. Temptation. That's what she felt, too. A desire far too dangerous to act on. She pushed back her chair and stood.

"Where you goin', Miranda?" Josie hopped up, too. "We aren't done with our game."

"Your uncle's here now and I should go. It's past your bedtime and mine, too."

"Stay, pretty please?"

Miranda froze, torn with indecision.

Trey's chair scraped as he stood. "Miranda's right. It's past your bedtime, young lady. Run and brush your teeth."

The little girl darted off, brace clacking. "Don't leave yet, Miranda."

"I won't. Promise." But now she was alone with Trey. Alone with the one man she couldn't resist.

If she closed her eyes, the memory of last night came back to her, stark and real. She could feel the luxury of his chest against her back, hear the reliable *thump-thump* of his heart. Smell his pine-and-leather scent. Feel the heat of their bodies together beneath the soft flannel and heavy wool.

What would it be like to be held like that every night?

Snug and protected in Trey's arms? She swallowed, fighting the rise of fear and the pull of desire.

"The walk to the inn is going to be long and cold." He knelt to add wood to the stove. "I can bank the fires and leave Josie alone for a few minutes, if that's what you want."

His eyes asked a greater question. He wanted her to stay.

Yes, part of her answered. She wanted to stay here in this paradise, where little girls were loved and treasured, where chocolate pastries and gumdrops were commonplace, where Trey could hold her through the night.

But it wouldn't be right. It couldn't be forever.

She didn't deserve his affection.

She reached for her cloak.

"The thermometer outside the mercantile read thirty-seven below when I rode past."

"I've got a warm cloak."

"You can't walk through town alone."

"The sheriff says there isn't a bounty hunter in this town. And if that's true, then I'm safe." She didn't look safe, staring up at him with hurt lining her face, her beautiful face he wanted to kiss over and over again.

"I'm not afraid of the dark," she insisted.

"Maybe I am."

Inches separated them as he reached to turn down her collar. He only had to lean forward to slant his mouth over hers. That's all. Just two inches and their lips would touch. Two inches and he could wrap her in his arms.

She didn't move away, her gaze steady on his mouth, her lower lip trembling. Did she want his kiss? His mouth tingled with anticipation. His chest ached with wanting.

Only the fire illuminated the parlor. The flickering light

grazed Miranda's mouth with the same lingering brushes he ached for.

One inch. Another. His mouth met hers in a soft brush of breath and lips, of desire and flame. He was lost in the sensation as pleasure tumbled through him, and he felt as if he were falling.

A small moan vibrated low in her throat as he wrapped one hand around her nape. His fingers twined through her silken hair and held on. She moaned again and pressed closer, her willowy body swaying against his. They clung together, man and woman, need and comfort. He deepened the kiss, pushing past the satin sweetness of her lips to taste more of her.

Chocolate, woman and heat. She filled his senses. She filled his need for more than a touch in the night and more than the briefest of kisses. His lips moved over hers, seeking, demanding.

And she answered. Her arms curled around his neck and she held on tight. She felt good, so good. His senses spun with her scent, her taste, the sound of her moan against his. He couldn't get enough of her. He slid his hands down her neck, over the slender curve of her shoulders, along her side where the soft flesh of her breast met the ridges of her ribs.

Then she broke away. Her hand covered her mouth, as if she was shocked by his touch. She stared at him breathlessly, with eyes so wide that he crumpled inside. He was no longer falling, his feet were planted firmly on the ground. Had he gone too far?

She visibly trembled. Shadows and light warred over her as the flames in the grate danced and receded. Silence stretched between them, longer and longer.

She let the shadows claim her, a woman afraid to trust, afraid to believe. "Where's my scarf?"

"Here." He knelt to pick up the fine wool garment from the floor. "I must have pushed it off your collar when I kissed you."

"I didn't notice." Her touch spread sizzling heat along the tips of his fingers. She took the scarf, the light briefly illuminating the fear on her face.

"I don't know what you've been through, but I can read the fear in your eyes. Your fiancé's hurt you, and once a man harms a woman, a fragile trust is forever broken."

She turned away, pulling her gloves from her cloak pockets.

"I think there are many layers of trust, each more difficult to earn than the next. You don't have to be afraid of me, Miranda."

"I've heard that before."

"Not from me."

She couldn't trust him, even now, not to hurt her. She kept her shoulder to him as she tugged her gloves into place, her jaw tense, her top teeth biting into her lush bottom lip. The warmth of their passion and the spark of their connection buzzed in the air between them.

"Let me walk you home."

"I can't." She glanced past him to the couch, and flushed. "You probably think… I don't know what you think."

"Miranda." He cupped her face with both hands. "Can't you see? There is nothing to be ashamed of about last night. Because this way I feel, here in my heart, it's something I've never felt for any woman."

"You can't mean that." She shook her head, taking a step back.

"Then let me show you."

How could she endure another kiss? Her heart felt split

in pieces between the tug of the present and the pull of the past.

Trey's lips closed over hers in a satin-smooth caress. Passion blazed like an explosion, the force rocking through her body, leaving her weak.

Trey held her up, one arm clamping around the small of her back, the other never leaving the side of her face. Tenderness governed his touch, but his kiss was pure passion.

How could it be? Lewis's kisses had never been like this. Trey's kiss was a breathless melding of lips and tongues, and something more. Something greater.

His breath came fast. She was trapped in his arms, clasped to his chest. He was relentless, and she liked it. He wanted her willpower, he wanted her control. He wanted a passion she didn't have. He frightened her and excited her and left her feeling on the verge of something...

She tore her lips from his and buried her face in the hollow of his throat. His heart thumped crazily beneath her brow. He held her a long time before he let her go.

"Wait, and I'll take you home."

She nodded. He walked away, and she unbuttoned her cloak. Trey's low rumble was answered by Josie's soprano. The sweet harmony of a ballad sweetened the air, played on a guitar.

Soon, the light went out and Trey emerged from the dark, closing Josie's door. He didn't look at her as he disappeared into the kitchen. He came back with her roses.

"You shouldn't forget these." He cradled the pitcher into his gloved hands. "We'll stop and have Mrs. Stoltz come over to keep an eye on Josie."

How could she hold even a little doubt in her heart

about this man? Miranda turned away, stepping through the door he opened and into the frigid night. Tears froze on her cheeks.

Trey's touch wasn't Lewis's. So why did it hurt so much?

The night gleamed, still and silent. An ebony sky stretched overhead, polished with starlight. Darkness sheened on the thick mantle of snow. Not even a coyote howled in the distance. Peace reigned, and the crunch of their shoes seemed to echo down the street.

"I didn't thank you for staying with Josie today."

"It was such torture. We played in the snow and she beat me at checkers."

"I can see you're suffering." He chuckled, an inviting, low rumbling sound deep in his throat. Like his moan when they'd kissed.

Longing broke through her, like a wave reaching shore. She couldn't give into the current. "The sheriff and his deputies know we spent the night together. And Nellie's mother must have figured it out."

"You know what we shared. There's nothing to be ashamed of."

"But your reputation—"

"Isn't going to be harmed by holding a beautiful woman in my arms."

"Now your charm *is* showing." She'd never known such powerful feelings. She couldn't help the way her heart thudded. "When you were up on the pass today, did it look like the crews were making progress?"

"A little, but with all the snow falling between storms, they still have a long way to go. This happens sometimes."

"I've never been anyplace that's snowed this much. I

need to keep traveling, but a part of me can't complain about being stuck here.''

"Why's that?"

"This is the happiest I've ever been."

"You're having that much fun running from bounty hunters?"

"That's it. It has nothing to do with you."

"Really? I thought it was my dash and charm."

"Not a chance." It wasn't his charm that drew her. No, it was the gentle lure of his masculine voice, both warm and strong. It was a thousand things, all impossible to measure.

"Here's the inn." She dug the key out of her pocket. All but one light shone in the parlor. The streets were otherwise dark, the town shut up tight against the bitter temperatures.

"I guess it's good-night, then." He took the key from her and unlocked the door. "Will I see you tomorrow?"

"Bright and early. I have that doctor bill to work off."

"You don't owe me a thing, Miranda."

"No, I owe you everything." He had no idea. Her entire body sang with a strange freedom.

"That's the way I feel about you. As if I owe you everything." His gloved hand cupped her jaw, the heated leather soft against her skin. "I never thought the day would come when I would welcome a blizzard, but for as long as those storms keep you here, I'll be forever grateful."

How she wanted him. He drew her against his chest. She could smell the faint scent of tobacco in the wool and the wonderful fresh scent of winter.

She laid her cheek against his sternum. His hard body pressed hers full length, and it felt so good, so *right*. Even if it wasn't.

"Doc." A man's voice broke through the silence, his step crunching on the iced-over street.

"Sheriff." Trey turned away from her to greet his friend, but his hand remained possessively on her shoulder. "Is someone hurt?"

"No, this is about Miranda." The lawman hopped up onto the boardwalk and into the faint light from the window. "I've left word with the boarding houses and hotels to let me know if a stranger checks in. They help out like that, from time to time. It makes for a safer town for all of us. Seems like we've got a new man in town."

"New?" Trey ground out. "A bounty hunter?"

She *knew* it was. Her pulse drummed in her ears. The skin on the back of her neck pricked.

"Could be. Now, my men have combed this town. Whoever it is has been lying low. Real low. The cold probably drove him out. I've got a deputy keeping an eye on the stranger, and I'll station another man outside your door for tonight, ma'am. The gunman hasn't committed a crime yet, but if he tries, my deputies and I will handle it."

Speechless, Miranda could only nod. A bounty hunter could have found her, and she wasn't terrified. Could it be? Did she truly have someone to help?

It was true. She wasn't alone anymore. She had people she could count on.

Trey's fingers squeezed her shoulder gently, his touch a reminder of the closeness they'd shared. A promise of all the intimacy they could share.

"I'll stay with Miranda," Trey offered.

"No, you've been up most of last night without sleep." Miranda faced him, no longer afraid. "I'll be safe. Thanks to you."

His smile warmed her, and it felt like everything had changed.

Chapter Twelve

The tap of snow and whisper of wind blended like a symphony in the still morning. Trey pulled his mare to a stop outside the inn.

The doors opened and the sheriff strode out onto the icy boardwalk.

"Mac. How's your aunt? I mean to stop by later this morning and check on her."

"She's doing better." The sheriff waited while Trey climbed out into the cold and tethered his horse. "Miranda made a real impression on her. This town's been missing a good nurse since yours headed for warmer weather."

"That's the truth." Trey had thought the same thing. What would it be like if she could stay? Was there a way to keep her in his life?

"Thought you might want to know the bounty hunter is still in his room. My men have been keeping watch. I want Miranda to take a look at him this morning."

"There she is." He squinted through the frosted window of the diner. She sat at a table in the back, alone and reading a book, one hand wrapped around a steaming mug.

Golden lamplight surrounded her, cradling her with tenderness. Her dark hair shimmered; her crafted profile looked soft and beautiful.

Everything inside him stood still, every fear, every uncertainty. He was a cautious man, both in his practice and in his life. But the feelings bright and resonant in his heart were far from cautious.

Just love her. Let her know she has a reason to stay.

Every step took him closer to her. The bell jingled above the door.

She turned, eyes wide. Then she smiled. "You're already starting your rounds?"

"No, it's too early. I wanted to make sure you were okay." He pulled out the chair next to her, but his gaze never left her face. "Kelley told me what he needs you to do. I want to go over with you. I want to be by your side."

"To see if it's the same bounty hunter?" Her eyes shone. It mattered to her that he'd come. "Thank you."

He ached to touch her, but here, in the diner, wasn't the place.

Miranda tilted her head back to gaze up at Kelley, but only appreciation shaped her smile. "I'm almost ready to go, Sheriff. I want to see if this man is the one who's been making my life miserable."

"Fine. I'll be waiting in the lobby." He left them alone.

The waitress thunked a steaming cup of coffee on the table. Without a word, she ambled away, casting Miranda a hard look.

What was that about? Trey covered her hand with his. "You are surprised I'm here, aren't you?"

"A little. It's pretty early." She finished her tea and set the china cup into its saucer with deliberate care. "You didn't have to come."

"Of course I did. You're not alone. If I have my way, you'll never be alone again."

She smiled, and the trust she gave him shone kind and true.

"It's him." She recognized the hard cut of his face through the window. She'd never forget that jagged profile and those lifeless, cruel eyes. She leaned back against the wall, out of sight, and afraid.

Heart pounding, she took a few deep breaths, trying to stay calm. She hated how hard she started to shake. Anger rattled through her, fast and hot. "I saw him get back on the train that night. Where did he come from?"

"Maybe he hiked back up the tracks between storms, a cold hard ride. But maybe I was wrong. You weren't as safe as I promised." Trey's hand settled on her shoulder.

"But I'm safer than I've been in my entire life." When she wanted to lean into his arms, cherished and sheltered against his chest, she took a step away. "He can't hurt me now, thanks to you."

The sheriff nodded to his deputy, who strolled into the small, dingy diner. "Miranda, after we get him in a cell, I want you to come down to the jail. Look through the wanted posters. I've got reams of them. Most hired guns are wanted for some crime. We just have to find it, and then he's through hunting you for good. It's the best way, and then, before he has the chance to ask questions, he'll be behind bars."

"Are your men going to arrest him now?"

"Before he can start talking about you. Trey, take her to the clinic. When we're ready for her, I'll send a deputy down."

Trey held out his arm, offering to walk her back to the

sleigh. An invitation stood between them, what he offered and what she was afraid to take.

Wishing she had more courage, Miranda slid her arm through his.

She stretched the knotted muscles in her neck, lifting her eyes from the stack of wanted posters she was going through.

It seemed unbelievable that after so much running and a heart load of fear, that she might find safety. Even for just a little while. The hope floundering in her chest burned a little brighter.

She wouldn't always be running. One day she would have the life she wanted. A place to call home. A child to love. A man to believe in.

Trey. Look at how he'd stood by her, kept every promise he'd ever made, created more happiness for her than she'd known in her whole life.

No one, ever, had done that for her. Not her father. Not her fiancé. Not one of her friends. But this man, who'd not long ago been a stranger, had.

How could she not want him? Love him? He was a combination of heart and might that intrigued her, left her breathless and left her wanting. How could she keep denying that want?

She'd felt it last night, and she felt it now, a budding need for more than brief touches, more than the friendship he'd offered her.

The outside door creaked open, and through the cracked door of the sheriff's office, Miranda could see the familiar cut of Trey's jaw and the brim of his Stetson.

How could she ever deserve such a man?

The sheriff's door squeaked open, and Trey stood in

the threshold, handsome enough to make her eyes hurt and her blood sing.

He leaned against the doorframe. "How's it going?"

"No complaints." She felt light as air just looking at him. "It's taking more time than I thought. There are hundreds of faces, and most of their features are beginning to look the same. Are you done with your rounds?"

"Yep, and now I'm all yours."

"Lucky me."

His eyes crinkled in the corners, his humor as easy as springtime even on this winter's day. He tugged a hard-backed chair across the floor and set it in front of the sheriff's big desk.

"Miranda, Trey." A deputy ambled into the room with another armload of notices. "The sheriff wanted you to look through these, ma'am."

Sunlight poured through the slats of the window blind, limning Trey with a golden glow. He bent forward to take a handful of posters. A dark shank of hair tumbled over his brow as he bent to thumb through them.

Miranda itched to reach out and brush that stray lock from his eyes. The memory of his kiss, the feeling of being held against his chest, the luxury of falling asleep in his arms all hammered through her, leaving her weak.

The deputy left them alone, and Miranda tried to concentrate on the notices. The charcoal sketches and smeary daguerreotypes blurred together, and she rubbed her eyes.

Every time she looked up, there was Trey. He made her dream. He made her wonder what it would be like to be loved by him.

She turned the page. Recognition speared through her. "This is it."

Trey leaned across the desk. "Are you sure?"

"I would know them anywhere." She shivered at those

cold, lifeless eyes and then at the headline running across the page. Murder. He was wanted for murder. For killing a woman.

What would he have done to her, if he'd caught her? In what kind of condition would she have reached home? And for what? Her father didn't care what happened to her, as long as she was returned. Or he wouldn't have enticed every lowlife in three territories with his outrageous reward.

Fury beat in her chest, growing with each heartbeat. What kind of man was her father? She'd been raised to respect him, but she could see once again that he wasn't the man he claimed to be.

For all his wealth and regarded position in the community, he wasn't a fraction of the man Trey was.

"Sheriff." She pushed back her chair, wanted notice in hand. It was stiff and yellowed with age, but it was all she needed. She would put this criminal behind bars and keep him there. And any others that came to this town.

Trey couldn't help twining his fingers between hers, walking with her hand-in-hand down the boardwalk. He wanted everyone to know what lived in his heart. Especially Miranda. "How does it feel to be free from that man?"

"Unbelievable." The shadows had vanished from her face, the lines eased, the heartache gone. Her step was buoyant and she seemed to float as they crossed the street. "That man and his gang have been following me since the Dakotas."

"And now you've put an end to it."

"With your help." Sunlight sparkled on the snow behind her as she stepped over an icy rut in the street, graceful and willowy.

She's free. It's all he could think of. Every step, every breath, every beat of his heart. She was filled with hurt, and he wanted to show her the way a real man loved a woman. To show her she had a reason to stay.

"It's a slow day, so I thought we might take some time off." He helped her into the sleigh and took the biggest risk of his life.

"We?" She lifted one delicate brow.

"Me and Josie. We're going to kidnap you." He tucked the blanket around her, her rose scent intoxicating him. "We're going to take you against your will and force you to have fun. You don't look very afraid."

"Believe me, I am. What are you going to do to me?"

"I'm going to show you what life is like without bounty hunters on your tail. What life would be like with me and Josie."

He couldn't look at her, but he felt her happiness and knew he'd done right. He circled around the sleigh and climbed in beside her. "But first, there's a little matter of my daily quest."

"What? You're on a quest?"

"Haven't you noticed?" He gave the reins a snap, and the horse and sleigh shot forward. "I've decided to spoil you so much you can't deny it any longer."

"Deny what?"

"The truth."

"What truth?"

"That you're worth the world to me, Miranda." He stopped in front of a house a block behind Main Street and left her waiting.

When he returned, he was carrying another dozen pale pink roses and a love in his heart that would forever burn.

Dulcet chimes rang through the sun-kissed air, merrily above the sounds of the birds, scurrying to gather food while the good weather held.

"Miranda, look!" Josie's glee sounded as free as a breeze. "I'm not scared. Well, not much."

"You're doing very well, Josie." Miranda brushed her fingertip across the gold locket at the little girl's throat. "You're safe as can be."

"I know." Trust shone as bright as the sky, and when Trey's gaze fastened on hers over the top of Josie's knit cap, she felt full to overflowing.

"I never crash, Red." Trey slowed the horse as they approached the intersection. "Did you know I'm the best driver this side of Bozeman?"

"How do we know he's telling the truth, Josie?" Miranda couldn't hide her happiness. "He makes all these outrageous claims but doesn't have any proof to back them up."

"You're ruining my reputation, Miranda. Question it, and it's bound to disintegrate."

"You're all charm, dash and hot air, is that it?"

"Shh. Don't let that get around." He winked, and they laughed together, their breaths rising in great white clouds in the chilly air.

Trey slowed the sleigh on the residential street to avoid the children playing. Little boys chased each other with snowballs, and little girls were busy making snow angels in the front yards. Older children were sledding down an incline, their merriment rising in delighted shrieks that drew Josie's wistful gaze.

Miranda's happiness faded a notch as she realized that while Josie had mastered walking, her leg wasn't strong enough to run and play like the other children. Yet.

Trey ruffled Josie's bangs, affectionate as always.

"Don't worry, Red. By this time next year, you'll be out-running them all."

"I wish, oh, I wish I could have a sled." Josie twisted in her seat to watch longingly after the children.

"Well, Christmas isn't too far away." He knuckled back his Stetson. "Maybe you should ask Santa Claus. Old Saint Nick just might have room in his toy sack for a little girl's sled."

"Santa won't find me this year."

"Why not?"

"'Cuz I don't live at home anymore."

Sympathy built in Miranda's chest, burning like flame. She reached out and brushed soft red curls from Josie eyes, filled with heart-breaking sadness. "That's not true. Santa knows where every child is, all the time."

"Even if they moved away?"

"Absolutely." Miranda felt Trey's hand on her shoulder, warm and comforting. His fingers squeezed and she knew what he was trying to say.

He cleared his throat. "Did I ever tell you about the time I met Santa?"

"Santa?" Josie gasped. "Really, Uncle Trey?"

"It's the one-hundred-percent truth." He snapped the reins. Main Street, sleepy and quiet, whizzed by in a blend of colors and light. "It happened last winter, just before Christmastime."

Miranda watched the light in his eyes beam and his saucy grin flicker.

"In fact, it was the day before Christmas Eve. Santa was out checking his list, making sure all the children in Montana Territory were behaving when he climbed out of his sleigh and twisted his ankle on Gertrude Murray's roof. Lucky for him, I made a house call and wrapped up his foot. I did such a good job, he was able to deliver all his presents the very next night.''

"How do you know?"

"Because he told me. Now and then he stops by and checks in with me. His ankle healed up just fine."

Josie leaned back with an awed sigh. "You really are the best doctor in Montana Territory, Uncle Trey."

"Darn right." He flashed her a scintillating grin.

Miranda's blood sang with the knowledge, her body trembled. He was like flame, drawing her closer. She wanted him. More than she'd wanted anything.

Their mood was light as they sped out of town. The sleigh runners squeaked on the glazed ice, and the wind brushed her face. The winter world, so crisp and new, sped by in brilliant, dazzling white.

The horse gained speed, and they soared over the ground like birds in flight. Fast and free, skimming up and down over every incline and gully, the wind whispering, the cold bracing, the merry bells celebrating.

"This is wonderful," Miranda breathed. "I've never done this before."

"Ride in a sleigh?" Trey winked at her over the top of Josie's hat.

"No, flew in one."

"Don't go any faster, Uncle Trey." Josie's fingers curled around the polished dash, her little body braced.

"I won't." He slid one arm around Josie's neck, and his hand settled on Miranda's shoulder, creating a dizzying connection between them.

Snow began falling, airy, sugar-spun flakes tapping to the ground, flickering from the partly clouded sky. Snow shrouded the tops of the silent firs and pines.

Why, from here the entire mountainside looked white and evergreen. The mountains rose steeply on all sides, hemming them in, their rugged peaks hidden by the fast-moving clouds.

"This is what I wanted to show you." Trey pulled his mare to a stop.

"It's like we're on the edge of the world." She began to climb out of the sleigh, and Trey was there, taking her hand. She stepped toward the edge of the bluff, gazing out at the steep river valley below, etched between mountains.

The shrouded peaks looked close enough to touch. The clouds wisped along the ground, laden with snow. A great vast silence filled the landscape.

Trey crunched through the snow, the end of the reins in one hand. His gloved fingers curled around her shoulder, solid and steady. "Look, you're in paradise."

"For as long as I have you." She knew it to be true. He was thunder and wind, earth and sky, and when he touched her, she felt new.

"This is one of my favorite places, as long as a blizzard isn't blowing." He lifted his thumb to brush away snow from her face. "Sometimes I need to get away from all the demands."

"What? The best doctor in all of Montana Territory feels demands?"

"More than you know." There was no teasing, no glint of humor, no sparkling grin. Just the intense light in his eyes, like flame and night, burning just for her. "I never thought there would be room in my life for anything but my work."

"And you admit to being wrong?" Why did this hurt, when it should tease?

"I know, it doesn't happen very often."

"Not often at all." Heaven help her, she loved him.

Loved everything about him. "You're a good man, Trey Gatlin. You've made a home for Josie, a real home."

"Which you helped me with. Look at her." He nodded toward the child gently knocking snow off a baby fir tree. "She's the little girl I used to know. She's always going to miss her parents, but at least I think one day I can be what she needs."

"You already are." She knew that he could be those things for her. "You have all my faith, Trey. Every last bit."

"Oh, you make me feel." He gazed off at the forest, where peace hugged the world in a mantle of white, where heaven fell to earth in tiny, perfect flakes. "How you make me feel."

There was no teasing, just a flesh-and-blood reality. He wanted her as much as she wanted him.

"You make me feel, too." Why was it so hard to admit?

Trey took her hand, his fingers threading between hers, his grip firm and protective, but not imprisoning. His touch made her feel as peaceful as the mountain forest, free like the sleigh skimming the earth.

No one had ever made her feel like this. Miranda held him tight, wishing she never had to let go.

Trey pulled the mare to a stop in front of the house. Mrs. Stoltz glanced out the window, then disappeared. The front door opened, and she came out to fetch Josie.

"You did good, Red." He couldn't keep the pride from his voice. "Real good."

"I was hardly scared at all." Josie bit her bottom lip, trying hard to make her words true. "Well, not much. We didn't crash or nothin'."

Miranda's locket winked in the light, and Josie's hand covered it. Everyone needed something to believe in.

He ruffled her hair. "I think this calls for a celebration."

"Yes!"

Over the top of Josie's head, Miranda's eyes brightened. The cold air had painted her face a glowing, healthy pink. She looked wind-tousled and beautiful and more than he could ever deserve.

"You go put your leg up for a while, Red, and Miranda and I will plan something special."

"Like a surprise? For me? Oh, boy." She let Mrs. Stoltz lift her out of the sleigh.

"What trouble do you have in mind now?" Miranda asked.

"You wait and see." He snapped the reins. "Although I have a different kind of celebration in mind for you."

"Now you're too confident. What if I'm not prepared to celebrate with you?"

"What? And miss out on the best kisses this side of the Mississippi?"

He could live the rest of his life like this, making Miranda smile.

"Doc!" An alarmed call rang down the alley. "Hey, Doc!"

"Looks like I've got work to do." He halted the sleigh in front of the stable. The plans for Josie's celebration would have to wait for a bit. And so would his need to be with Miranda. "I'm sorry."

"It's all right." Miranda touched his arm, tender, so very tender.

His chest tightened. He wanted to draw her into his arms, but instead he stepped out into the cold away from her. Someone was ill or injured and needed him. He had to go.

"One of my hired men was moving the hay in my barn." Mr. Tate, the blacksmith, hurried up the slick street, breathless, worry tight on his face. "He cut his hand pretty bad."

Trey reached for his bag, but Miranda already had it out for him, her quiet regard unmistakable.

"Do you need any help?"

"It's just a cut. Go in and warm up. I'll be back soon."

Snowflakes clung to her rich, dark curls, flirted with her lashes, brushed her pinkened cheeks and nose. He craved her kiss. And more, much more.

"Miranda, will you tuck me in?" Josie limped across the parlor, her injured leg obviously hurting from the cold ride. But she looked brighter, less grieving. "Baby Beth is all ready for her nap, too."

"Then we'd better not leave your baby waiting." Miranda crossed the parlor, where Mrs. Stoltz was dusting Trey's messy desk in the corner. "What do you think your uncle has in mind for tonight?"

"For my surprise? Maybe chocolate cake?" Josie crawled into her pretty bed, frothed in delicate roses and lace. She tucked Baby Beth under her arm.

Miranda knelt on the braid rug and released the clasps on Josie's leg brace. "I think I should bring my roses in here, so you can smell them while you rest. Would you like that?"

"Oh, yes."

"Then I'll be right back." Miranda set the brace on the floor, then grabbed the throw from the foot of the bed. She draped Josie and Baby Beth with care.

Mrs. Stoltz didn't look up when she stepped into the

parlor. Trey's roses sat in a fat pitcher on the table. She lifted it, drinking in the delicate fragrance. The fragile pink buds were already opening.

Trey was courting her the old-fashioned way, with tokens of affection. Had Lewis shown her this courtesy? Not once. Lewis had acted as though she were lucky to have his attention.

Not Trey. He would never treat her that way. Today on the mountain he'd looked at her as if she were a priceless treasure, one he was lucky to hold.

I'm the lucky one. She had no doubt. Mrs. Stoltz gave a huffing sound, her disapproval tainting the room's happy, cozy atmosphere.

She stalked past Miranda without looking at her, and she remembered the woman's previous words. *Always looking out for others, that's our doc.* Implying Trey's care and regard was nothing out of the ordinary.

But it was. She knew it. He'd told her, and she believed him because his every word, every look, every action told her.

Then she remembered Mrs. Stoltz had probably been the one to take the sheets off the sofa, the night she'd spent here in Trey's arms. She would have also noticed Trey's bed hadn't been slept in.

She pushed open Josie's door. The little girl stirred, her doll hugged tight. She looked sleepy, so Miranda didn't say a word as she set the flowers on the nightstand near the bed. She pressed a kiss to Josie's brow and left the room, careful not to wake her. Careful not to care too much.

"Doc, glad you could help me out. If I let the wife see I tried to cut off my hand, she'd make me sleep in the barn." Sanderson winked.

"Then you're lucky I was nearby. I'd hate to treat you for frostbite." Trey finished bandaging the man's injury. "Keep that dry. Stop by tomorrow and let me look at it. I know your brother works on the snow crews. Is there any news about the train?"

"There's a chance it'll be running tomorrow."

"And none too soon." Tate grabbed his pitchfork. "Sanderson, I don't want you moving that hand. Go home and let your wife fuss over you."

Trey grabbed his medical bag and headed for the door.

"Doc." Sanderson trailed him. "Any word from those specialists you know back east?"

"I'm still waiting for all the telegrams to come in." Trey stepped out into the alley. "I haven't lost hope. I'll find an answer for your son."

On his way home, Trey decided to stop by the depot and send another telegram to his one-time mentor, Dr. Mitchell, who ran the children's hospital in Philadelphia.

It gave him something to think about other than Miranda. If the trains could run as early as tomorrow, then she would want to be on it. And she could be in danger.

He had to convince her to stay.

Joy glimmered inside her like the starlight on the snow outside. The frosty window cooled her over-warm face, flushed with happiness as Trey's guitar sweetened the air. A ballad vibrated on those strings, soothing and stirring. Miranda closed her eyes, unable to believe this luck.

In a way, she had her father to thank for his hardheaded way of trying to control her life. Because all the heartache had brought her here to this shining, perfect happiness.

If only she could seize this moment, this day, and make it last forever.

"The music is working like a charm." Voice low, Trey

closed Josie's door tight. "She went right to sleep without a single worry."

"Of course, the wonderful evening we shared had nothing to do with it." She turned from the window, away from the darkness and shadows, to the gentle light where Trey leaned his guitar against the edge of a chair.

"She liked going out to a nice meal, didn't she?"

"Yes, and stopping by the mercantile on the way there and buying her a brand-new tea service."

"Hers was too fragile to move with." He shrugged one magnificent shoulder.

Her fingers ached to touch him there. And other places.

"I guess we should talk." He grimaced, looking down at his clenched hands. "The train could be running tomorrow. As long as there isn't a blizzard big enough to stop it."

Her heart fell to her toes. "I heard."

"I was hoping the snow crew would be courteous enough to give us more time."

"They weren't lazy enough, and now I have to leave."

"But you're here tonight." He held out his hand, palm up. His gentle, healing hands.

"I am."

He wanted her, the same way she wanted him. Miranda shivered with that knowledge. She took a step, closing the distance between them. Her hand met his and he guided her to him. The fire crackled, radiating heat. The mantel clock ticked the seconds it took for her to step into his arms.

The first brush of his lips to hers sparkled. Powerful feelings tore through her, sharp and overwhelming. Could this be true? Could this be happening to her?

"Miranda." His moan against her mouth told her that

he felt this, too, this thrilling, frightening affection that made them both far too vulnerable.

His tongue caressed her lower lip. His hand curled around her nape to hold her to him. She brushed his tongue with hers, and he moaned again, drawing her against him. She curled her arms around his neck, drinking in the exquisite sensation of his hard male body that felt like heated iron against hers.

"Here, on the sofa." Barely breaking their kiss, he guided her through the shadows.

Somehow he kept their bodies flush, his firm, unyielding heat scorching her from chin to ankle. She felt the ridge of his arousal rock-hard and unmistakable as he hauled her onto his lap.

It was far too intimate this way. Heaven help her, she liked it. His mouth found hers, and this kiss was like a storm at sea, a crash of waves and battering rain, trying to pull her down.

"You taste like chocolate cake." His chuckle came breathless against her lips.

"So do you." She spoke as they kissed, his mouth covering hers, flexible and sensational. Oh, she could lose herself in this thrilling, vibrant pleasure.

"I bet you didn't know I was such a great kisser."

"No, but you *think* you are."

His laughter rumbled, flavoring their kiss. "I'm wagering that mine are probably the best kisses you've experienced in Montana."

"You're the *only* man I've kissed in Montana."

"I must be the one you couldn't resist. I guess that makes me irresistible."

"Just another one of your many flaws, huh?"

"That's right."

A great rending in her heart left her vulnerable, as if

the rope holding her to shore had severed and she was free. Free to go where the current carried her.

"Your skin is as soft as those roses." His lips grazed her throat with a slow, molten heat that left her quaking. "You taste like them, too."

His tongue teased the sensitive hollow between her shoulder blades. On a sigh, her fingers curled through his thick locks, holding him there. Sensation battered her, like waves on the shore. Over and over the pleasure rippled as his hands caressed up her rib cage and down, up and down.

Carried away on a tide of pleasure, she pressed kisses along his brow. Her hands traveled down his broad back as she discovered the way his muscles bunched and stretched beneath his blue flannel shirt. Oh, he was one-hundred-percent pure wonderful. Her fingertips tingled with the pleasure of touching him.

"This is nice." His words fanned against the exposed skin as he unbuttoned her collar. His free hand caught her around the hips and lifted her. In one fluid motion, he laid her on her back and stretched out over her. "This is better."

"Much better." She felt two more buttons pop.

"I'm glad you agree." His kisses warmed the top curves of her breasts, and then her bodice gave way to his persistence. His mouth covered one bared peak.

"Oh!" Her spine arched and she came up off the sofa cushion, but Trey pressed her back down, gentle and reassuring, his tongue creating tiny flicking sensations against her overstimulated nipple.

It was too much. Pleasure speared through her abdomen and quaked low, deep inside. Sensation skidded across every inch of skin and vibrated in every nerve ending. She felt as if she were drowning, as if she could never get enough air. Intoxicating. Thrilling. Terrifying. All at once.

Trey's hand closed over her other breast and began kneading as his mouth continued to suckle. Oh, she couldn't bear this. Her spine stiffened. Every muscle tightened, tension mounting.

She couldn't take much more. She couldn't... Her back arched off the cushions. His hips caught hers, pressing her back down. She could feel the hard ridge of his erection. Excitement pounded through her.

His tongue plucked at her nipple, sending sharp, tightening waves of pleasure. Her fingers curled around his nape, cradling him to her breast. She felt restless. The place between her thighs felt achy and hot.

She wanted him, how she wanted him. But fear stopped her. Fear, and something else.

"Trey." She pressed a kiss to the crown of his head. His dark hair tickled her nose, soft and faintly scented with wood smoke.

"I've found heaven." His breath flicked across her damp, aroused nipple. "And you're going to make me stop."

"Truthfully, I'm undecided." His tongue curled around her nipple in a long, hot caress. "Oh, that might have swayed me."

"How about this?" He drew her deep into his mouth and suckled.

He caressed her with both hands and his mouth, nudging aside her fear with his gentle strength. Her hands snaked down his broad back, then up again, curling over his shoulders where his muscles bunched beneath her fingertips. Satin and iron.

Then he lifted his mouth, his eyes dark with desire. He caught her lips with his in a slow, tender caress that lit her up from inside, filling the empty places in her soul. It was an exquisite give-and-take that left her breathless.

The Regulator clock chimed the hour, and Trey moaned as he tore his mouth from hers. A sigh grated in his throat, and he laid one hand across her sternum, where her heart beat only for him.

"I don't want you to go home tonight." His thumb rasped across her bottom lip. "Stay here, in my arms. I don't want this heaven to end."

"I want to, believe me, but if I leave tomorrow…" She closed her eyes. She didn't want to leave. Not tomorrow. Not ever.

"Then I'll go hitch up the sleigh." He pressed a kiss to her cheek, tender, always tender, and stood. His step knelled in the silence that stretched long and tenuous inside her.

It was for the best. Trey Gatlin wasn't hers to love. Not truly.

Tomorrow the train would come, and she'd never see him again.

Chapter Thirteen

"I don't care what you heard." Father's anger pounded like thunder. *"Lewis Nelson is the greatest man I've ever known. The best damned doctor I've come across. He's got what it takes, and by God, I won't hear a word against him. I won't have it, not from you."*

Miranda refused to cringe as he slammed his door shut, the sound like a gunshot in the room. "But he tried to—"

"I know what he tried to do. You're always so damn difficult, girl. Selfish, that's what it is. From the day you were born. Selfish, lazy, I don't know why I've bothered trying to find you a good husband, but believe me, you will marry him."

Miranda sat up, remnants of the dream lingering like smoke. Wind howled against the wall, rattling the windows. A blizzard had set in, battering the hotel with inhuman force.

She tossed back the covers and walked to the window. Only darkness stared back at her. The snow striking the glass was as black as the night. As black as her future.

What if she *could* leave tomorrow? In truth, she'd be running away from Trey. From the chance to love a magnificent man. She was more afraid of that than the bounty hunters.

That's how much Lewis had hurt her.

Tonight Trey had quietly offered to love her, the way a woman dreamed to be loved. And he'd just as quietly accepted that she couldn't. Did he understand her fear?

Fear or not, she was alone. She let the curtain fall back and looked around her room. Enough embers still glowed to cast faint shadows across the half-read book on her nightstand, the empty bed and the satchel already packed and ready to go.

When she left here, this is what she would take, few warm memories and her satchel. Was that good enough? Was that what she wanted? Plenty of empty nights stretched out ahead of her.

Why shouldn't she make memories now to see her through whatever lay ahead? Her body thrummed with the need for him, not just suckling her breasts, but more. She wanted to love him completely.

Tonight could be her only chance to love Trey. Never, in her life to come, would she find so great a man. Or one she could love with all her heart.

How could she sit here, alone in the dark, and turn her back on that gift?

He could barely hear the knock on his door above the blizzard's fury and his guitar. He leaned the instrument against the couch, wondering who needed him now.

For the first time, he felt too weary of heart to go out into that bitter cold. And yet he knew he had to.

He pulled open the door. ''Come in and get warm,'' he said to the huddled, snow-covered form on his porch.

''Trey.''

He knew that voice. Miranda flew into his arms and held him tight. So very tight.

"Are you okay? Is everything all right?" He wrestled the door closed with one arm, holding her with the other.

She nodded, her teeth chattering, too cold to speak.

"Something has to be wrong. Is it another bounty hunter?" He pushed back her hood, stiff with ice.

Her dark eyes gazed up at him, luminous and full. "Well, you could say a man drew me here."

And then he knew. She'd come for him.

Unable to find the words, he loosened her scarf and stripped away her frozen cloak. She shivered hard, and he drew her against his chest again, this time warming her. He led her to the hearth where the fire crackled. He eased her down on the warm stones.

"You're as cold as ice." He lifted a blanket from the back of the sofa and draped it over her trembling shoulders. "I can't make love to you if you're frozen like an icicle."

"Who said I came here to make love to you?" Her eyes sparkled, teasing.

She drew him, her brightness and her shadows. Unable to hold back, he pulled her into his arms. Breathed in her scent and sweetness, gave her his warmth. She shook so hard, and not only from the cold.

A soft orange glow brushed her face and highlighted her slim, ripe woman's body. She leaned into him, when she could pull away.

He pressed a kiss to her temple, tasting her skin. Snow, woman and roses, always roses. Desire for her sizzled in his blood and thrummed in his groin. His feelings drove him now.

He pressed another kiss to her hair. "Miranda."

"Trey, you're so warm. As hot as the fire."

''I know.'' He brushed wind-tangled curls from her brow. ''Look what you do to me.''

''I see.'' She had to feel his erection firm against the small of her back. She had to know what he wanted. What he wanted to give her.

''You do the same thing to me, Trey. You make me as hot as fire.'' She twisted in his arms, gazing up at him, reaching for him.

Thrilling need filled him. He caught her mouth with his, the kiss so tender it brought tears to his eyes. He loved her. More than he could bear.

''We don't have to make love, if you're not ready. You could just lie in my arms and sleep, Miranda. I understand. I would be happy just to be with you.''

''But I'm not feeling sleepy.''

''Are you sure?''

''More than I've ever been about anything,'' Miranda breathed, then kissed him.

Her lips were heated velvet against his. Sweet desire pumped through his veins, and her arms wound around his neck. He tipped her head back, kissing her deeply, taking pleasure as she moaned.

He tore away, breathing hard. ''You're shaking harder.''

She closed her eyes. ''I guess I can't hide how I feel.''

''Don't try.'' He leaned his forehead against hers. ''You don't ever have to hide anything from me.''

''Then you know I'm nervous. A little scared.''

''I won't hurt you. I would never hurt you.''

''I know.'' Her words shone with wonder and she pressed kisses the length of his brow, down his cheekbone and along the rough curve of his jaw.

''I am afraid of getting pregnant,'' she confessed, her words fanning against his kiss-damp skin.

"Not a worry." He smoothed his hands down her spine, feeling the faint knobs of bone through the fabric. She was small, for all her strength. Vulnerable. "Fortunately for you, I'm a knowledgeable doctor."

"As opposed to an unknowledgeable one?"

"Exactly." He lifted his chin so she could press kisses soft like hot satin against his whiskered throat. "I'm often asked questions by brides-to-be, or their mothers drag them to me. I'm aware of the latest in contraceptive devices."

"And you can admit it without blushing." Her tongue teased his Adam's apple.

"Usually." He tugged the blanket off her shoulders. He traced his thumb along the lush curve of her bottom lip. "Come, let me love you."

Her eyes widened. Her bottom lip quivered against his touch. He held out his hand, palm up. Her warm hand covered his, a question asked.

He answered with a kiss, tender and loving. He helped her to her feet. His heart hammered as if he'd run ten miles. Somehow he led her through the dark and into the privacy of his room.

He reached for a match.

"No." Her hand stopped his. "I'm nervous enough."

"You have no need to be." He lowered her to the edge of the mattress. "This is for you. All the loving, and all the pleasure. If you're not sure, you tell me. What you want matters, Miranda. You could never disappoint me."

His words were like no magic she'd ever known—love and respect and caring. How could anyone feel these things for her? She didn't know, but she felt filled to the brim inside with a strange, thrumming happiness.

He moved out of the room and came back. He laid something on the edge of the nightstand. Oh, the contraception device. She'd never seen one and had only heard the faintest of whispers. Even in this, he was taking care of her.

Denim rasped as he knelt before her. His hand caught her heel and he loosened her shoe. Her body felt on fire as she waited for him to undress her.

"I bet you didn't know that I'm the best lover this side of the Dakotas." He slid off her shoe and sock, then removed the others.

"The best lover? No, I don't believe it."

"It's true. I'm not one to brag."

"I noticed that about you the moment we met." She jumped when he touched the pearled button at her collar, then released it.

"I'm a modest fellow, so I try not to boast. I'm only telling you so you won't have one single worry."

"I haven't noticed your modesty before."

The last button gave way. His fingers scooped the fabric off her shoulders and down her waist. "It's a virtue, too. I try to keep quiet about them."

Miranda felt light as air as her petticoats and dress slid down her thighs. "Like being the best lover this side of the Dakotas?"

"Exactly." His hands curved around her shoulders and slipped the straps of her chemise down her arms. "If word like that got around, a fellow could be inundated with needy women seeking him out, crazy for pleasure."

"That's me." She gasped when he reached around and loosened her corset. "Crazy for pleasure."

"I noticed that about you right off." He brushed his lips down the curve of her neck the same moment her corset gave way.

Cool air drifted across her bare breasts. She felt their tips pinch and her skin tingle. She felt self-conscious, but his gentle humor and steady presence kept her from darting out the door. Could this really be happening?

It was. His hands cupped her bared breasts. His thumbs caressed slow circles over her nipples. Pleasure twisted through her, tightening with each flicker of his thumb.

Then his mouth was there, hot and demanding. He suckled, and keen, crisp pleasure twisted through her. She closed her eyes, lost in feeling.

His fingers grazed her hip as he untied the ribbons at her waist. She could barely reach the surface of her thoughts to stop his hands. "I feel naked enough."

"You're only half-naked. Trust me, that's not nearly enough." Her drawers slid over her hips. "*That's* more like it."

"I'm shivering again."

His hand splayed across her thigh. "You're not cold. If I had my way, you'd never be cold again."

"Oh, Trey." Every doubt, every fear, every memory melted like ice to sun, and she reached out to unbutton his shirt. Her fingers fumbled as he drew her breast deeper into his mouth.

"Trey." Sensation pounded her. His mouth worked her breast, his hands caressed her stomach, and twisting fire pummeled her. "I can't get your shirt unbuttoned."

"Stop trying. Like I said before, this is for you."

He turned down the sheets, the rustle echoing through the darkness. Even above the storm's fury, she was aware of every sound in the room—the soft rhythm of his breath, the rasp of her skin against the sheets, the creak of the bed ropes as she stretched out on the feather mattress.

His bed. It smelled of soap and winter. She lay on her back, staring up into the dark. She was aware of Trey's movements—the thud of his boots as he set them on the floor, the jingle of his belt buckle, the crisp rustle of his denims as he stepped out of them. Her eyes were adjusting to the dark and she could see his shadowed male body approach the bed.

She shivered as his gaze raked her nakedness. She ought to feel exposed or embarrassed. Maybe even ashamed. But right now she was too excited.

He stood there, gazing down at her. She couldn't breathe. She couldn't think. Slow, sweet aching spread through her as the mattress shifted with his weight. He kneeled over her, naked and proud, his chest a hard plane of delineated muscle and bronzed skin.

He's magnificent. Like sculpted stone. Shivers of need rippled through her. She reached up, aching for him to cover her. "Please."

His mouth claimed hers. Like the wind was to the sea, he drove her, guiding the give-and-take of lips and tongue. Desire punched through her, leaving her shaking so hard, she knew he could feel it.

"Miranda," he rasped, his fingers covering her breasts, kneading and tugging. "You like this?"

"Yes." She arched again into his touch and pulled him against her.

His weight pinned her to the mattress, his strength made her feel not small, but cherished. The hard ridge of his shaft thrummed against the curve of her stomach, hard and amazing, and she wanted to reach out for him.

But he moved, suckling one breast, then the other, easing his hands down her stomach in light caresses. Her fingers curled into the sheets. Pleasure built, unbearable just from the pressure of his mouth.

How could this be? Her senses filled with him, her body felt sensitized because of him, and it was so beautiful she couldn't breathe. His kisses trailed across her belly and his fingers burned against her inner thighs. He inched down, and his erection nudged like steeled heat against her lower thigh.

"Just relax." His fingers swept up her inner thigh and higher, to that private place that felt hot and melting.

At his first touch, she moaned, gasping in surprise. White-hot streaks of pleasure shot through her, and she opened up to him, letting him touch her more. His fingers spread heat and dew, and then found a spot that made white light burst behind her eyes.

"I thought you might like this." His words tickled her right hip. "Was I right?"

A gasp tore from her throat. She couldn't breathe, she couldn't bear it. Pleasure became sharp, fire became agony. She couldn't take this. The sensation was too much, growing blade-sharp.

She grabbed his shoulders. "Trey, I can't—"

"Trust me, Miranda." Trey's words came broken, as if this giving gave him enjoyment, too.

"Love me, Trey. *Now.* I want you inside me."

"It would be my pleasure." Resonate and tender, sincere and true.

He leaned away, and she heard a rustling, then a muted snap of rubber. She flamed, heat pulsing through her veins, waiting for him.

Then he was back, covering her with his body, drawing her against his chest. Wonder burst through her. He felt like steel, and yet his kiss was a ripple of want. His fingers touched her again, and she was caught in a swift current, pulling her under.

Adrift, she clung to him. His shoulders were solid beneath her fingertips, his chest an unyielding plane. His hard thighs pressed hers, and she opened to him. His swollen shaft nudged against her there, where she felt so vulnerable. He felt hard and far too big. She arched her hips just enough to deepen that contact, to feel him stretch the opening of her body.

His muscles hard beneath her fingertips quivered as he pressed inside her. Exquisite sensation rippled through her. She waited for it to hurt, leaning her forehead against the hollow of his throat.

But there was no pain, only a small snap. She could feel his hardness deep inside, stretching her, filling her up. They were joined, and wonder burst through her.

"Are you okay?" His lips grazed her temple.

She nodded, she couldn't speak.

He drew her tighter to his chest, cradling her, his thick hardness pulsing inside her. She pulsed, too, there, where they joined. Heat built in her chest, spreading outward. Simply from holding him within her.

She breathed in his strength and the scent of winter and salt on his skin. He smelled good and felt even better. His hands caressed her back, and she tasted tears in her throat.

How could this man, so fine and honorable, want her?

He arched against her, a slow, tender pressure, then withdrew. Friction sliced through her. She reached out for him, to draw him back, and he did, thrusting full length. Pleasure twisted tighter. Heat spread through her chest.

He set a rhythm that left her restless. Every thrust and withdrawal pushed and pulled at her like the tide, building faster and higher until she was helpless against it. She could only cling to him and endure the white-hot pleasure. The heat in her chest spread up her arms and down her legs until she felt aflame.

Trey's weight pinned her to the mattress, his hardness moving within her and against her. Bright, sharp, the tension grew. Bigger, brighter, too much to bear, and then she exploded with a keen-edged, spiraling pleasure.

Thrilling waves of pain-sharp heat tore through her

body, rippling the muscles that clenched him. She cried out, clinging to his shoulders, helpless to stop the blinding sensation.

He cried out, too. His hips rocked against her, driving deep over and over again. She could feel him grow even thicker inside her, feel him pulse and surge. Breathless, he wrapped his arms around her. He kissed her gently, as if he treasured her above all else.

She kissed him back, clinging to him. To this man she loved with all her heart.

She woke up in heaven, wrapped in Trey's arms, tucked beneath his chin. The storm raged, but its wrath couldn't touch her, not here, snug in Trey's bed, sated in his arms.

"Good morning, gorgeous." His kiss warmed her brow.

"It is a very good morning."

How could it not be? She was nestled against his iron-hard chest, wrapped in his sensational arms. She could hear the thump-*thump* of his heart. She felt full, complete, tingling with happiness, spooned against him.

His hands crept up her stomach to cup her breasts. She moaned, pressing into his touch. Already he was hard against the back of her thigh, and she was wet with wanting him.

He rolled her against him, onto her back. "I loved last night."

"So did I." She ran her hand over the curve of his shoulder and down the front of his chest. Soft downy hair tickled her fingertips. "I don't think I've ever slept so well."

"Me, neither." He dipped his head and laved her right nipple with his tongue. "I guess making love with you is a better sedative than red gumdrops."

"It's good to know lovemaking has its medicinal purposes." Her spine arched, and her head tipped back in the soft pillow. He drew more of her breast into his mouth. Sweet, heavenly sensation spilled through her.

"I want you," he rasped, his touch thrilling and demanding.

The night had only increased Trey's desire for her. He eased his thigh between hers and felt her wetness. She moved against him, breath ragged, hips arching.

He reached across her, his mouth licking a heated trail in the valley between her lush breasts. He tore open the waxed-paper packet.

Thick shadows covered her, but he could still see her. Head thrown back, mouth slightly open, the round curves of her breasts shadowed and full, she looked like a woman well loved. A woman who wanted to be loved again.

"Trey." She sat up. Her kiss was pure passion, pure want, without shame. Her creamy thigh brushed his, the outer curve of her breast felt like velvet heat against his biceps. She reached out and curled her fingers around his shaft.

He gritted his teeth against the pleasure. Her forefinger traced him, leaving a fiery trail of sensation that gathered at the base of his spine. Somehow, he managed to roll on the condom and press her into the mattress. She wrapped her arms around his back, urging him between her parted thighs.

"I want you inside me," she whispered against his mouth.

"I want nothing more." He ran his hand down her face, just to touch her. Her hand curled around his wrist, and he could see the dark sheen of her gaze, wide and wanting.

He wanted her, too. More than his life. With love burning in his heart, he gave her all he had. His mouth grazed hers, tenderly so that she would know. She was wet and soft against his shaft and he thrust into her. A groan rocked him as he sank hilt-deep into her gloving tightness.

"Oh, Trey." She lifted her thighs and her knees clasped his hips, welcoming him more deeply inside.

He trembled, not sure he could endure the bright, sharp pleasure that twisted through his spine. Or the way his heart wavered, dangerously vulnerable.

Surrendering, he gave into the uncertainty, into the frightening way that he loved her. He drove into her with a rhythm that made her cry out, that made her come once and again, her tight muscles rippling around him.

Over and over again, he moved inside her, until the pleasure became a bright, blinding light that tore away the last of his control.

He came with a shout and a pulsing sensation so great, it left no doubt. He loved her. How he loved her.

Not even the storm's frigid temperatures could chase away the warmth inside. As he faced the bitter winds to feed the horse and milk the cow later that morning, the warm glow of loving Miranda remained.

Remembering the feel of her, he nearly lost his way in the gale-force wind. His blood zinged with the memory of her breasts creamy and rose-tipped, firm like ripe peaches in his hands, and the feel of her tight sheath around his shaft. He tripped up the bottom step, a load of wood in his arms, eager to see her again.

He pushed open the door and there she was at the stove, the lamplight surrounding her with a gentle glow. Her dark hair shimmered like rare silk and her dress shivered around her, hugging her soft woman's curves. She spun, her dress twisting around her hips. Her eyes brightened in welcome.

"Uncle Trey!" Josie dashed across the kitchen. "Miranda's gonna cook breakfast. We're gettin' hungry waitin' for Mrs. Stoltz."

He shouldered the door closed. "She's not here yet?"

"Nope."

"I hope you like eggs." Miranda reached into the cabinets and found a bowl. "Josie's been a big help this morning. Sweetie, now I need a slotted spoon."

"I'll get it!" The girl pulled out a drawer and began digging through it. Mrs. Stoltz's new organization became instant chaos, but Josie's happiness gleamed like a gem, and that was all that mattered.

"See what I mean?" Miranda sparkled with quiet mirth. "I hope Mrs. Stoltz has a sense of humor."

"I guess we'll see when she gets here. It's not like her to be late." He brushed off the moss and bark from his jacket sleeve, trying to act casual. But desire hammered through him with the force of a speeding train. "I didn't know heiresses could cook, too. You're full of surprises."

"I've got my uses." The edge of her skirt swirled as she returned to the counter, cracking an egg with a practiced snap.

"I found it!" Josie produced the necessary spoon and sidled up to Miranda to watch her work.

He watched, too. He couldn't help looking, couldn't help admiring this woman. Even now, as she whipped eggs with the snap of her wrist, she made the ordinary magic.

"I'm going to wake up Baby Beth." Josie leaned against Miranda's hip for a quick hug. "She needs her bottle."

"I think I hear her crying." Miranda smiled as Josie

took off, dashing through the house. She whipped the eggs in the bowl. "You look half frozen. I have your coffee ready."

"I was hoping you would warm me up instead." He wrapped his arms around her waist, pulling her against his chest and hips. "The same way you warmed me this morning."

"You're going to have to settle for coffee, buster. I have eggs to fry." She leaned back against him when he nuzzled her neck. "Maybe later, when a certain somebody isn't around."

"I'm going to hold you to that promise."

She melted against him. The way he held her felt right, as if they belonged together. His arms rested at her waist, his chest and abdomen spooned her. It would be easy to get used to this. Far too easy.

She flipped the sizzling eggs and added sausage links in the corner of the pan. Maybe if she concentrated on cooking she wouldn't think about the man holding her intimately. Or the love they'd made together.

He kissed her neck, just below her ear. "How did you learn to cook?"

"You mean, because I grew up the way I did?" She felt sad inside, remembering. He probably thought she'd had her heart's desire growing up, just because her father could afford it.

"When I was a little girl, my mother would spend most of every Sunday in the kitchen because it was Cook's day off. She was happy there, cooking and baking. She'd let me watch her and when I was big enough, she let me help."

"Your mother taught you. She must not have been an heiress."

"Actually, she was." Miranda flipped the sausages. "She was very practical, too. We were very close before she died. My father was always working."

"I work a lot, too." He stopped kissing her but didn't move away. "Of course, my mansion isn't as fancy."

"Well, who needs a mansion?" She lifted the eggs out of the splattering grease and onto a platter. "You have a wonderful house, Trey. A real home. That's more important."

"It's nice, but it's just a log home, like thousands in this territory." He leaned his cheek against hers. "You deserve better."

"Better?"

"Well, I'm not the richest man you've ever met."

"You don't think so? There are many different kinds of riches." Then she realized what was troubling him. Trey didn't know poverty could be in the wealthiest of homes, a poverty of love and heart that no money could buy. Or replace.

The cold, empty house she'd grown up in couldn't hold a candle to the bright cheer of this home.

"So, this is about money." Her heart twisted, sad again. "I don't care how much you make, Trey. Do you think it matters to me?"

"It could." He stepped away. "Your fiancé must be wealthy."

"I no longer have a fiancé." She scooped the sausages from the pan. "I don't have anyone but you."

He nodded, strong and silent, just out of her reach. "Could that be enough?"

"What? I thought you were the most charming man this side of the Badlands." She set the pan off the heat, holding her heart still. Was he regretting last night? Was he trying to find reasons to push her away?

She opened the breadbox and counted out a half dozen slices.

"You're an heiress, Miranda. I'm a small-town doctor. I'm never going to be more."

She faced him. "Is that what you're afraid of? That I want a rich man? Do you think I'm that shallow?"

"No." He raked a hand through his dark locks, tousling them, looking rugged and handsome, powerful and dangerous.

"Truth is, I'm not sure that I'm the kind of man you want." He met her gaze, his eyes dark, pinched in the corners as if in pain.

"You're the best lover this side of the Dakotas, so I ought to be privileged to be in your bed," she said, teasing and turning away, anything to escape this terrible rending in her heart.

"Then I guess you are lucky." His hand settled on her shoulder, warm and tender.

"I sure am." Her entire body felt hot as a desert's sun and her love for him just as bright.

His mouth crooked into a smile. "I'm falling in love with you. I just want you to know that. I loved last night and I don't want to disappoint you. Ever."

"You couldn't."

Truth. The power of it cracked open the deepest chambers of her soul. She felt dizzy, full and bright with wanting.

She spun into his arms and held him with all the strength in her heart.

Chapter Fourteen

Dr. Lewis Nelson had never heard of such a pathetic excuse. "What do you mean the train can't run? Because of a *storm?*"

The country yokel with the nose longer than his chin behind the ticket counter gave a wide-eyed nod. "Happens all the time, mister."

"*Doctor.*"

"You're a doc? You must be a big-city fellow." The clerk lit up, his nose shiny. In fact, the whole of him could have used a good scrubbing. "Whatcha doin' out here? We already got us a town doc."

What was with these country people? "I am inquiring as to when the next train will be running."

"No tellin'."

"Is this not a schedule?" He tossed the folded pamphlet on the cheap-looking counter. "Does this not suggest a regularity of railroad travel in this territory?"

"Huh?" The clerk scratched the top of his head. "Like I tole ya, the train might run if the blizzard ain't too bad a one."

"What has that got to do with it? Surely the train won't blow off the damn track."

The clerk gasped. "No, uh, the snow crews went ahead and finished clearing the snow off the tracks up at the pass yesterday. But there's no tellin' if this storm'll drop enough snow to fill up the gullies."

Damn it. Lewis snatched both his ticket and schedule from the counter. This was the end of the line. *For now.* He was stuck here in this godforsaken corner of Montana Territory.

Miranda wasn't dead. The lowlife bounty hunter had told him so. He'd received word from one of his men just before the trains shut down.

He stopped at the telegraph office and took umbrage at the lazy clerk who moved toward the window like molasses. "I need to send a telegraph to Philadelphia. To Dr. John Mitchell. I want to tell him his daughter is alive and well and I'm on my way to fetch her."

That is, as soon as this damn storm ends.

"Your turn, Miranda," Josie announced after strategically capturing three checkers.

"You're beating me again." Miranda pretended she didn't see the obvious move and sent another black checker in jeopardy.

"You gotta have a do-over." Josie planted both hands on her hip. "Look, you should've moved that one right there. Do it over."

"If it will make you happy."

"Yeah, 'cuz if I beat you too much, you won't wanna play with me anymore."

Miranda complied. She captured two of Josie's checkers, then waited while Josie took one of hers. The storm raged outside, making the small home snug and safe. Lamplight cast a golden glow around the parlor and dining room, and the crackling fire kept them warm.

How could Trey think she wouldn't love this beautiful place? With shining wood floors, comfortable furniture, books lining the walls, the house felt more like home than anywhere she'd ever been.

Besides, the two people she loved most lived here.

Trey shut the medical text he was studying with a mild thud and pushed away from his desk. He rubbed his tired eyes.

"Did you find what you were looking for?"

He shook his head. "I have a sick child I'm trying to treat. I can't make a diagnosis with his atypical symptoms. I keep in touch with doctors I know back east, but I haven't received any real help on this one yet."

What Trey did mattered. And it made her proud. "Did you want me to get you some tea?"

"No, I need to start my rounds soon." He pushed back the chair with a scrape and stood. "Looks like Josie's beating you again."

"She's too good for me."

"Me, too." He ambled closer, tall and strong.

Desire spun through her. This morning felt so far away, only five hours. Too long to go without making love to him again. Too long without the tenderness of his kiss, the heat of his touch, and the fire of their joining.

"Sounds like the wind's letting up some." Trey curled his hands over the back of her chair. "Maybe the storm's almost over."

"I hope not." Some of the happy glow inside her ebbed at the thought. "If the storm ends, then the trains will eventually run again."

And I'll be forced to leave. She left those words unspoken, but they buzzed in the air as the clock bonged the hour and Josie squealed.

"I win. Again." She clapped her hands. "Miranda, can we play another game? Can we, please?"

"Oh, no." Trey's voice rumbled behind her. "It's nap time for you. Some little girl I know still has an injured leg to heal."

"Do we gotta do my exercises?"

"You bet we do. Go on ahead, I'll be there in a minute."

Josie sighed, displeased her winning streak was at an end. She snatched Baby Beth from the table and tromped across the room, her gait not so different from any other little girl's.

Trey swung into the chair next to her. "I have a soft spot for bad checker players." He winked—he knew she'd been throwing the games. "I have another soft spot for a beautiful woman I know."

"Two-timing me already, huh?" She leaned forward and their lips met.

His hand cupped her jaw, holding her mouth to his. He tasted like chocolate and smelled like pine. When he broke away, his eyes were black with desire. "What are you going to do if the storm is over? Would you stay?"

Could she? Her heart soared at the thought. If only... No, her problems weren't going to go away. She couldn't hide forever. "I don't see how I could."

"With the bounty hunters after you?" He nodded. "Seems to me we can deal with them the same way we did with the others."

She closed her eyes against the memories. The first one had been killed in a shoot-out. The second was locked up awaiting a trip to the territorial prison. "If only they weren't such violent men, maybe I could stay."

"Kelley and his men can handle it, have you considered

that? I'm sure they wouldn't mind. And you know this town needs another nurse.''

"I'm not a real nurse.''

"You're real enough to me.'' His hand touched her arm. "Just think about. Think about staying. I can keep you safe, I swear it.''

His chair scraped as he stood. He walked away, leaving her confused and torn. She couldn't stay, could she?

A knock drummed on the front door and Trey rerouted his way across the parlor. She'd stopped watching for bounty hunters, but her heart skipped a beat as he swung open the door.

A swirl of white drove into the parlor along with a snow-covered man. She didn't recognize him. Miranda stood and began gathering up the checkers.

"Doc, one of the telegrams you were waitin' for came today.'' He reached into his jacket and withdrew an envelope. "I figured, since it's about the Sanderson's sick boy, I'd bring it right over.''

"I appreciate it, Conners.'' Trey reached into his trouser pockets and searched for a tip.

Correspondence about a patient. Miranda folded the game board and put it away. She was proud of this man and his work. She knew Lewis had never been troubled over a sick child. Neither had her father.

The more she knew Trey, the more honorable he became.

She cleared the clutter from the room. As she worked, she could hear the low rumble of Trey's voice coming from Josie's room and Josie's sweet-toned answers.

This is what a family would be like, she realized. She carried the empty mugs, one of hot chocolate and one of tea, to the kitchen. Mrs. Stoltz hadn't shown, probably because of the storm, and she had the room to herself.

Miranda ran her gaze over the polished cabinets and counters, over the blackened stove spitting heat, and to the curtains at the windows.

If she stayed, her days would be spent here, in his house. And like this—caring for Josie, looking after Trey, sharing his bed at night. It seemed too much to hope for.

But if she could have one wish, then this would be it. To love Trey for the rest of her life.

Trey closed Josie's door, stopping at the sight of Miranda tidying up the parlor. She worked with graceful efficiency, humming as she picked up Baby Beth's blanket, bottle and a stray sock. He warmed from head to toe watching her.

"Trey." She folded up the small pink blanket. "Is she resting?"

"Asleep. Her exercises are going well."

"I noticed her running around here. Her leg's stronger." She laid the folded doll blanket on the arm of the sofa. "Will she need that brace much longer?"

"Maybe not." He held out his arms and she stepped into them. He pulled her to his chest and held her there. Desire pulsed through his veins, but he held her. Breathed in her rose and honey scent. "Josie loves you, you know."

"I love her, too." Her voice rumbled against his chest.

"She'd really like it if you could stay."

"You mean, move out of the inn?" She tilted her head back to look at him. "I've already done that. Didn't you notice I brought my satchel when I came through the storm?"

"I noticed." How could he tell her about the way he felt? About how much he wanted her? He couldn't find the words. "I didn't want to assume, considering what we shared last night."

"Yes. Last night." She breathed the words, burrowing her cheek against his chest.

"Should I not have taken advantage of you?" He closed his eyes, knowing what had to be said. "Are you still sure I'm what you want?"

"You didn't take advantage of me."

"You said that you're still planning to leave. I admit it, I wanted to love you so much that I wasn't thinking. All I wanted was to love you the way you deserved. I'm afraid I didn't do that. Maybe that's why you're determined to leave."

"Oh, Trey." Her knuckles traced the shaven curve of his jaw. "Maybe you didn't notice, but I wanted to make love to you."

"I noticed." How could he forget? The sight of her bathed in darkness, head thrown back, crying out in pleasure. "But I'm the man. I should've had more self-control."

"Oh, and a woman by nature is lacking in self-control?"

He shook his head. "That's not what I meant."

"Then stop being so noble. And stop feeling guilty for taking my virginity. Because it was freely offered." Her thumb traced his lower lip. "I'm glad that the only man I've loved is you."

He held her tighter when he should let her go. "The wind is dying down."

"Dying down? It's still beating at the window."

"Yes, but it might get worse. There are some patients who need me to check on them today." He kissed her, and need for her thundered through him.

The front door banged open, driven by the wind. A

white-clad figure tumbled in with the twisting snow. Trey stepped away from Miranda.

"Mrs. Stoltz." He caught the door. "I'm glad you made it."

"It looked to me like I was *interrupting*." The woman met his gaze. Judgment burned there, but Mrs. Stoltz said nothing more. She struggled with her snow-driven wraps.

"Here, let me hang those by the fire." Miranda was there, helping, as always. Fresh as spring on this cold winter's day. "The water's hot on the stove."

"I can take care of myself," the housekeeper said, this time without acid in her words. "I woke up with my gout so bad, I just couldn't make it over earlier."

"Let me take a look at your ankles before I go." Trey offered his arm. With a measuring look, Mrs. Stoltz placed her elbow through his and took a painful step. "I appreciate that you made it. I sure am getting used to your cooking."

"Stop trying to sweet-talk me, young man." Mrs. Stoltz almost smiled. "How is Josie today?"

There was no mistaking the fondness in her voice, and for that Trey gave thanks. "Napping. I think her leg is healing well enough. When she wakes up, she'll need her brace."

He caught Miranda's gaze across the length of the room. She held a broom in both slim hands. Snow melted at her feet. Loving her felt so right, as if they were made for each other. And the thought of her leaving...

He tucked his emotions back into his heart.

She'd hungered for Trey's touch all day. Between rounds, her duties with several of his housebound patients and the evening reading, it seemed as if they would never be alone together.

Finally, Miranda tucked the little girl and her doll into bed and sat in the near dark while Trey played his guitar. One sweet love song after another strummed above the crash of the storm.

Lulled by melody and harmony, by verse and chorus, she couldn't take her eyes from the man bathed in shadows, making music with his hands the way he'd made love to her last night.

"Finally." He stilled the instrument's strings with the flat of his palm, then waited.

Beneath her frilly quilt, Josie didn't stir. She breathed in a relaxed, quiet rhythm, lost in good dreams. Miranda resisted the urge to press a kiss to the girl's brow. After all, Josie wasn't hers to love, not forever, anyway.

What would happen when the storm came to an end? Would the trains be able to run? Or would she be able to stay awhile longer? Please, she prayed. Just a little longer.

Trey followed her into the parlor, closing the door after him. They were alone. *Finally.* The day had been filled with sweet happiness, but being alone with Trey, why, nothing could compare.

"Come to me." He drew her against him, his mouth slanting over hers. His kiss was tender, but it was passionate, too. A give-and-take of heat and rhythm that made it clear what the night would bring.

She felt satisfied, whole, just with his kiss. But there was more to come. He backed her into his room, never breaking his kiss. Harder and deeper, she clung to him. Desire coiled through her, twisted harder and tighter. She fisted her hands in his shirt and held on.

He filled the empty places in her heart. He chased away every drop of loneliness. Somehow, he made her whole. She needed him like the air she breathed.

As Trey's mouth moved over hers, satin heat and daz-

zling sensation, she couldn't think. She could only feel.
Her worries vanished. The fears of tomorrow faded away.
Deep down in her heart, where it hurt the most. Where
she was most vulnerable.

He lowered her to the bed, never breaking their kiss.
Wilder and more passionate, she clung to him. His big
gentle hands helped her out of her dress, then her corset.
Light from the parlor caught on her breasts as he removed
the last garment. She watched his eyes darken as he studied her pebbled nipples.

He shook with need. With need for her. The realization
left her shaking, too. She ran her hands over the outer
curves of his arms. He felt amazing. The texture of his
muscles delighted her fingertips.

Then his mouth captured one sensitive nipple, and she
arched with pleasure. His hands were kneading her as he
suckled. She closed her eyes against the exquisite pleasure
coiling ever tighter and rained kisses along his brow.

Trey slid one hand to her waist and untied her drawers.
She felt like warmed silk beneath his hands as he caught
her hips and helped her back onto the sheets.

A faint slash of light cut across the aroused tips of her
beautiful breasts, the slight curve of her stomach and the
creamy length of her thighs. Desire glazed her eyes. Her
mouth was swollen from his kisses. Her pearled nipples
were wet from his tongue.

Hunger pulsed in his groin, and he was rock hard. He
quickly unbuttoned his denims and stepped out of them.
As he grabbed a condom, she settled onto the pillow, her
thighs slightly parted, and reached for him.

He climbed onto the bed, hard and heavy. She curled
her fingers around his forearms and pulled him over her.
She knew what she wanted, and she made it clear as her

thighs cradled him. His shaft settled against her damp folds and tight curls.

''I need you.'' He rasped the words. He would go slow later, next time, after this need was slaked.

But right now, he couldn't slow down. She was moist heat, and when she arched against his shaft, his control snapped. He lifted up just enough to notch the entrance to her body. She closed around the head of his shaft, silken heat and gloving tightness.

''Yes,'' she hissed in his ear, voice heavy with desire, and arched again.

He thrust into her to the hilt, joining them together in one long glide. She cried out her thanks, rocking against him, lost in the passion of their love. He withdrew, and she cried out again, and he plunged deep into her sheath. With a long, quick stroke he brought them together over and over again. Her nails bit into his back. Her knees lifted, taking him more deeply.

He held her tight, too, buried as deep inside her as he could get. Release ripped through him, a tidal wave of pleasure that rocked him clear to his soul. She cried out, her tight muscles pulsing around him. They collapsed together, breathless, bodies locked together.

He couldn't find the words, but he hoped she could feel it in his kiss. Hoped she could feel how much he loved her.

The blizzard found new strength with the dawn, and the temperatures dropped even lower. Even with the fire lit and pumping out heat into the cozy log house, Miranda shivered as she washed and dressed. But she wasn't suffering. Her body thrummed from Trey's lovemaking, and she faced the empty kitchen with a smile.

On the way out to the stable, Trey had lit the stove,

leaving the door ajar to feed the new flames. She added more wood and closed the door. The fire blazed, beginning to warm the cold room. She pulled the curtain aside and a wall of snow stared back at her.

The drifts had buried the house. What had it done up on the mountain pass?

Her heart filled with a bigger hope. She'd been blessed with a few more days in this paradise. With a few more days of loving Trey.

She ground his coffee and put on her tea water. Josie called to her, needing help with her brace. The little girl greeted her with an ardent hug and, like a newly risen sun, warmed the chill right from the room.

"I'm real happy you're here, Miranda," Josie said while choosing the barrettes for her hair. "Every morning is happy now."

"It is, isn't it?" She ran the brush through Josie's strawberry locks, gossamer fine against her hand.

A knock rattled the front door. "Maybe it's Mrs. Stoltz. I know Trey hasn't unlocked the front door yet. You wait right here."

She wondered if the snow had drifted as high on this side of the house. She unbolted the door and opened it. Snow rose in a tall bank above the porch roof, but Trey had already shoveled a tunnel from the door.

Conners from the telegraph office held out a folded sheet of paper. "Another telegram come for the doc this morning, *ma'am.*"

The way he emphasized *ma'am* told her he didn't approve of finding her in Trey's house at this time of morning.

She blushed, knowing full well what he must think. "Thank you. If you'll wait a moment, I'll get you a tip."

"Don't bother." One side of his mouth turned down in

censure, his eyes unflinching. Then he shoved the paper into her hand and disappeared up the tunneled path.

She wouldn't feel ashamed. She might not be married to Trey, but loving him was *right*. She knew it. It was the only happiness she'd had since her mother died, and she wouldn't let anyone tarnish it.

A corner of the telegram had curled back when the clerk had jammed it into her hand. She didn't mean to see, but the word *Philadelphia* jumped out at her.

Philadelphia. Who did Trey know in Philadelphia? A cold shiver skidded through her chest. She folded the corner back into place, but her curiosity grew. Trey was a doctor. A lot of doctors knew Father....

No, it wasn't her message. It wasn't hers to read.

She carried it across the room and laid it on the center of his desk. Where another telegram lay, face up, her father's name catching her eye.

A wave of cold splashed over her, and she gripped the edge of the desk to keep from falling. It couldn't be. She closed her eyes, certain she was wrong. She wouldn't believe it.

Trey *wouldn't* betray her. He wouldn't have lied to her.

He was a man she could count on. A man, true and honorable.

Then why had he received a message from her father?

She opened one eye, then the other. The lamp on the nearby table cast enough light to see the words, face up on the desk for anyone to see.

"Trey, I'm pleased you contacted me," she read. "I'll be leaving for Montana Territory—"

It was true. Her knees gave out and she sank into the chair. She looked again, and the telegram was still there, her father's name at the bottom.

"Miranda, are you gonna come braid my hair?" Josie called from her bedroom.

"In a minute," she promised, her entire body shaking.

Father was on his way. What was she going to do? *Trey had lied to her.*

Tears stung the back of her eyelids. Her gaze traveled to the door. A great rending tore through her chest, leaving her quaking with the truth.

Trey had written to her father. He knew her father.

This can't be true, her heart kept telling her. But she knew it was. Another chill shivered down her spine. This room where she'd felt so safe minutes earlier now felt like a prison.

She looked at the telegram again. *Trey, I'm pleased you contacted me.* How could this be true? Her mouth was still swollen from his kisses, her body deliciously warm from their lovemaking.

The back door slammed. "I've been shoveling for nearly an hour, but I've got us tunneled out, both front door and back."

Trey's step knelled on the floor. "If we go outside, we'll have to carry Josie up. It's too slippery for her to handle with her brace."

She knew he was standing in the arched doorway, staring at her across the dining room. She couldn't look at him. Not with tears in her eyes. Not with this pain in her heart.

She'd made that mistake before. With Lewis. With Father.

She turned away and let a cold sheet of ice wrap around her heart.

"What's wrong?" He sounded as if he cared. So warm and tender, as if he were a man true to his word.

She knew the truth now.

"A telegram came for you." Her voice trembled. "I put it here, with the other one."

"Good. I sent out a few questions about the Sanderson boy." He ambled closer.

He didn't sound worried that she might have seen the message and figured out what he was up to. Somehow that made the pain worse. Did she seem that easily fooled? Ashamed, she bowed her chin, refusing to look at him. At this man who'd lied to her. Who'd made love to her last night and *lied.*

There was no other explanation. Not one she could think of.

He took her by the hands, as if to lead her away from the desk. "You're white as a sheet." He laid one hand across her brow. "Are you all right?"

"Fine, considering."

"Good. Maybe I kept you up too late last night." Affection warmed his voice, letting her know how much he'd enjoyed making love with her into the wee hours of the morning.

Tears filled her eyes. Had all of it been a lie? Every kiss? Every caress?

She bit her lip, willing the sadness back into her heart, back out of sight.

"Hey." Tenderly, he knelt before her. As if he cared more about her than anyone in the world. "I see those tears. Tell me. What's wrong?"

He doesn't really love you, Miranda. The realization hit her like a brick, bruising her to the bone. "It's the telegram."

"What about it?" His face clouded. "Oh, I see. Conners saw you here this morning and realized you'd spent the night. What did he say? How did he treat you?"

She bit her lip. He seemed to care so much.

"I should have realized." He kissed her tenderly, as if he intended to kiss away every pain in her heart. "Having you here is going to cause gossip. That's the last thing you need right now."

"I don't care about gossip." She pushed away from him.

"I don't know what has you so upset, but let me hold you." Trey held out his arms, ready to draw her close to his heart. "I bet you didn't know I'm the best listener this side of Canada."

"Humor won't work this time. I'm too upset." Her eyes looked huge and shimmered with tears. Pain seemed to fill her up. "You've been corresponding with my father."

"What?" This wasn't what he'd expected her to say. Trey let his hands fall to his sides. "I don't even know your last name. How could I know your father?"

"Where did you go to medical school? Wasn't it someplace back east?"

"Philadelphia. Nice city, but I'm not fond of cities. Give me the great Rockies any day." Now it was making sense. Maybe she'd seen that he was corresponding with several doctors and she worried about that.

She pushed the telegram across the desk blotter so he could see it. "You know this is my father."

He cocked his head to catch a glimpse. Her finger was next to John Mitchell's name. A cold chill blasted through him, like the leading edge of a blizzard.

"Dr. Mitchell?" He couldn't keep his voice steady. "You're Dr. John Mitchell's daughter?"

She nodded, tears filling her eyes, but they didn't fall. Her mouth was a thin, controlled line. And the way she looked at him...

As if he were the worst piece of crud on the planet. "This can't be. You're not his daughter."

"You can stop pretending now, Trey." Gone was her softness, the glow that lit her up inside. She was like the night, cold and dark. "I know what you've done."

"I write John for help. I do it now and then, whenever I need advice. He's not the only doctor I ask. Look, you can see the other telegrams."

"I see." She sounded so quiet, as if all her emotions had simply frozen solid.

How could she doubt him so easily?

"You think I wrote to him about you." Trey fisted his hands, controlling his feelings. "Is that what you think?"

"You did write him, Trey. And he's coming."

"No." This couldn't be happening. This morning had been perfect, gently awakening in her sweet arms, making love to her when they were both still half asleep. He'd given his heart to her.

And she still didn't trust him.

"When is he coming, Trey? Will he be on the next train? Will he have Lewis with him?" She sounded angry. She sounded hurt. And so afraid, it vibrated in her rich alto voice.

In a voice that filled his dreams. "I wrote your father about the Sanderson's youngest boy. Standard diagnosis would be cancer, but there are some conflicting symptoms that lead me to think maybe there's another diagnosis. Maybe, with the right treatment, there's hope. That's why I wrote your father. And six other pediatricians I know who work with seriously ill children."

"You still wrote my father, Trey."

"No. You're upset. I understand that." True fear lived in her eyes. He remembered Dr. Mitchell well. A hard perfectionist of a man. Tough on his students, tougher on his patients. How hard was he on his daughter?

She'd known little tenderness in her life, he figured. He had to remember that now, when she needed him the most. He set aside the hurt and anger and dared to reach out, to pull her to his chest. She felt stiff but didn't fight him. Even though she believed he'd betrayed her, she still let him hold her.

She loved him. He hadn't been sure until now.

"It's going to be all right. I promise you." He pressed a kiss into the luxurious curls at her brow. He would protect her. He wouldn't let anyone hurt her. Never again.

"You didn't answer me. When is my father coming?"

He nearly crushed her to his chest. "I'm going to take care of you. I won't let him hurt you. I swear to it."

Once, she'd found shelter in Trey's arms. Now she felt only pain. She pushed away from him. How many times was she going to fall for the same promise?

Trey hadn't touched her in anger, but this injury was deeper than Lewis's. She wove around him, crossing the parlor. Josie, standing in the doorway, her hair loose around her shoulders, watched with worried eyes.

"Where are you goin'?" The child sounded afraid. "Aren't you gonna braid my hair?"

"I can't, Josie. I'm sorry." She truly was. She loved this little girl. She didn't want to cause her any harm.

But there was no way she could stay here. Not with a man who'd played with her dreams of love and family.

Trey's room was cool and dim. She shoved her few dresses into the satchel. Every movement she made tore at the wound in her heart. In her too-soft, too-dreamy, foolish heart. She never should have trusted him. She never should have trusted anyone. How could she have been so gullible?

She swiped at her tears and looked around the room. Nothing of hers remained. Just the bed she hadn't taken the time to make yet this morning, rumpled from their lovemaking. She could see the indentation of Trey's head on her pillow, where he'd held her safe while she slept.

She hadn't been safe at all. It had been a lie.

"Miranda." His step tapped outside the threshold. "I can see that you're packing. You think I contacted your father and told him to come here. But why would I do something like that?"

"His reward. Ten thousand dollars is a small fortune." She turned, facing him.

"Money. You think this is about money?" He felt stung. "Look around, Miranda. You know what money looks like, and it isn't a modest log house in a forgotten corner of Montana."

"Don't raise your voice to me." Her chin lifted, and she was fighting for something he didn't understand.

"Then listen to me. I'm telling you the truth. If I want money, I can earn it. I can move to a bigger city. I don't have to be here waiving fees. That's my choice. Just like this is your choice. Please believe in me, Miranda. I love you."

"I've heard that before." She snapped her satchel shut. "Lewis told me that when he tried to rape me in my own home."

He could see the pain in her. How could he help her? "Miranda, I'm not Lewis. I don't know Lewis. In fact, I don't know one doctor named Lewis."

"That's a relief." She grabbed her satchel and approached him. Her eyes were filled with distrust.

Her distrust hurt like a blow. "Please. I only want to love you."

"Love." She steeled her heart. "That's not possible. Would you move aside?"

He shook his head. "There's a blizzard out there. It's cold and it's dangerous, and I don't want you to leave."

"I have to." She pushed past him, amazed he would let her go.

Josie's gait clomped across the floor. "Miranda, wait. How come you're all packed up? You can't go."

Miranda lifted her cloak from the coatrack. "I need to go back to my room at the inn."

"But you're gonna stay with us now and help take care of me." Tears twinkled in Josie's eyes. "We gotta play checkers today and make new clothes for Baby Beth."

"I can't, Josie. Maybe your uncle can explain why." She couldn't breathe, her chest hurt so much. She pressed a quick kiss to Josie's cheek, wishing she could do more.

She felt Trey's gaze, heard his sad silence. He'd seemed so sincere, but she couldn't trust him. She *wouldn't*.

Her hand fumbled with the knob. Would he try to stop her? Fear sliced through her, sharp as a blade. She pulled open the door, listening to his step ring louder and closer.

Just take one step. Then another. She forced her wobbly legs to carry her across the threshold and into the eerie tunnel of snow.

"Miranda, you can leave, but it won't change the truth." He followed her outside, hands clenched. "I didn't do what you think. I'd never do one thing to hurt you."

He looked worn, on the edge of tears.

That almost stopped her. Almost.

Father's words flashed through her memory. *Trey, I'm pleased you contacted me. I'm on my way to Montana Territory.*

It didn't matter what she wanted to believe. Father was

coming. And Trey had written him. She'd trusted the wrong man.

That was her mistake. One she wouldn't make again. Ever.

"This isn't a misunderstanding, Trey." She turned and walked away. She could feel his gaze on her back. She could feel his silent plea.

She climbed up the slick ramp to the street, now several feet higher. A blizzard raged. The bitter wind sheared through her. The world was a mix of white and gray as she stumbled down the street.

Stop her. Trey headed after her, but Josie's sobs stopped him. Miranda was running as fast as she could—he could hear her quick step on the glazed snow.

He couldn't leave Josie alone with the fires going. He couldn't leave her crying. But how could he let Miranda go, either?

Torn, he stepped back into the house and closed the door against the cold. What had happened? Why wouldn't she believe him?

"Why'd M-Miranda l-leave like that?" Josie clutched him around the knees in a vise grip, her need so great, her heart uncertain.

He scooped her up in his arms and settled her on his hip. "She thinks I did something and she's upset."

"Then s-say you're s-sorry." She wrapped her reed-thin arms around his neck and held him with bruising force. "I l-love Miranda."

"I do, too." He pressed a kiss to her brow, his own heart ready to split in half.

He wanted to chalk this up to his theory of romance—love just couldn't survive in this trying world. Love was idealism, but real life had flaws.

But that wasn't it. It was something more. He'd seen Miranda's heart. He knew she was gentle all the way to her soul.

She believed he'd hurt her. That he'd pretended to love her so he could turn her in for the reward money.

You should have been more careful with the telegram. Her accusation grated through his mind. He looked down at his desktop, Josie still on his hip. Pressing a reassuring kiss to her brow, he looked over her shoulder at the telegrams.

Mitchell. The man had taken the time to write a colleague when his daughter was missing? Trey leaned closer to read the great doctor's message.

"I'll be leaving for Montana Territory concerning personal matters. I can spare some time to discuss this case with you."

Personal matters. He had no doubt what that meant. Someone had let him know Miranda was here. Maybe one of the bounty hunters had managed to get a message out. He didn't know.

He felt gut-punched. He'd made love to John Mitchell's only daughter. Taken her innocence and her trust. Hell, there was no strong resemblance between father and daughter. He hadn't even known her last name.

Now it was too late. He had to go after her. Maybe Josie could stay with Mrs. Stoltz—

A loud knock rattled the door, interrupting his thoughts. "Dr. Gatlin! Come quick."

Not now. He actually thought about not answering his door. He was the town's only practicing physician. He had an obligation. There were two seriously ill patients in this town, and Mrs. Mason was ready to have her baby any time.

He had to go.

Chapter Fifteen

Frozen to the bone, Miranda stumbled up the inn's dark staircase. She felt shaken to the core and not just from battling the blizzard all the way across town.

"Miss! You, there." The innkeeper's high voice sounded tinny in the narrow stairwell. "You can't go up there."

"It's me, Mrs. Howell." Miranda turned around, pulling down her hood. "You weren't at the front desk."

"No, don't get much business in a storm like this." The woman looked nervous. "It was my impression you had checked out."

"Yes, but I've changed my mind. I came to ask if you still have a room available."

"I'm sorry. We rented our last bed."

The inn wasn't full to capacity. Miranda knew that. She saw the steady gleam in the woman's eye and understood. Mrs. Howell knew where she'd been spending her nights. "Fine. Thank you for all you've done for me. I'll try somewhere else."

"You do that." The innkeeper lowered her gaze.

Miranda climbed back down the stairs, careful not to

slip. Ice crinkled off her cloak with every step. "Take care, Mrs. Howell."

The old woman merely nodded.

She couldn't bring herself to blame this woman who'd tried to save her from the bounty hunter. The bell jangled overhead as she opened the door.

She tried three places before she found someone who would rent her a room. Tough-looking Mildred Ruben ran a clean boardinghouse at the edge of town. It was a little shabby, but it was safe and warm. Mrs. Ruben didn't look at her with judgment pinching her eyes.

Cold to the bone, Miranda sat in front of the blazing fire in her new room. Slowly the chill eased, replaced by an overwhelming sense of grief. Mrs. Ruben brought up a hot cup of honeyed tea. The woman's concern touched her, and Miranda couldn't thank her enough.

Alone, in the silence of her room, she let the tears fall. One after another. For every kiss she'd given Trey. For the love she'd given him. And the love she'd believed in.

A false affection.

All she'd wanted was the love of a good man. A child to care for. And a home, safe and warm. She trusted him because she'd wanted this loneliness in her heart to fade.

After a while, there were no tears. And in that silent, cold place, she decided to look ahead and not behind. To leave the dreams of her childhood in pieces, where they belonged. To stop wasting her time wishing for someone to love her. For a man great enough to believe in.

Her time would be better spent figuring out how to elude her father, Trey's friend.

He closed the bedroom door. Mrs. Cavendish, face drawn with worry, hurried down the hall, her silk brocade robe drawn tight around her.

"Your husband's chest pains have eased. I have him on some medication that should help." Trey hated delivering bad news. "I'm going to need to keep close watch on him. I'm taking him to the clinic."

"I can't allow that."

"I know it's cold outside, but it's a short drive and he needs constant care."

"No, I won't do it." Mrs. Cavendish held up one jeweled hand. "Not without a second opinion."

"Fine. But your husband needs care now." He reached for his jacket. "Let me send word to my housekeeper to light the stove in the clinic."

Mrs. Cavendish looked uncomfortable. She pursed her lips, fidgeted, then glanced at her daughter for help. "I mean, we want a second opinion now."

"There's not another doctor in town."

"There is a retired one." Meryl Cavendish lifted her chin. "Yes, I think that's what I'll do. I'll have old Doc Brown come and take a look at Herbert. It's for the best."

Trey understood. Sometimes bad news was difficult to take. "For your husband's sake, let me stay until you contact Dr. Brown."

"Fine." She turned her back on him and stalked away.

"Mama is very upset." Daughter Florence stepped forward, explaining quietly. "She takes things to heart. Surely you can understand."

Trey got the feeling Florence wasn't talking about her father's heart attack. "Is this about Miranda?"

"That nurse who's staying with you?" Florence blushed, staring hard at the lush carpet.

"She's not staying with me." Not like that, the way it sounded. "Are you saying your mother wants a second opinion because of Miranda?"

"Because of your behavior." The young woman

blushed harder. "If you'll excuse me..." She hurried into a room and shut the door.

Not knowing what else to do, Trey returned to the old man's side, checked his pulse and listened to his heart.

A cold feeling settled into the pit of Trey's stomach. He couldn't help feeling as if his whole life was unraveling.

Doc Brown came an hour later, crooked with age and grumbling about having to be out at an ungodly early hour. Trey did his best to fill the old man in, but he got the distinct impression Dr. Brown didn't care.

Since Meryl Cavendish made it clear his services were no longer needed, Trey headed out into the bitter cold.

The storm battered him, but he hardly felt it. The town streets were dark, and the buildings locked tight against the subzero temperatures. His step crackled in the ice-glazed snow.

Howell's Inn was locked up tight. When he rattled on the door, Willa Howell bustled into sight and turned the lock. He stepped into the warm foyer and shucked off his hat.

Mrs. Howell's face pinched. Her eyes widened. "You've come to see your woman?"

He could tell by the old woman's face that she'd heard rumors. How gossip traveled so fast was a mystery. His heart sank when the old woman told her Miranda wasn't here.

"I hope you don't plan to hurt that girl anymore, Doctor," Willa said as she held the door. "A woman alone in this world has it tough enough. I should know, trying to keep my place respectable."

The blizzard felt harsher, colder as he stumbled down the icy boardwalk. A light glowed in the sheriff's office, and he banged on the door.

"Doc." Mac Kelley looked up from feeding the pot-bellied stove. "You're out and about early."

"Cavendish had a heart attack."

"Then what are you doing in my office?" The lawman stood, eyes curious.

"I think you know the answer to that. Old Doc Brown is treating him now that he's not dying." Trey knuckled back his hat. "I've got a problem."

"You sure do, friend. Don't worry, I know where she's staying." The sheriff grabbed a battered coffeepot from the top of the stove. "Sit down by the fire and have a cup with me. I have a feeling it's going to be a long day."

Trey had that feeling, too.

The blizzard was disorganized, the veil of snow falling and lifting, allowing glimpses of passersby. Even though she was on the second story, the new street level was just beneath the sill.

She saw him through the window walking down the side of the street. Her heart reopened like a raw wound, hurting worse than before.

A tear fell on the map spread out in front of her. She wiped it away, refusing to let the others fall.

The memory of his touch skidded across her skin. His tenderness haunted her. Why had he tricked her? Why had he made her believe in him?

Footsteps creaked on the floorboards in the hallway. Was it him? Then a knock sounded on the door. Did he think she would forgive him? Or was he worried about keeping her here until Father arrived?

He'd studied under Father. A lot of young doctors had, most she'd never met. Father was very strict about her meeting young men. Could Trey have known who she was from the start? From the moment she'd boarded the train?

"Miranda?" The door rattled again. "Miranda. I know you're in there. Mrs. Ruben told me."

He doesn't love you, Miranda. Remember that. She traced her finger across the ridge of the Rocky Mountains marked on the map. Her eyes ached from the unshed tears in her throat. Those tears gathered and grew bigger, more painful.

He knocked on her door again, louder this time. "I didn't mean to hurt you."

She closed her eyes. *Please, just go away.*

"Miranda, I know you're hurting. I know what you think about me." He paused, his fist contacting the door, a sound of frustration and pain.

How could he be hurting, too?

"Please, open the door. Let me prove to you I'd never hurt you."

Emotions stretched so tight in her chest, she couldn't breathe. She leaned her forehead against the door. She wanted him to hold her. She hurt so much only his touch could drive away the pain.

How could that be? How could she still want him after this? How many times was she going to make the same mistake? To seek affection from men capable of hurting her?

"I'm not opening the door. Not for you. Ever." She splayed her hands against the flat wood. "The longer you stay here, the more gossip there's going to be. Please, just leave me alone. That's all I want."

"I can't do that."

A scraping sound caught her attention. She looked down and saw the distinctive colored parchment slide under her door. Four sheets of paper. Four telegrams.

"You'll see I'm telling the truth. Those are the doctors I wrote to about Tommy Sanderson's illness." Even though his voice shook, he hadn't lost his temper. He hadn't lashed out at her.

She didn't understand why. She knelt and folded open the first sheet from a doctor in Baltimore, then another from Chicago. They all mentioned the Sanderson boy's symptoms.

They were clearly legitimate.

"Your father was just one of the men I asked for help. That's all." He paused. "Can you see that now?"

She could only stare at the telegrams. In her mind, that wasn't enough proof. She didn't doubt he would ask for help in figuring out a tough diagnosis, especially when an ill child was involved.

"Nothing has changed, Trey. I don't want you here."

"For once, I'm not going to do what you say, Miranda." He sounded confident. "From the moment I met you, I've tried to do whatever you've needed. Be what you needed. I love you enough that I'm not going to stop now."

Tears sliced up her throat, and Miranda silenced them on her sleeve. Great sobs welled up.

On the other side of the door she heard a snap, and then the twang of guitar strings. The sweet blend of an A chord hummed through the wood, mixing with Trey's cello-smooth voice.

"Pledge to me only with your eyes," he sang. "And I'll promise love with mine."

She recognized the ballad as one he often played to Josie. She knew the words by heart. Just like she knew the sound of his footstep and the texture of his kiss.

She could not open the door. Her heart hurt too much.

She listened to the strum of his guitar and the melody of his songs until the afternoon passed and darkness fell.

Then he walked away, leaving her with silence.

"Uncle Trey, when's Miranda comin' back?" Josie pushed the food around on her plate.

Trey stared down at Mrs. Stoltz's stew and stirred the spoon around in his bowl. His stomach felt too bunched up to eat. "I don't know, Red. I upset her pretty bad."

If only he could have talked with her. But she'd been hurt before and thought... He just wanted her love. He wanted her to believe in him. How on earth could he make this right?

Mrs. Stoltz cleared her throat as she crossed the room. She plopped the bowl of steaming potatoes on the table. The look she gave him could not be misunderstood.

"I want you to understand, Dr. Gatlin. I won't cook and tidy up after a woman like that. I won't do it again."

Josie tilted her head to one side. "A woman like what, Uncle Trey?"

His hopes sank another notch. Did the whole blasted town have to be so quick to pass judgment? He'd lived here five years. Didn't his neighbors know him better than this? Than to believe he would use a woman?

"I don't mean to be unkind, Doctor, but it's time to consider your reputation." The housekeeper plunked the butter dish on the table. "There are some people in this town who won't stand for it."

"I don't see how falling in love with a woman can adversely affect my medical training."

"If I didn't need this job so much, I would give you a piece of my mind." Mrs. Stoltz marched to the other side of the kitchen. "Love. What does a man know about love?

More like…well, I won't say it in the presence of a child.''

He rubbed his aching brow. Maybe he'd been too impulsive, but he loved Miranda. Still. Enough to marry her.

As if that could happen now. She was John Mitchell's daughter. One of the most esteemed pediatricians in the country. And not just respected, but wealthy, too.

Trey was a small-town physician.

What could he offer Miranda except his protection for as long as she needed it? His protection was also the one thing she no longer wanted from him.

He had only his love to give her. He feared it wasn't enough.

The blizzard died just after midnight. Miranda looked up from studying her map, her rented room dark except for the lamp at her side and the fire in the hearth.

Silence. It was a lonely sound.

Last night she'd been warm in Trey's bed, discovering love in his arms. Well, what she thought was love.

She hadn't touched his telegrams again, only piled them on the little stand by the door. They didn't matter now. The storm was over, and she would have to leave town. Somehow. Before the trains brought the bounty hunters and her father.

The map before her blurred. She was exhausted, but the minute she stopped concentrating, her mind would drift to Trey. *Just think about what you have to do, Miranda.*

When she crawled between the clean sheets, they were cold. Infinitely lonely. Her flesh ached for Trey's touch. For the hot, spiraling pleasure only he could bring her.

She found no solace in sleep. She woke off and on, dreaming of bounty hunters, dreaming of Lewis's hands at her throat.

* * *

The morning was bitterly cold. The town, practically shut down for three days, bustled with activity. Sleighs slid by, shoppers crowded the boardwalks and teamsters hauled fuel and hay in tall sleds. The streets were so busy that crossing them was a trick.

Miranda noticed that several women turned their shoulders to her on the boardwalk. Others shook their heads at her as they passed by. She kept walking, but it wasn't easy.

The doorbell chimed merrily when she stepped into the mercantile. A group of men huddled hear the fire, deep in conversation. A little boy ran up and down the aisles, escaped from his mother. Women's voices rose above the crackling fire near the yard-goods counter.

Miranda remembered helping Josie choose the curtains for her room. Sweetness washed through her. There were good memories here, too. Memories she was grateful for.

"Miranda," Kayla Steiner called out, hauling her three little girls down the aisle after her. She must not have heard the rumors yet. "How good to bump into you. As you can see, Nellie's just fine, thanks to your help."

She shrugged. She'd done very little. "I'm glad Nellie's feeling well again. Did you ever find Santa Claus?" she asked the little girl.

Nellie shook her head and sighed. "I guess he can see little girls and boys all the way from the North Pole. He doesn't have to fly around at night."

Kayla Steiner winked. "I keep meaning to drop by the clinic and pay my bill. Trey's a fine doctor, no doubt about that. And a fine man." The woman's hand pressed Miranda's in a show of new friendship. "I'm glad you came to our town. How's Trey's little niece doing?"

"She's settling into her new home." Whatever he'd

done, he was a good parent. Miranda couldn't deny it. "Trey is taking fine care of her."

"I'm sure he is. Good father material, that man. Now, I have to get going, I've got an appointment to keep." Kayla led her girls to the counter to pay for their purchases.

She headed down the aisle, toward the back where books lined a quarter of the wall. Voices lifted and fell, women's voices. Their words became clearer and clearer as she strode down the middle aisle.

"Billie has a touch of the quinsy and it's getting worse. After what I've heard I'm not sure I should take him to Dr. Gatlin." The woman sounded torn by indecision.

"It's the right decision, Blanche." This voice sounded confident. "Mrs. Cavendish herself refused to put her husband in that man's clinic. Conner's wife said she was right there in the parlor, looking as content as you please. I don't want a man like that looking after my children's health."

Miranda couldn't believe they were talking about Trey with such disrespect. How could they turn against such a fine and caring physician? And because of her. Because he'd taken her into his home and his bed.

"Maybe it's time we find another doctor for this town." Another woman's voice rang with fury.

"Now, Gemma, you know that's rash."

"We simply need to organize. Boycott his services. Put him out of business and he'll have to move elsewhere."

The minute Trey opened the mercantile's front door, he heard Gemma Shaw's words. He held Josie tight, debating whether or not to walk back outside. She'd had enough heartache, with Miranda leaving. With losing her parents. She didn't need to be upset anymore.

But it was too late. Gemma caught sight of him and turned her back on him.

The other women cast him disparaging looks and did the same.

"Don't let it bother you, Doc." Old Mr. Whoppler patted Trey's shoulder. "I remember what it was like to be young. Don't tell no one this, but me and Rosie did a lot of dancin' before we got married, if you catch my drift. You make sure you marry that pretty woman."

"Thanks." At least that was one Willow Creek citizen who wasn't ready to tar and feather him.

Business had been down at the clinic. This morning he'd been refused at three houses where he knew he was needed. He could only hope old Dr. Brown would see to their care.

"What are you women doing?" A familiar voice rose above the crackle of the fire and the uncomfortably silent store. "How can you turn your back on him like that?"

"Miranda!" Josie called out.

Trey's heart fell to his knees when he took one look at her face. Anger darkened her complexion. Hands clenched, eyes aflame, she didn't even look at him. She was focused on the five women crowded around the yard-goods counter.

"Mrs. Shaw, did Trey turn his back on your husband when you couldn't pay your last bill? Mrs. Johnson, did Trey refuse to treat your son's broken wrist because it happened during his noon meal?"

"Miranda." Trey couldn't believe it. She was defending him. He handed Josie to old Mrs. Whoppler and hurried to stop her. "Miranda, this isn't helping."

"What? You're going to let them do this to you? Without even defending yourself?" She was willow slim, just a slip of a woman, but she stood with the strength of twenty men. "I can't take this anymore. I know you hurt me, Trey, but you're a fine doctor. The best I've seen. These people should be grateful."

"Miranda, this isn't your fight." But he loved her even more for it, for fighting for him even when she hated him.

"I know plenty of doctors who couldn't summon up a bit of human decency if their lives depended on it. But you treat everyone fairly and with respect. I know the good you do. Every day. I can't stand that these people want to hurt you."

When he didn't think he could love her more, she filled his heart again. "I don't need defending, Miranda. I've done nothing wrong."

"Did you hear that?" Gemma whispered to the woman at her elbow.

"Gemma, be careful." He stepped forward, not to fight, but to protect. "I keep a lot of secrets in this town. And I don't pass judgment."

He watched the woman, who looked ready to run him out of town herself, wither. "Compassion is a virtue. One I've shown you. No more disparaging remarks about Miranda, agreed?"

The woman nodded quietly, with secrets of her own to hide.

Shoes tapped on the worn wood floor. "Miranda!"

Trey watched as Miranda knelt to wrap Josie in a big hug. The women went back to their fabric choosing, shaking their heads and muttering quietly. But there was no helping that. What he didn't like to see was how hard Josie clutched Miranda, as if she never intended to let go.

Josie would only be hurt if Miranda couldn't forgive him.

He ambled closer, knowing at least two dozen shoppers

were listening. "I promised Josie a new book. We finished Huck Finn this morning."

"Uncle Trey got to read to me, 'cuz no one came to the clinic." Josie sank her fists into Miranda's skirts and held on. "Mrs. Stoltz is makin' fried chicken for lunch. She promised, 'cuz I was sad. Are you gonna come, too?"

Josie squeezed Miranda's hand so tightly. It was Josie who'd brought them together. Josie and her need.

Miranda quietly brushed those stray red curls from Josie's eyes. "I was going to come over to the clinic when I was done here. I planned on bringing you a surprise."

"I don't see a surprise." Josie wasn't fooled by Miranda's empty hands.

"That's because I haven't started to shop yet, you silly goose." She was like a rare, brilliant diamond, out of place in this lackluster country store. She shone like that gem, pure and true, radiating light.

"Uncle Trey, did you hear? Miranda's gettin' me a surprise." All the sadness was gone, Miranda's absence forgiven. What was he going to do now?

Miranda defended him, but she wouldn't meet his gaze. How did he take the first step? He couldn't do it here or now, not in public. Would he get another chance?

"I have some shopping to do, too," he said quietly. "Maybe we could do it together."

Miranda bit her bottom lip and nodded, but he could see it in her eyes. It was Josie she didn't want to disappoint. Not him.

"Goody!" The little girl tugged Miranda across the store, unaware of the disapproving glances from the women at the fabric counter.

He stayed back, giving Miranda plenty of room while she and Josie picked out books from the shelves.

Mr. Whoppler ambled by, heading to the back, and

gave him an obvious wink. *You make sure you marry that pretty woman.* Trey couldn't help smiling, remembering the old man's advice.

Miranda *had* defended him. Did he stand a chance?

Miranda felt every gaze in town follow her down the block to Trey's clinic. The windows glowed warm and welcoming, but there was no one in the waiting room.

"It's been a little slow." He managed a lopsided smile. "I can't figure out why."

"Neither can I. I heard some rumors."

He stood before her, not a stranger, but her lover. A man she'd made love to, trusted with her whole heart. She knew the granite-hard line of his shoulders and how his broad chest felt against the palms of her hands. She knew the feel of his weight on her body, the heavy, thick heat of him inside her, the tender strength of his arms.

"It's time for Baby Beth to wake up." Josie caught hold of the doorknob. "I'd better go get her dressed. Miranda, will you braid her hair?"

"Of course." How could she say no?

Trey caught the door before it banged against the wall and closed it.

They were alone. She reached inside her reticule and withdrew the four telegrams. "I wanted to return these."

"Did you look at them?"

"I believe you. I know you asked about the Sanderson child. I don't doubt that."

"Then tell me what you don't believe."

How could she say the words? "You know my father. That can't be a coincidence."

"Half the doctors in this country have read your father's publications, if not more. I've traveled to hear his lectures, just like a hundred other doctors. It doesn't mean

I recognized you on the train platform. Is that what you think?''

Her heart was breaking all over again.

"You can't believe that. I couldn't have known. And that means I couldn't have told your father. You defended me today. You must believe it."

"I would put all my faith in you as a physician."

"But as a man?"

All her faith, too. She took a shaky breath.

He pointed to the sheets of paper in his hand. "Did you see the dates on the telegrams? Two of these came before you ever stepped foot in this town. Did you notice that?"

"I don't doubt you."

"But I could have also contacted your father about you. Is that what you think? What you truly believe?"

What did she believe? What was beneath the tremendous pain in her heart? *You treat everyone fairly and with respect. I know the good you do.* Her own words haunted her now.

She had her answer. Trey was even a better man than she'd thought. A man who caused no harm, ever.

Not even to her, now, when she'd failed him.

The door banged open. Josie charged in with Baby Beth cradled tight. "I brought her brush and ribbons and everything."

"Look what I bought." Miranda withdrew a wrapped package from her pocket. The paper fell open to reveal a set of matching gold barrettes. "A surprise for you and Baby Beth, just like I promised."

"Oh, *thank* you." Josie clomped close to take the package, her eyes shining like a newly risen sun.

"I'm *so* glad you finally came." Josie's hand slipped trustingly in Miranda's. "Mrs. Stoltz was very grumpy this morning."

"Let's hope her frown doesn't sour the fried chicken." Trey winked.

"Chicken doesn't taste sour, Uncle Trey." Josie shook her head.

The warmth touched Miranda's heart, but she wasn't part of this family. She took a seat near the warm stove, avoiding Trey's gaze. She could feel his presence like a touch to her soul, and she couldn't face him. Couldn't stand to admit the truth.

She wasn't worthy enough to be loved by a man like Trey Gatlin. Or maybe, loved at all.

Just like Lewis said.

She looked beautiful. Her dark hair was down, cascading over her shoulders and breasts. Trey remembered winding his fingers through those curls in his bed. She'd been naked beneath him, crying out with the force of her release.

Now she looked withdrawn, unhappy, without light. She sat on the sofa beside Josie, comfortable in the shadows of his office. Her voice was gentle as she rearranged the barrette in Baby Beth's hair.

"Uncle Trey!" Josie hopped to her feet, then spun in a slow circle. She lifted a hand to her French-braided hair secured with her new barrette. "Look what Miranda did."

"You look beautiful, Red." That's what Josie needed, someone to fawn over her like a mother would, braid her hair, buy her trinkets, who understood the importance of caring for Baby Beth.

Could Miranda be that person? Hope rekindled inside him. "Mrs. Stoltz has your fried chicken ready and waiting."

"Yippee. Come on, Miranda."

Miranda stood slowly, her mouth unsmiling. "Maybe I could come see you later."

"But you gotta come to the house. You're gonna stay with us now, right?" Need. It vibrated, thin and wavery, quivering in the air.

Miranda's brow furrowed. She didn't look at him. She looked at the door, then at Josie. "What you do think Mrs. Stoltz will think of that?"

Trey stepped forward and offered his hand. "It doesn't matter what Mrs. Stoltz thinks. You're welcome in my home."

Every instinct told her to leave, but she laid her palm against his. His fingers laced through hers, binding them together. "I don't belong in your home, Trey. Or in your life."

"I disagree." His fingers tightened around hers. "Josie, why don't you on go ahead to the house? Be careful on the snow. I'll bring Miranda in a minute."

Josie didn't seem happy, but she obeyed, hauling Baby Beth with her.

Alone with him, the room felt so small. She felt small as he towered over her. She was ashamed of all the ways she'd failed him. There were no words powerful enough to mend the damage.

"Why are you pushing me away this time?" His voice rang with a quiet strength, a tender question. "You know now that I didn't betray you."

"My father is still coming to see you."

"That doesn't matter. I'm not going to allow anyone to hurt you. Ever." He lifted their joined hands and laid her fingers against his chest, over his heart. "I will defend you and protect you with my life."

"I believe that." Her chest fluttered, and she wanted away from his tender, intimate gaze. From his words that felt as if they could tear her apart. She couldn't love him, not now. "I was wrong about you."

"It's okay." He pressed a kiss to her mouth, tender and questioning. A soft caress of velvet heat and promised passion.

She wanted to love him. Completely. She wanted to forget her heart was damaged beyond repair. She wanted to close her eyes and pretend Trey was hers to love forever.

Chapter Sixteen

"Josie's waiting." Trey nuzzled Miranda's neck and breathed in the rose-and-woman scent of her satin-smooth skin. Images of loving her flashed through his mind, the feel of her in his bed and the depth of emotion they'd both shared. "Let's go back to the house. I'm starving, and not for lunch."

"I can't." She bit her bottom lip, pain huge in her eyes. "You don't understand."

"Then tell me."

"I failed you." She stepped away, lost amid the shadows in the corner of his office. "When it mattered, I didn't believe you. You've done nothing but care for me, love me, show me a respect I don't deserve, and I couldn't find it in my heart to trust you."

"It's okay." He followed her. He wanted nothing more than to fold her in his arms and never let go. To love her forever. "Something tells me you haven't had much experience trusting the men in your life. But that's about to change. I am the man you can count on. Always."

"How can you say that? You hardly know me. You don't know the kind of person I am inside. The choices I've made." Her face crumpled with pain.

"I know what matters." He pulled her against him. He wished he could protect her from the hurt inside. She leaned against him, tense and stiff, unable to surrender. To give him the last of her love and trust.

But he would earn it. If he could. All he wanted was the chance. Miranda had brought light to his dark life, love to ease his loneliness. She'd cracked open the defenses around his heart, and now he would do the same for her.

"Let it end here, Miranda. The hiding and the running. We'll face your father together. I'll make sure he backs down and leaves you alone, whatever your problems."

Her hands fisted in his shirt. "I can't put you at risk like that. I won't. It's over, Trey."

"There's no risk, Miranda. I've got the sheriff and his men behind me. And I have you."

His kiss was like dawn, a gentle heat, a new light. Tears pricked Miranda's eyes. She held him tight, kissing him back deeply, passionately. Feeling the depth of the promise he'd made.

He needed her. He loved her. She felt it in his every breath, in every fluttery beat of his heart beneath her hand. He would stand up for her, fight her father and any enemy. For her.

Her love for him shimmered deep within, a bright, lustrous secret she could never share with him.

"My father is a powerful man, Trey." She stepped away from the warm shelter of his arms. "He's used to having his way. And he wants me to marry Lewis."

"Why Lewis? I don't understand." Trey watched her retreat farther into the shadows. "You're a grown woman. You have your own life."

"Yes, but Father is determined to force the issue."

"This is a free country."

"If you know my father, then you know that doesn't matter to him." She stared down at her hands, fisted tight. "He's made Lewis in his own image, his favorite protégé, the son he never had. He's adamant about it, and he doesn't care what it costs him."

Trey remembered the man well. Cold, relentless. But one of the sharpest scientific minds he'd ever met. "Power is important to your father. He likes to be seen as a great man."

She nodded. "He could hurt your career, Trey."

"He can't hurt me."

"But Lewis would. He's probably traveling with my father. And Lewis has made it very clear he wants to marry me."

For her trust fund. Fury battered him, but Trey took a deep breath. Miranda didn't need his anger, she needed his strength. "I'm not afraid of Lewis. I am the toughest doctor in the territory."

"The only one I've ever seen wearing a six-shooter." Her lower lip wobbled. "You're a noble man, Trey. You don't deserve the trouble I'm bringing you."

"I just want to love you, Miranda. I'll do whatever it takes."

"There's nothing you can do." Couldn't he see? What did she have to do to change his mind? To prove to him that she wasn't free?

And even if she were, she'd failed him. Failed to trust him. Lewis had hurt her so much, she couldn't even trust herself.

"I love you, Miranda." He didn't relent. His faith in her shimmered like the brightest star in the night. He couldn't see that she didn't belong there, that his misplaced faith in her was undeserved.

"I love you with all my heart and soul." He stood so

strong, steel and heart. ''All that I have and all that I am are yours, Miranda.''

''What do I have to give you in return? I thought I loved Lewis at first. He was charming and handsome and attentive. He was an important doctor. I just wanted someone to love me, and look how that turned out.''

His touch was pure comfort along the side of her face. She leaned into the palm of his hand, craving his warmth. Shame felt like darkness inside her, like a shadow no light could penetrate.

Trey didn't know what she'd done, how she'd excused Lewis's behavior. How the first time he'd lost his temper with her and frightened her with his raised fist, she'd excused it. He hadn't harmed her, not really, and he was under a lot of stress at work.

Excuses didn't stop the comments he made. Until one day, she realized what she was to him, what she'd become by making less of herself for his benefit.

She'd only wanted Lewis to love her, but now she was something no man could love. Not truly. Every cruel word, every slap, every bruise had taken something from her. Laid a shadow across her soul.

''I do love you.'' His kiss was a lifeline. And she clung to him, even knowing he couldn't save her. Couldn't change the shadows inside her. ''You don't have to tell me anything, Miranda. Lewis is behind you. Your future is with me.''

How could he be so unfailing? So determined to love her? ''We don't have a future together, Trey.''

''What? You want to deny me a lifetime of nights in your bed? An eternity of mornings waking up in your arms?'' His love beckoned her, offered her light.

''I'm like a package damaged during delivery. You can strip away the torn paper and hope what's inside is going to be perfect.'' She stared hard at her chipped nails, because she couldn't look him in the eyes. She couldn't bear if he saw her deepest secret, yet he had to know. ''Once you unwrap that package, you see what's inside is damaged beyond repair. There's nothing to do but send it back.''

''Oh, Miranda.'' He held her with a tenderness she didn't deserve. With strength she couldn't call her own. His kisses against her mouth pledged his love. The forever-kind-of-love she'd always longed for.

And could never be worthy of.

''I've had enough of this nonsense.'' Dr. Lewis Nelson could taste the dark rage building in his chest. He hadn't suffered through medical school and years under John Mitchell's thumb to stand here and take this treatment from an uneducated yokel who couldn't spell his own name.

The storm was over. He was through with excuses.

''Sharpe.'' He found the bounty hunter gambling in a filthy pit of a saloon and dropped a half eagle on the table to cover the tab. ''You're finished with this game. *Now.*''

The ratty gunman sneered around a cheap cigar. ''I work for you, Doc. You don't own me.''

''Sure I do.'' He pulled the Colt from his hip, cocked it and thumbed the trigger.

That got the lazy bastard out of his chair.

''I'm crossing those mountains on horseback if I have to.''

''But the avalanche danger—''

''I don't care,'' Lewis bit out. ''Find a guide who can get me to Willow Creek by dawn.''

A knock sounded at the kitchen door. Miranda's fork clattered from her fingers. She didn't know why she felt jumpy. Maybe it was the weight on her conscience.

''Since Mrs. Stoltz took off in a huff, I'd better get the door.'' Trey winked at her, letting her know he'd forgive her anything. ''It's probably for me, anyway.''

Miranda looked down at her plate. She'd hardly touched the food, Josie's favorite meal.

''Can your little girl come out to play?'' a child's voice asked, sweet as spun sugar. ''I gotta new sled and my cousin's gonna pull it.''

Surprise snapped in Josie's eyes. She held her breath, waiting for her uncle's answer.

''Sure, Nellie. I'll bundle Josie up and send her right out.'' Trey closed the door. ''Want to go sledding, Red?''

''Boy, do I!'' Josie jumped off her chair and dashed across the kitchen.

Miranda watched from her place at the table while Trey helped Josie into her wool cloak. He wound the scarf snug around her neck. He made sure her warmest mittens covered her hands, and that she had on two pair of socks in the watertight boots. With care, he tied on a warm cap, then pressed a kiss to her cheek. Just the way a father would.

Josie headed out the door, and Miranda slipped to the window, heart cracking. Little Nellie Steiner held out her hand, and the two girls waddled down the alley, so well bundled they could barely walk.

''She's going to have a lot of fun.'' Trey pulled her snug to his side. ''She's been wanting to go sledding ever since she got here.''

''I'm so glad she's making new friends.'' Miranda watched Josie reach the end of the alley. Two other little girls waved hellos. ''She's settling into your life very well.''

"She is." His lips grazed her temple. "So could you."

The power of those words shook her to the core, and she leaned against him, taking solace in his arms. In his loving arms. She couldn't say the words in return.

"Do something for me." His request rumbled through her, warming her down to her soul. That's how deeply he touched her.

His fingers threaded through her hair, cradling her head, tender, oh how tender. "Let me cherish you. Let me show you exactly how a man loves a woman."

His lips grazed her brow, then nibbled down her nose. His mouth slanted over hers, his kiss deep and open. Breathless, touched beyond words, she clung to him.

A fork fell to the floor as he shoved the plates out of the way. His eyes were black with desire, his breath choppy, and the way his kiss sealed her mouth made it clear what he wanted.

She couldn't deny him this. His hands smoothed her skirt up her thighs. Trembling, she laid back on the sturdy table. His touch blazed like fire. Desire spread like flame. He moved between her thighs, unbuckling his denims, and his breath was as ragged as hers.

He fumbled with a condom and then his erection surged against her inner thigh. He gazed down at her, a question in his eyes. So much love swelled in her heart. She waited, pulse hammering, body aching for completion.

"Say the words, Miranda," he rasped, his shaft nudging her apart. "I want to hear you say it."

He waited, her body quivering with need, the blunt head of his shaft thrumming against her. She lifted her hips, trying to draw him inside.

"Say the words, Miranda." His eyes were black, intense, filled with undisguised need.

The truth tore through her, sharp and keen. Her hand

clasped around his lower back, urging him to fill her. "I love you, Trey."

His kiss was a smile, and he joined them together with one slow thrust.

She spent the afternoon with him straightening up the clinic, fetching bandages when a patient arrived and organizing the drug cabinet. Josie came in, glowing from the fun she'd had.

Supper was a joyous affair. Miranda made chicken pot-pie, and they talked around the table until the food was cold and the lamps needed lighting. Trey brought out his guitar and played the evening away.

Miranda stored every moment in memory. Savored it so that she would never forget. Throughout the evening Trey told her how much he loved her with every word, every smile, every touch.

After putting Josie to sleep, Trey led Miranda to his room, where he undressed her with quick care. They made love over and over, each time more passionate than the last.

Spent, she snuggled against him, cheek resting on his chest, listening to the beat of his heart. "Do you think you can sweet-talk Mrs. Stoltz back to work tomorrow?"

"I'll try. I am the most charming doctor this side of Wyoming." His caressed one hand down her spine. "If Mrs. Stoltz is resistant to my supplications, I'll hire someone else."

"Someone who will take good care of Josie." She knew that.

"You sound as if you're not planning on staying." He lifted his head to look at her. "I thought we came to an agreement on the kitchen table."

She remembered the way he'd loved her. "I'm leaving in the morning."

"I know you don't belong here." His voice broke. "My life is a modest one. I can't provide you with what you're used to."

"It's not that, Trey." She swallowed past the grief and the tears knotting in her throat. "It's me. I don't belong here in your bed. Look how it's hurt your reputation."

"It will survive. And I don't plan on being a bachelor for much longer." He kissed her.

She nestled against him, holding on with all the strength in her heart. "Just love me one last time. I need you to love me."

Need coursed through him and he reached for a new condom. Love was in his touch as he knelt over her and caressed the curves of her breasts. She gasped, then moaned with abandon. He'd loved her thoroughly and still she was eager for him.

Control snapped, and he bent to catch one pebbled nipple with his tongue. She cried out, her fingers winding into his hair, plucking lightly at his scalp. Her back arched, and she opened her thighs.

"Please," she whispered.

He had only this last night as her lover. She'd said it and he felt it as sure as the winter air. He was already settling between her thighs, nudging against her damp folds, seeking entrance. She rose up, taking him into her gloving tightness. Like heated satin, like no home he'd ever known, he stretched out over her and thrust deep.

She folded her body around his, her knees clenching his hips, her arms wound around his back. He could feel her trembling, on the brink of surrender. Then she cried out, clamping tight around his shaft, and took him with her. Into a release of searing heat and pain-sharp pleasure.

He held her to him, still sheathed in her body, kissing her with all of his being. Love washed through his soul, love without measure.

Maybe she couldn't stay, maybe he wasn't enough for the precious diamond she was. But he was not letting her face her father or her fiancé alone. He would protect her to hell and back if he had to, regardless of what it cost him.

When the underworld froze over, it wouldn't be this cold. Or this damned miserable. The skies had cleared after midnight, and a quarter moon had made traveling through the mountain pass easier, but Lewis figured they'd be dead of hypothermia before they reached his destination.

Then he could never slake his thirst for Miranda's sweet body. That realization kept him in a rage, and the rage warmed him enough to keep on going through the wee hours of the morning.

Miranda, all delectable curves and willowy grace. Like a sugary treat of marzipan all ready for him to taste. Her breasts had been that sweet between his teeth and her thighs as smooth against the palms of his hands.

Lust surged through him, heady and raw. He'd waited long enough to take what was his. And he was still waiting. Who would have thought the quiet, dutiful mouse of a woman would be so hard to tame. Or this damn hard to get to the altar.

Lewis couldn't wait to get his hands on Miranda. She'd caused this delay. She'd caused this hardship. If she'd done what she'd been told, they would be married by now. And he'd have his one million dollars.

One million dollars. Enough money to buy that damned detective's silence. That was the real problem. The greedy man was growing greedier. He'd threatened to go to the authorities, and Lewis feared he already had.

He needed Miranda and he needed her money.

Pain hammered through his too-cold body in sharp, slicing waves. When he caught up with the little shrew, he would show her a few things, like how a real man loved a woman.

And this time, she would learn to like it.

A loud knock shattered the silence and drew Trey away from their kiss. Miranda sat up, clutching the blanket to her. Cold air skidded along her overly warm skin.

"It's for me." He pulled away from her with a regretful kiss. He fumbled around in the dark and she reached for the lamp.

"I'm almost dressed." He sat down on the edge of the bed. His boots thunked against the floor. "Stay where it's warm."

Tender, his words, rich with love. She hugged the beauty of it to her heart. This would be the last time she ever saw him.

The banging resumed, at the window this time, right above the bed. She jumped, but Trey, apparently used to it, pulled back the curtain.

A lantern lifted, illuminating a thin man's worried face. "Dr. Gatlin! Come quick. The midwife said to fetch you. The baby ain't comin' right."

"I'll be right there, Mr. Mason," Trey answered through the thin glass. He let the curtain fall into place.

"Do you need help? I can come." And stay for a little longer.

"You can't help with this, and the midwife is used to assisting me." He buttoned his trousers as he headed for the door. "If all goes well, I'll be back for breakfast."

"I love you, Trey." More than her freedom, more than her life.

Already he was running through the house. She heard the rustle of wool as he snatched his jacket, then the click of the bolt turning. The door creaked, and he was gone.

The sheets were scented with their lovemaking. She lay back, remembering. She wanted to memorize every touch, every taste, every feeling.

I'll defend you with my life. His promise had rung without compromise. He fully intended to protect her at any cost. Always noble and honorable. That thought was enough to force her out of his bed.

She shivered into her clothes. Josie slept soundly, sweet as an angel. Miranda took a rose from her pocket, one she'd pressed from the flowers Trey had given her, and laid it on the lace-covered nightstand. The faint fragrance calmed her, and she knew she'd made the right decision.

She refused to let any harm come to this child. Her father was coming. The trains would be running soon, bringing danger. She had no real choice, no other decision to make, because she loved Trey and Josie with all her heart.

She brushed a kiss along Josie's brow before leaving the room. Brushing the tears from her eyes, she walked through the parlor. It was hard to close her heart against the pain.

She took one look around. She'd known love and peace, acceptance and security in these rooms. But she'd known it couldn't last.

This place was a dream, too good to be true, a fairy tale that had come to an end. Happily-ever-afters only happened in books, not to her. But for this brief time she'd had the chance to know love, deep and abiding and real. And if deep down she'd hoped—

Well, she should have known.

She would never forget him. Never stop loving him. He would always be her whole heart.

It took all her strength to open the door, walk through it and keep on going.

"We're being tailed," the pockmarked guide said when he'd returned from checking their back trail. "Three men, look like federal marshals to me. You in some kind of trouble?"

"Hell, no." Lewis swung the horse around, but the reins tumbled from his right hand. It was this damned weather. Cold enough to freeze the fingers right off a man.

He was a surgeon, and he was starting to worry about his hands. He hadn't been able to feel them since dawn. But each time he checked, the skin beneath his gloves was pink. Just cold, not frostbitten.

Miranda was going to pay for this, too. "How long until we find her?"

The worthless bastard just swiped the snow from his eyes like an imbecile too lackwitted to think. "Hard to say with this kind of weather. Doc, you might wanna keep your voice to a low roar. We got a lotta new snow up on them peaks. Won't take much to bring it down."

What kind of answer was that? Lewis was a respected physician and was going to be a wealthy man. He didn't need to put up with this kind of insolence. "I asked, how long?"

The scruffy man didn't cower. "Her trail is fresh. Can't be too far," he answered, his mouth a twist of disdain.

Disdain. From a ragged little nothing like him. Lewis felt his rage build with every step, and his hands shook with the force of it. All he wanted was to marry the woman. That's what mattered right now. Taking what belonged to him.

"Look. There she is." The guide gestured.

Sure enough, there she was, one of two figures dark against the pristine snow. Victory was in sight. A cold wind caught him mid-chest as he crested the hill, cutting through him like a glacier.

He pulled off his gloves to check his hands again. Pink, not bloodless. He wiggled his fingers. They hardly moved, and he still couldn't feel them.

He slid one hand inside his coat, to warm it against the heat of his chest. "Who's that with her?"

"Looks like a mountain man to me, doc, meaner than a riled bear. That gal of yours couldn't have better protection."

"He'll die from a bullet just like any man."

The guide lifted his lip in a sneer. "But only a citified fool would think about drawin' a gun up here. Avalanches." He gestured to the tall peaks mantled with deep snow. "Now, if you want to get that woman, you'll do it my way."

For one million dollars and the pleasure of bedding Miranda, Lewis controlled his temper. But it wasn't easy, and it wouldn't last for long. He followed the gunman down the dangerous ravine.

This was the only way to keep Trey safe. Miranda repeated that thought in her mind, hoping it would ease the pain in her heart and chase away the empty feeling that she'd failed him again.

But she found no comfort as heavy clouds rolled in from the north, shrouding the peaks just overhead, close enough to touch.

"Looks like a storm's blowin', miss." The mountain

man who went by the name of Bear spoke low as a whisper. "Like I told you, we take this slow. Gotta have respect for these mountains. We'll hole up in my cabin, up north a ways. If the weather clears, we'll snowshoe the rest of the way."

She'd never showshoed, either. Surely it couldn't be as hard as riding a horse astride. Her inner thighs burned and her bottom felt bruised. She ached from head to toe, and if she got any colder, she knew she couldn't take the pain of it.

She wanted to go back to Trey. She wanted to feel the warm, strong haven of his arms.

This is for Trey, she reminded herself, sitting straighter in the saddle.

A gunshot exploded behind them. Bear fell like a rag doll against his horse's neck. He lay there, unmoving. The horse pranced, eyes wild, but didn't run. Terror shot through her and she raced to the injured man's side.

"Miranda, there you are." It was Lewis's voice that rang along the slope. "You can't imagine how hard I've been looking for my bride."

"I'm not your bride, Lewis. I don't marry men who shoot innocent people." Hated boiled deep inside as she tore off her glove. She unbuttoned Bear's fur collar. A pulse beat against her fingertips, fast but steady, and she slumped with relief.

Hatred boiled over, filling her up. She refused to look at the man capable of doing this—this cowardly, heartless act. She had to help Bear. But how?

Horse hooves struck the iced snow behind her, bringing Lewis closer. She'd been right to run from him. Right to leave Josie and Trey behind. Look what he would have done to Trey.

Her heart ached for Bear, so apparently lifeless. She

whipped off her scarf and wrapped it tight around Bear's chest. Blood already stained his fur coat.

The mountain man opened his eyes. His hand moved to his hip.

"Just slap my horse on the rump, and she'll head to town on her own," he whispered brokenly. "You ride hard, miss. Into the tree line."

Horse hooves clipped on the snow directly behind her. Lewis laughed, saying something she didn't listen to. All she saw was Bear lift his revolver. She leaned to her side and wheeled her horse away.

A gunshot exploded in her ear.

"My hand! I'm a surgeon, and you shot my hand! I'm going to kill you, you—"

"Go!" Miranda slapped the knotted ends of her reins against the mountain horse's rump. Bear's mare took off, running hard down the slope.

She saw Lewis's gun on the snow, the walnut grip bloodied. She thought about trying to grab it, but she couldn't waste the time. Murder glinted in the doctor's eyes.

She dug in her heels and the mare took off, churning through the deep snow.

Exhaustion battered him as he finished cleaning up. Marie Mason had lost a lot of blood. With a healthy baby girl in her arms, her husband at her side and the midwife keeping a watch on her, she would be fine. He was grateful for that.

He found a fresh pot of coffee on the stove. He poured himself a cup and washed up in the basin. He checked his bag to make sure all his instruments were wrapped, ready to be boiled when he reached the clinic. He made sure he had his bottles of morphine, chloroform and carbolic spray.

The back door rattled, and Sheriff Kelley walked in. "We have a problem, Trey. Bear MacAllister just rode into town with a bullet in his back."

"Good thing I'm done here. Get him to the clinic. Did you see the wound?"

"I had Deputy Richards take him over to Doc Brown. It's a bad wound, but it's clean. I figure old Doc can patch him up good enough until you return. I figure you'd want to go with us."

A bad feeling wrapped around Trey's chest. "Okay. Tell me."

"Miranda's taken off for Pine Bluff Pass. Bear said she'd hired him early this morning."

"Hired him? How did she know..." Then it occurred to him. Bear had come to the clinic to have a festering knife wound cauterized, and Miranda had bandaged him.

"Bear could barely talk," Kelley continued. "But he wanted you to know. Miranda's fiancé is the one who shot him. And he's up there on the mountain with her right now."

"I'd like to get my hands on that bastard." Black rage roared in his chest.

That lowlife had put great fear in Miranda's heart, had abused her, attempted to rape her and destroyed her sense of self-worth. That was why she'd left. Why she couldn't trust him enough to protect her.

The rage in his chest exploded.

"My men are mounting up. I've got my best tracker already on the job. We'll find them."

"I'll be saddled and ready in less than a minute."

Miranda was alone up in those mountains with a wife abuser. Somehow, some way, Trey was going to save her.

* * *

Miranda's horse stumbled through the unstable snow and then sank down to her hip. The animal struggled, exhausted. Miranda was exhausted, too. The cold wind stabbed through her like a thousand icy needles. She couldn't endure the pain.

She'd lost Lewis in the forest, but she knew he could easily follow her tracks. The mare whinnied in fear as the snow gave way again and she sank all the way to her belly.

She hated running. She hated being afraid. And after tonight, after she crested this mountain and found the next town, she was going to stop.

The horse struggled up a ridge, only to balk at the sight of a vast slope. It stretched all the way up to the peak and down, out of sight. They had to cross it. Miranda dismounted, biting her lip to keep from crying out with pain.

Her boot lost traction on the steep slope, and she tumbled onto her face. She skidded a few yards, gliding to a stop. She climbed back up onto her feet and managed to struggle back to her horse.

"Come on, girl," she soothed. "You and I are going to get through this. When we reach Pine Ridge, you're going to get a warm, comfortable stall and a big bucket of steaming oats. And I'm going to get a hot bath and the softest bed I can find."

Miranda wasn't going to die on this mountain. It was that simple. She was going to hire a good attorney and she was going to fight her father and Lewis. Neither of them was going to hurt her again.

She wanted her dreams back and she would fight for the right to them. Because without dreams, life was only an existence, a grim and lonely place. Just like this slope, desolate and frozen.

"Miranda," a man's voice called out, the echo sounding and resounding across the vast mountain.

The snow cracked beneath her feet and she dropped to her knees. It felt like the whole mountain shook.

She spun around and laid her finger over her lips. "Quiet, Lewis. You'll start an avalanche."

There was nowhere to run, so she faced him, this man who'd tried to hurt every part of her. Fear curled around her heart, but it was anger that lifted her chin.

Because of Lewis, she might never have a life with Trey. She might never be his wife. Never again fall asleep in his arms or wake up to his warm humor. Because of Lewis, she might have lost the only man she'd ever wanted.

He marched toward her, confident on the snow. He was always confident. But she wouldn't be fooled anymore. He was a coward, he wasn't a man. She spied a broken branch lying on the ground and grabbed it.

"Come on." He grabbed her by the back of the neck, as if she were a dog on a leash he could lead around. "You and I are going to find the closest preacher and we're getting married."

"Not on my life." She swung with all her might. The flexible pine bough slammed into his wounded hand.

He let go of her, shouting with pain, his fury reverberating along the solemn, mighty peaks. Blood sprayed, and she didn't wait, she ran. But the snow beneath her feet crumbled, dangerously unstable. She skidded down the slope on her knees.

"No, you don't. You aren't getting away from me." He lunged toward her, skidding on his belly across the snow.

She tried to scramble out of the way. But he grabbed her from behind and hauled her across the length of his body. She fought, but his bruising strength held her captive.

"I've waited long enough for my money," he whispered in her ear. "And the pleasure of bedding you."

Blood spilled down her cloak, and he didn't seem aware of his serious wound as he pulled the belt from his trousers. "I'm going to tie you up if I have to, but make no mistake. I'll have what I need before this day ends."

A horse's whinny shrilled across the vast field of snow. They both looked up to see a group of armed men riding into sight. The blue coat of a federal marshal shone dark against the endless white.

But it was another man who drew her gaze and held it. She knew by heart the lean slope of his hat and the wide line of his powerful shoulders. *Trey.*

"You're under arrest, Nelson," the man in blue called out as he broke through the line of trees. "Drop your weapon and release the woman. Now."

The six lawmen with him and Trey drew their revolvers.

This is what she'd left Willow Creek to avoid. She should have known Trey meant what he said. That he would protect her at any cost.

"I came to get my bride," Lewis called out, almost amicable. He could be a very charming man. He tossed a revolver onto the snow. "There's no law against that, is there?"

"One, and it's called kidnapping." Trey nudged his horse closer. "The lady doesn't want to be with you."

"Trey! No." Did he have to stand out front, make himself a target? The hard handle of a second revolver knocked her in the back as Lewis withdrew it from beneath his jacket. "Get back. He's got a—"

Lewis drew and fired with his injured, bloody hand. She

heard someone cry out. Trey? Fury hammered through her, like a jolt of lightning, and she hit Lewis with all her might. He cocked the gun again, and she struck again, this time aiming for his injury.

''Miranda, no!'' Trey's strangled shout rose above the fray. Boots pounded on the snow, approaching fast, but Lewis wouldn't let go of the gun. He fired as she tried to hit the weapon from his hand.

Cold arrowed through her ribs.

She looked down at the blood staining her hands. Her blood.

A strange inhuman roar sounded on the mountain above them. The snow trembled beneath her knees. A gray mist rose on the peak as a giant wall of snow broke loose.

Death streaked toward them. Miranda watched Lewis try to run across the slope, as if he could outrun an avalanche. The roar magnified. The ground shook like an earthquake. A wave of snow swallowed him, and then he was gone.

''Miranda!'' Trey's shout thundered above the deafening avalanche.

She tried to move, but her legs wouldn't work. A wall of snow hit her with a killing force. Something as solid as steel curled around her waist and everything went black.

Chapter Seventeen

The thundering roar exploded behind Trey as he drove his mare hard into the line of trees. Branches snapped across his face and arms. He felt the cold whoosh of the wind from the avalanche, slicing across his back. He spurred his mount and leaned over Miranda's limp body, protecting her, always protecting her.

In another second, the avalanche was still. Thunder continued reverberating across the high mountain peaks. Snow like dust flickered in the air, beginning to settle. Trey breathed a sigh of relief. He couldn't quite believe he'd managed to live.

Miranda lay slack in his arms. Her blood stained them both. Too much blood. He hauled his mare to a skidding stop and dismounted, cradling the woman he loved in his arms.

''Trey?'' Her voice came so weak, at first he thought it was the wind. ''Trey?''

Thank God. He dropped to his knees and laid her down on his jacket.

''Wh-where's Lewis?''

''He's gone, love.''

She was pale, her pupils dilated, her lips blue. She was

hypothermic and hemorrhaging. She clung to him, weak as a kitten, so very weak.

When he turned her over, he saw the bullet wound in her back, and it was bleeding profusely. New, red blood.

"Don't die on me, Miranda." He grabbed his medical bag from his saddle. "Do you hear me?"

"I'll try not to." She licked her lips with the tip of her tongue, as if she were thirsty. "I'd hate to ruin your reputation."

"That's right." He cut the fabric away from the wound in her back, and his heart fell.

It was bad. The entry wound was ragged. The bullet had damaged a lot of muscle and broken through a rib. It was all he could see, but it was enough. His hands shook as he pulled out the carbolic spray.

"I trust you, Trey. Whatever happens." She managed a faint smile, short-lived and bittersweet. Sadness filled her eyes, and love shone there like a polished gem so rare, he'd never seen its like.

Only felt it, in his own heart.

They both knew she could die here on the barren slope, as the sun faded and snow began to fall.

"You just hang on long enough for us to get you to a town. We're not far from Pine Ridge. I know the doc there. He's got a good clinic."

"Of course I'm going to make it. I have you, my good-luck charm." Then she closed her eyes.

She trusted him with her life. Not as a doctor, but as a man.

Kelley pounded across the rocks in the treeline. "Trey, we gotta go. A storm is ready to hit, and if it turns into a blizzard we don't have much time."

"I just need a few minutes. I have to stop the worst of the bleeding before we move her."

A gust of wind blew cold across them. The sheriff was right. There wasn't much time.

The storm held off until they reached the edge of town, then it hit hard. Not a blizzard, yet. Trey protected Miranda the best he could from the bitterly cold wind. She lay motionless in his arms, her breath a light flutter against the hollow of his throat.

"Is she still alive?" Kelley took the reins from Trey's numb hands.

"For now." Grim, he dismounted, gently keeping Miranda cradled against his chest. The winds hammered them as he climbed up the porch steps and pounded on the door.

Dr. Urich answered. He took one look at Miranda and swung the door open wider. "Gatlin, it's good to see you. Come on in. My clinic's in the back of the house."

Urich was a good doctor, well schooled and methodical. The kind of man Trey trusted.

Even then, there was no certainty Miranda would live.

Trey laid her on a clean table, the scent of carbolic spray strong in the air. He shucked off his jacket and searched for a wash basin.

"I know she's important, but this is my clinic." Urich clasped Trey's shoulder. "I'll take it from here. Go sit with your friends in my parlor, warm up, and I'll do my best for her."

"I can't leave her."

"You can't help her, Trey. Your hands are stiff from the cold. Do the best thing for her and put her in the care of the second-best doctor in the territory."

Trey pressed a kiss to Miranda's cold brow. She didn't stir. Just this morning she'd been warm and safe in his bed, snug in his arms. He could still hear the sigh of contentment she always made, snuggling against his chest. His arms ached with emptiness.

This is how he would feel without her, from this day forth. Empty, alone and without hope. His heart cracked into a thousand pieces. He stepped into the hallway and closed the door.

Trey's voice rumbled over her like spring sunshine. "I bet you didn't know that I'm the best snowman maker in this entire territory."

"I dunno, Uncle Trey. You aren't doin' his head right."

"What?" His grin was jaunty and slow, lopsided and sexy. Enough to warm Miranda all the way to her toes.

Light snow fluttered between them, delicate flakes that were as dizzying as she felt.

Trey hefted the snow head and placed it dead center on the portly snowman's body. "Look at that. Perfection."

"His head's shaped like an egg, Uncle Trey."

"Well, now, I meant for it to look like that."

He was her forever hero, a fairy-tale knight Miranda never thought could exist. His mouth found hers with a sizzling kiss, a promise of passion yet to come, and she knew it beyond a doubt. She could love this man until the end of time.

Pain interrupted her. It hammered down her back and through the ribs beneath her shoulder blade. Sharp, strident beats that tore through her dreams.

She opened her eyes. Light burned, bringing tears. A shadow leaned into her field of vision. A warm, strong hand brushed across her brow. Tender, soothing.

Trey. Tears burned in her throat. He'd stayed with her. He'd risked his life to rescue her from Lewis and from the avalanche. He'd saved her life on the mountain when she could have bled to death.

"Hey, sleeping beauty." His voice strummed like music, harmonic and so very welcome. "I've been kissing your brow, but you didn't wake up. I must be the wrong prince for you."

He was so close, he was touching her, yet he felt so distant. Felt a world away. His eyes were dark as night, without a sparkle or twinkle, and she wondered what that meant. Why he would be here, at her side, when he didn't want to be.

Then she knew. Trey couldn't be anything less than honorable. He wouldn't leave her alone, not without anyone to care for her.

"You're in Doc Ulrich's clinic. He's not bad, for a sawbones."

"Hey, I heard that, Trey," a man's voice answered from farther away, warm and humorous.

Trey's hand brushed the side of her face, a tender yearning touch that made her throat ache. "You're going to be fine. You just keep fighting that fever."

He removed his hand and wrung out a cloth. Water splashed into a basin by her head. The sharp, bitter scent of quinine lifted with the stream. He laid a warm damp cloth across her brow.

Exhaustion pulled her down. She didn't want to close her eyes. She wanted to keep looking at this man who'd saved her. In every possible way.

His hand covered hers. She saw the loneliness in his gaze. A connection telegraphed from his hand to hers, and she felt his sense of loss. The desolation.

Even though he tended her, he knew it, too. She would never again spend another night in his arms, never again know the tender gift of his love.

Morning came with a harsh light and a starker reality. Sheriff Kelley's boots thudded in the hallway outside Miranda's room. Trey stretched the knotted muscles in his back as he crossed to the door.

"Eastbound train's on its way." Kelley nodded toward the bed. "How is she? Can you leave?"

"Planning on it. How's Bear?"

"Doc Brown said he'll pull through." Kelley rubbed his brow. "Got a telegram for you. Want me to pick you something up at the diner?"

"I'd appreciate it." Trey took the folded telegram. "Black coffee. As much as you can carry."

"I'll do my best." Kelley ambled away, heading out into the bright sunshine.

Trey checked over his shoulder. Miranda was still asleep, so he leaned against the wall and read the note. It was from Mrs. Stoltz, on Josie's behalf.

"I miss you lots, Uncle Trey," he read. "I don't like you bein' gone. Bring me back lots of presents."

Warmth filled him up. Funny, he missed her so much. He missed reading to her after supper, playing the guitar so she could fall asleep, and seeing her cherub's grin at the table every morning.

He felt Miranda's gaze like a touch against the back of his shoulder. He turned, and there she was, sitting up in bed, her dark hair tousled like rare silk around her soft face. The brush of sunlight peering between the closed curtains somehow found her and worshiped her with a tender glow.

"You're still here." Her voice trembled like a flute's gentle melody. "Somehow I thought you would be gone this morning. That you'd stayed by my bed like a guardian angel of mercy and would disappear when I woke up."

"I'm just flesh and bone. Sorry to disappoint you." He strode into the room, regret like a heavy weight on his heart. "Your color is better. Any streaking pain down your back or right leg?"

"No streaking pain." She bit her bottom lip, a vulnerable gesture. "You don't have to be my doctor, Trey. I'd rather you were my friend."

Friend. Not lover. Not future husband. Just friend. He shrugged away the disappointment. He'd known it would come to this. "Lewis Nelson's body was recovered. I wanted you to know so you wouldn't be afraid anymore. It's over, the running, the fear. You can go home."

"I can." Sadness hung in the air between them, and she didn't mention her father. She would not burden this man one more time.

She had Sheriff Kelley's offer of help, and she would accept it now. With a deputy to protect her, she felt confident she could reach the territorial capital safely.

There was so much she wanted to say to him, but the words dried up on her tongue, leaving her with silence.

"Josie is going to miss you," Trey began, and he felt more distant than ever, miles away. "She's gotten pretty attached to you. Maybe you could send her a letter now and then to let her know you care. If you get time."

"You know I can't forget Josie." Miranda couldn't bear to look at him. Not even her private longings, her private love for him could change their situation.

If she reached out to him, she would only complicate his life. He hadn't offered marriage, and in a small family town, many more people would scorn their living arrangements.

Besides, until she could settle matters with her father, she wasn't free to love anyone.

"You could write me, too." Trey leaned one powerful shoulder against the wall. He looked like an outlaw with his dark hair tousled across his forehead and that lopsided grin teasing his mouth. "Maybe you don't know this, but I'm one of the best letter writers this side of the Mississippi."

"Just *one* of the best?" That made her smile. "You've grown more humble since I met you."

"It's one of my virtues." It hurt to tease, but the truth hurt even more. "I can stay if you need me."

"I can take care of myself." She set her chin and met his gaze. He could read the answer in the solemn confidence that glistened in her eyes.

"Then I guess it's goodbye." He'd feel foolish kissing her cheek, after the sweet intimacy they'd shared, so he simply tipped his hat to her and walked away. At the threshold, he looked back and for a moment almost told her.

But what would be the point? She didn't need him anymore. He would keep his confession to himself, of how much he loved her. He'd always be grateful she'd walked into his life and changed him.

The morning breeze blew crisp, sharp and cold. Trey lifted his face to the sun and breathed in and out until the pain eased.

He almost went back into the clinic, but the truth was, his love could never be enough for an heiress. He could follow her to Philadelphia and try to change.

But how would that work? How would that make either of them happy? He loved Montana. He loved his practice. He would never be content in a fancy hospital, where money was more important than the medicine he loved.

Besides, she didn't want the love of a small-town man.

Miranda heard the whistle blow. The trains were running again. She eased out of bed, gritting her teeth against the pain.

Sunlight glowed behind the drawn curtains, teasing at the edges. She pulled back the heavy, slightly dusty fabric to squint through the sun-kissed glass.

Twinkling snow mantled the town. A vivid blue sky stretched cold and cloudless and touched the heavy snow-capped peaks that were so close, she could see the rugged cuts of their faces.

Children's merry shouts lifted in the still air. The approaching train, heading east toward Willow Creek, chugged to a stop at the crowded depot.

She watched the milling people, eager to greet waylaid travelers or to board the rumbling train. She waited, the air wedged in her chest, until she caught a glimpse of him.

His eyes were dark, but a grin touched his mouth. He spoke to the sheriff, and they both chuckled. He moved out of her sight, boarding the train.

When the engine pulled away, she watched until the last car turned the bend and disappeared. Trey was the only man she'd ever loved. Could ever love.

And now he was gone from her life.

Every mile that passed added another wound to his heart, but Trey kept telling himself it was for the best. His heart didn't believe it, but his mind knew it was true.

The train chugged to a noisy stop at the Willow Creek depot. He saw Josie on the platform below, holding tight to Mrs. Stoltz's hand. Her face lit up when she saw him and she waved wildly. Baby Beth waved, too, tucked in Josie's left arm.

He waited to disembark with the other passengers, many grumbling about the rotten train service. He climbed down into the crisp winter sunshine and there was Josie, a bright beaming light of a child, running to meet him. "Uncle Trey! Uncle Trey!"

He held out his arms and she launched into them. He lifted her up and swung her around and around. Her laughter rang above the rumble of the engines and the drone of voices.

Then she held him tight and pressed a sweet kiss to his cheek. "Boy, I sure missed you, Uncle Trey."

"I missed you something terrible, Red." He kept her in his arms for a few seconds longer. "You're running pretty good on your hurt leg."

"Yep. Mrs. Stoltz made me do my exercises while you were gone. I missed your guitar." She tilted her head back, the question wrinkling her face. "Where's Miranda?"

"She'll come see you later."

"Not now?"

His heart twisted. "I know you were counting on seeing her today. But maybe you and I can ride the train and visit her sometime."

"I'm not afraid. Well, not *too* afraid." Josie looked down, touching the gleaming locket on her chest. "I got Miranda's good-luck charm. It's filled with her mama's love, you know."

"I heard that."

She sighed heavily, a sound of grief and heartache. "I'm real sad."

"Me, too, Red."

He took her by the hand. He hadn't thought it could happen, but he loved Josie like a daughter. She was a piece of his heart.

And all because of Miranda.

Chapter Eighteen

Three weeks later

Miranda's palms were damp when the door opened. Her heart skipped rapidly as her father entered the attorney's somber office.

He looks old. She hardly recognized him. He no longer looked strong and invincible, a man used to hiring, firing and managing hundreds of people. Gray marked his black hair, and bags of loose skin sagged beneath his watery eyes. He stood lopsided, shoulders down, his spine no longer straight.

"You weren't at Lewis's funeral service," he admonished, and authority still rang in his baritone. "You can't imagine how that made me look. People asked questions and I was forced to make excuses. Of course, I couldn't tell them the truth."

"No, I suppose not." Anger, fear, lost adoration and disdain all melded together into a confusing, stomach-twisting knot. This man had fathered her, had provided for her. But that didn't mean he owned her. That wasn't love. Trey had taught her that. "Aren't you going to ask about my health?"

"You look fine to me." Her father's hands fisted, big, healing hands. "I don't know why Lewis did what they said, but you made matters worse. He was a great man, the greatest I'd ever known."

"He fed your ego, Father. And that was more important to you than protecting your daughter." She bit her lip, old hurts a lifetime long aching in her chest, but she hadn't asked her father here to try to resolve them.

The past could never be fixed. And she didn't want a relationship with this man. He couldn't love anyone but himself. He had nothing to offer her that mattered. He'd failed to do so her entire life. He didn't look ready to change now.

She gestured toward the lawyer seated behind the cherry desk. "My attorney is here to discuss with you the terms of my trust."

Fiery anger flared across his face. "So, this is all about the money. You wanted it for yourself. You didn't want to share it with the man I'd chosen for you. The man to take my place in the hospital I'd built from nothing. Is that why you lied about him?"

"I never lied, Father, and you know it. This is about how you treated me all my life." She would not let him hurt her. Not anymore. "I disown you. From this moment on, you are no father to me."

"That's ridiculous. Where do you get these notions? From those books you read?" His face twisted with disgust. "If you think I'm handing over the trust to you, you can forget it. Not your lawyer, eavesdropping behind his desk, or a court order from a judge is going to change my mind."

The disdain remained on his face. A disdain she'd

grown so used to, she'd failed to even recognize it over the years.

"I'm declaring my independence, Father. I want an end to the reward notices. I want my trust fund because it is the only way I'll be rid of you."

She stood up, letting the attorney know she was done and then turned to face her father. "Goodbye, John. I hope you enjoy your lonely, colorless life."

Her father's temper flared in a curse that echoed off the walls, but he couldn't control her now. The attorney handed him enough legal documents to distract him, and she walked through the door.

Finally free.

"Hey, Doc," Sanderson called out across the busy mid-day traffic. "I just picked up a delivery at the depot. Maybe you should hurry on down there and take a look at who got off the train."

Trey looked up from untethering his horse. "I'm not expecting anyone."

"I think you'll want to see her." Sanderson tipped his hat. Ever since his son was recovering with a new course of treatment, thanks to Dr. Mitchell's brief visit two weeks earlier, he'd had a bounce in his step. "I've got one name for you—Miranda."

No, it couldn't be. Trey whipped around, staring down the street. He could see the line of cars at the depot, and the plumes of coal smoke, black against the pristine sky.

"Did Miranda come? Oh, goody!" Josie stood up on the sleigh's seat and craned her neck to get a view of the train. "Hurry up, Uncle Trey! We don't want to miss her."

Miranda was back. Just for a visit, probably. She'd said

she would visit Josie. That had to be it. Trey calmly sent the mare in a very fast trot down the busy street.

"Slow down, Doc!" Sheriff Kelley called from the boardwalk. "Any faster and you'll cause an accident." Then he laughed.

The lawman thought he was funny.

There she was. Trey's heart hitched, filling with love and longing. She looked good, tall and slim, like a willow in the wind. Her dark rose dress shimmered in the brisk winter breeze. She looked like an out-of-season blossom against the ordinary world.

"Miranda!" Josie launched from the sleigh before it was even stopped. She hit the ground running, and this time he didn't admonish her. She pounded up the wooden steps and flew into the woman's arms.

Miranda, the heiress. She looked like one, too. Her dress was pretty, but not obviously expensive. She didn't wear any sparkling jewels. It was in her manner, bred into her like her grace and gentleness.

"I missed you so much." Miranda knelt, hugging Josie ardently. There was no denying the love she had for the girl. "And look at you. Where's your brace?"

"Don't need it anymore. I can run and play and everything."

"So I see." Miranda brushed curls from Josie's eyes. "I'm so glad. Why isn't your uncle coming up here to greet me?"

Trey stepped forward. "Because he figures you're a dream and in two more seconds he's going to wake up alone without you."

He shouldn't have said that.

She stood, confident, back straight. "I'm feeling the same way."

Light shone in her eyes, a love so powerful she couldn't hide it.

She'd come back. That had to say something. Hope kindled in his heart, and he held out his hand. ''I know there isn't a blizzard and there are plenty of inns in this town, but I'd like to offer you shelter from the storm.''

''But it's fair weather.''

''I'm not talking about the weather.''

''Neither am I.'' She laid her palm across his.

At the first contact of her skin, fire streaked up his arm, snapped down his spine and left him breathless.

''My father is dealt with, and Lewis is gone. There's no reward and no bounty hunters. Would you still love me even if I don't need your protection?''

''What kind of question is that?'' He slid his hands up her forearms, drawing her closer. ''I think I fell in love with you the first moment we met. When you put yourself in danger to help Josie. I love you, Miranda, without condition, without end. Only you.''

''That's the way I love you.'' It hurt to say the words, to be this vulnerable. But it felt good, too.

She could see the future, happy as Trey's wife, caring for Josie, helping him with his work. There would be babies one day, a little boy with a jaunty grin and a little girl with sparkling eyes. With Josie, they could be a family, just like she'd dreamed.

She felt a tug on her skirt.

''Miranda, are you gonna marry him? That would be good 'cuz I don't want you to leave. Not ever again.''

''I suppose I just might,'' she admitted through the sweet mix of emotions wedged in her throat. ''He is, after all, the most handsome man this side of the Badlands. I'm lucky to know him.''

''No, *I'm* the lucky one.'' Trey's mouth covered hers

in a tender kiss that promised a lifetime of loving. He whispered in her ear. "And you already know I'm the best lover in the territory."

"I'm going to make you prove it. Tonight."

He brushed his hand along the curve of her jaw, caressed his thumb against her satiny cheek. It felt like heaven to touch her again.

He'd missed her, how he'd missed her. "I want you to marry me, Miranda. Please, do me the honor of becoming my wife. Because it *would* be an honor, to share every day and night with you. If you'll have me the way I am."

That precious light in her eyes didn't dim. "I love the way you are, Trey. Don't you know that by now?"

"I'm a small-town man." He wasn't ashamed of it, but was it enough for her? "I'm a doctor who's never going to be rich. I have a house that can't be called a mansion. And I don't have a trust fund to match yours."

"That's a relief. I was once engaged to a man like that. He was horrible." She looked up, without regret, without compromise.

"This is important to me, Miranda. If I'm not good enough—"

"Good enough?" she interrupted. "Trey, you are a better man than I deserve. But I'm going to hold on to you with all my strength and never let you go."

"This isn't Philadelphia."

"No, and it's a good thing. Because while I was staying here with you, I learned something important, and it's changed my whole life. I'm a small-town woman at heart. And if I have your love, then that's all the riches I need."

He was the one, valuable beyond price. And she would spend her life proving it to him. To this Montana man made of tenderness and might, who'd given her his heart.

* * * * *

If you liked her Regencies,
you'll be sure to love
the first Medieval from

Deborah Hale

The Elusive Bride

When a marriage is arranged between
the Lord of Ravenscroft and Cecily Tyrell
of Brantham, the proud knight must
battle her scorned suitor to keep
the lovely lady for his own!

The Elusive Bride

Available in bookstores December 2000!

Harlequin®
Historical

Visit us at www.eHarlequin.com
HHTEB

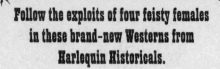

Follow the exploits of four feisty females
in these brand-new Westerns from
Harlequin Historicals.

ON SALE NOVEMBER 2000

THE LAW AND MISS HARDISSON
by **Lynna Banning**
Lawyer Irene Hardisson defends a rugged
Texas Ranger when he's framed for murder.

MONTANA MAN
by **Jillian Hart**
On the run from her domineering fiancé,
Miranda Mitchell finds love
with a caring doctor.

ON SALE DECEMBER 2000

THE LAST BRIDE IN TEXAS
by **Judith Stacy**
A handsome stranger falls in love
with Elizabeth Hill, the last unmarried
woman in town.

PROTECTING JENNIE
by **Ann Collins**
Fleeing an arranged marriage, society girl
Jennie Andrews goes west and lands in
the arms of a rancher.

Visit us at www.eHarlequin.com   HHWEST10

If you enjoyed what you just read,
then we've got an offer you can't resist!

Take 2 bestselling love stories FREE!

Plus get a FREE surprise gift!

Clip this page and mail it to Harlequin Reader Service®

IN U.S.A.	IN CANADA
3010 Walden Ave.	P.O. Box 609
P.O. Box 1867	Fort Erie, Ontario
Buffalo, N.Y. 14240-1867	L2A 5X3

YES! Please send me 2 free Harlequin Historical™ novels and my free surprise gift. Then send me 6 brand-new novels every month, which I will receive before they're available in stores. In the U.S.A., bill me at the bargain price of $3.94 plus 25¢ delivery per book and applicable sales tax, if any*. In Canada, bill me at the bargain price of $4.19 plus 25¢ delivery per book and applicable taxes**. That's the complete price and a savings of over 10% off the cover prices—what a great deal! I understand that accepting the 2 free books and gift places me under no obligation ever to buy any books. I can always return a shipment and cancel at any time. Even if I never buy another book from Harlequin, the 2 free books and gift are mine to keep forever. So why not take us up on our invitation. You'll be glad you did!

246 HEN C24S
349 HEN C24T

Name   (PLEASE PRINT)

Address   Apt.#

City   State/Prov.   Zip/Postal Code

* Terms and prices subject to change without notice. Sales tax applicable in N.Y.
** Canadian residents will be charged applicable provincial taxes and GST.
   All orders subject to approval. Offer limited to one per household.
   ® are registered trademarks of Harlequin Enterprises Limited.

HIST00_R   ©1998 Harlequin Enterprises Limited

You're not going to believe this offer!

In October and November 2000, buy any two Harlequin or Silhouette books and save $10.00 off future purchases, or buy any three and save $20.00 off future purchases!

Just fill out this form and attach 2 proofs of purchase (cash register receipts) from October and November 2000 books and Harlequin will send you a coupon booklet worth a total savings of $10.00 off future purchases of Harlequin and Silhouette books in 2001. Send us 3 proofs of purchase and we will send you a coupon booklet worth a total savings of $20.00 off future purchases.

Saving money has never been this easy.

I accept your offer! Please send me a coupon booklet:

Name: _____

Address: _____ City: _____

State/Prov.: _____ Zip/Postal Code: _____

Optional Survey!

In a typical month, how many Harlequin or Silhouette books would you buy <u>new</u> at retail stores?

☐ Less than 1   ☐ 1   ☐ 2   ☐ 3 to 4   ☐ 5+

Which of the following statements best describes how you <u>buy</u> Harlequin or Silhouette books? Choose one answer only that <u>best</u> describes you.

☐ I am a regular buyer and reader
☐ I am a regular reader but buy only occasionally
☐ I only buy and read for specific times of the year, e.g. vacations
☐ I subscribe through Reader Service but also buy at retail stores
☐ I mainly borrow and buy only occasionally
☐ I am an occasional buyer and reader

Which of the following statements best describes how you <u>choose</u> the Harlequin and Silhouette series books you buy <u>new</u> at retail stores? By "series," we mean books within a particular line, such as *Harlequin PRESENTS* or *Silhouette SPECIAL EDITION*. Choose one answer only that <u>best</u> describes you.

☐ I only buy books from my favorite series
☐ I generally buy books from my favorite series but also buy books from other series on occasion
☐ I buy some books from my favorite series but also buy from many other series regularly
☐ I buy all types of books depending on my mood and what I find interesting and have no favorite series

Please send this form, along with your cash register receipts as proofs of purchase, to:
In the U.S.: Harlequin Books, P.O. Box 9057, Buffalo, NY 14269
In Canada: Harlequin Books, P.O. Box 622, Fort Erie, Ontario L2A 5X3
(Allow 4-6 weeks for delivery) Offer expires December 31, 2000.   PHQ4002

This Christmas, experience
the love, warmth and magic that
only Harlequin can provide with

Mistletoe Magic

a charming collection from

BETTY NEELS
MARGARET WAY   REBECCA WINTERS

Available November 2000

HARLEQUIN®
Makes any time special ™

Visit us at www.eHarlequin.com   PHMAGIC

CELEBRATE VALENTINE'S DAY WITH HARLEQUIN®'S LATEST TITLE—

Stolen Memories

Available in trade-size format, this collector's edition contains three full-length novels by *New York Times* bestselling authors Jayne Ann Krentz and Tess Gerritsen, along with national bestselling author Stella Cameron.

TEST OF TIME by Jayne Ann Krentz—
He married for the best reason.... She married for the only reason.... Did they stand a chance at making the only reason the real reason to share a lifetime?

THIEF OF HEARTS by Tess Gerritsen—
Their distrust of each other was only as strong as their desire. And Jordan began to fear that Diana was more than just a thief of hearts.

MOONTIDE by Stella Cameron—
For Andrew, Greer's return is a miracle. It had broken his heart to let her go. Now fate has brought them back together. And he won't lose her again...

Make this Valentine's Day one to remember!

Look for this exciting collector's edition on sale January 2001 at your favorite retail outlet.

HARLEQUIN®
Makes any time special ™

Visit us at www.eHarlequin.com

PHSM

**COMING IN NOVEMBER 2000
FROM STEEPLE HILL**

Three bestselling authors invite you to share in their

HOLIDAY BLESSINGS
by
New York Times bestselling author
DEBBIE MACOMBER
Thanksgiving Prayer

A young woman must decide whether she is willing
to brave the rugged wilderness of Alaska for
the man she loves.

JANE PEART
The Risk of Loving

During the holiday season, two lonely people decide
to risk their hearts and learn to love again.

IRENE HANNON
Home for the Holidays

A troubled widow finds her faith renewed on
Christmas Eve when she falls in love with
a caring man.

HOLIDAY BLESSINGS

Available November 2000 from

Steeple Hill™

Visit us at www.steeplehill.com   PSHHB

JILLIAN HART

grew up in rural Washington State, where she learned how to climb trees, build tree houses and ride ponies. A perfect childhood for a historical romance author. She left home and went to college and has lived in cities ever since. But the warm memories from her childhood still linger in her heart, memories she incorporates into her stories. When Jillian is not hard at work on her next novel, she enjoys reading, flower gardening, hiking with her husband and trying to train her wiggly cocker spaniel puppy to sit. And failing.

HHBIO538